# A Lifetime Love Affair

PJ Harris

ISBN: 0990015904
ISBN-13: 9780990015901
Library of Congress Control Number: 2013920650
CreateSpace Independent Publishing Platform
North Charleston, South Carolina

# *Acknowledgements*

First to my Lord and Savior, Jesus Christ, who gave me the strength and courage to continue my journey regardless how intense the task. Thank you for teaching me loss so that I would know how to accept and appreciate gain.

To the most important man in my life, AP; words could never express my appreciation for of all that you have done to make this book a dream come true. Thank you for listening, hearing, reading and being there when I needed you.

To my best friends, Shirley, Agnes, and Tyrone. There is nothing anyone can say when you've had a friendship like ours for over forty years. Thank you for your trust and inspiration.

To all of my aunts, Ann, Lois, Ruby, Bell, Mattie, Norma, Genovia, Marge, friends Celina, Renee, Chonita, Wanda, Alberta, Lynn, Milton and all of the Golden Girls your encouragement and support has been outstanding. Thank you.

To my editor, Rhonda Crawford, author, Jessica A. Robinson, and advisor, Yvette A. Carter a special thank you for all your education and coaching.

To createspace.com Rock On.

# *Chapter 1*

A regular Saturday event, Carita met her friend Marilynn at the LL (Langston's Lounge), a local bar owned by Marilynn's uncle, Walter Langston. Marilynn had taken over operations in the kitchen, selling bar-b-que chicken and rib sandwiches with French fries. The weekend crowd was usually more than one person could handle, so Carita didn't hesitate to assist her friend. Raised in a strict Christian home, Carita's grandmother would have a heart attack if she knew Carita was working in a bar. Marilynn, who had just returned from L.A. to care for her ailing mother, had a hard time finding employment in her profession. Selling dinners and sandwiches provided the income she needed until she could secure a steady job.

One Friday in particular, while working at the club with Marilynn, a young man approached Carita and asked her to dance. Being somewhat shy, she declined.

"No thank you," she said. "I need to help my friend and I'm afraid I won't have time."

Knowing all about Carita's shyness, Marilynn pushed her and said, "Go on girl, he's harmless. That's my cousin. He's home on furlough from the service. I think he'll be here for the next thirty or forty days. When he leaves, he's going overseas," she explained.

"I don't know," Carita said. "We'll see. I don't think I've ever seen him before. How long has he and his family lived here?"

"All of us were born here," she said.

Douglas, Walter's son stood tall and thin with thick brown hair. His light brown eyes were just heavenly and added substance to his keen nose and high cheekbones. This man was very handsome and his bowed legs added sexiness to his well-shaped body.

Once again, he came to the sales window and asked Carita if he could buy her a drink.  Again, she declined.  Throughout the evening, Douglas waltzed back and forth asking for dances or to buy a drink.

Finally Douglas said, "You won't dance with me. I can't buy you a drink. How am I going to get to know you?"

Carita pretended to be too busy and just ignored his comment.  Who did he think he was, she said to herself.

"Listen, Marilynn said, "aren't you good and legal, or are you just faking when we go out?"

"Marilynn, you know I'm twenty one.  I just don't know this guy and, although he's your cousin, everyone is not man hungry like you."

Marilynn giggled. Carita was telling the truth.  Her uncle warned Marilynn not to be in the bar flirting with the patrons.  The two were very close since her dad and Walter were brothers and she was her dad's only child.

Finally the night came to an end and Carita, for one, was glad.

Douglas looked at her and tried to figure out why she didn't like him. She was an attractive little thing.  Her stunning auburn hair came just below her neck and her face was round enough to hide the cheek bones.  Her dazzling brown eyes added a magnificent glow to her copper brown skin when she smiled.  She only stood about five feet with a tiny waist, making her truly petite.

Douglas, trying to make one last attempt to gain her attention, said, "Well, I guess you're glad the night is over but I'll be here next week to irritate you until you say yes to one of my requests."

The following week, Carita and Marilynn went to the club early to set up.  This week was the town's folk payday, which was estimated to bring a larger profit.  Upon their arrival, they immediately saw the same annoying Douglas.  Of course, he offered to help and Marilynn quickly accepted before Carita had the opportunity to politely decline.

He turned to Carita and said, "How are you?"

She gave him a quick "fine" and moved on to the kitchen with a box of paper goods and cookware.  As she approached the kitchen door, Douglas opened it for her.

"Wasn't that nice of me?" he said.

She just looked at him and rolled her eyes. What an annoying ass, she thought. He was so full of himself that it wasn't even funny.

Marilynn and Carita prepped the food in order to have everything ready by nine that evening. The lounge was usually crowded by then and the patrons' lips were tuned to eat off their liquored high. Soon the club got crowded with people dancing and drinking and of course, they wanted food. The girls predicted the profits would be good.

As Carita made change for a customer, the "Pain" Douglas appeared at the door.

"Girl, why won't you dance with me?" he asked, "It's only a dance. I won't bite you." He smiled convincingly.

Carita thought, "Why not. I'm sick and tired of him coming to this window. I might as well get this over with. Maybe he'll leave me alone." She also thought the music would have been something fast since that's what had been playing most of the night. However, a slow tune played and she had to be close to this guy she considered a fool.

As they danced he said, "Girl, I like you. I can't figure out why you don't like me?"

She looked at him as though he had lost his mind. "Do you think that it's because you are so full of yourself?"

"What's that mean?" he asked.

"You're conceited. You assume that everyone is supposed to be at your beck and call."

"Maybe. But all I really want to do is dance and spend some time with you."

As he talked, he pulled her a little closer to him and whispered in her ear. "I really like you girl. Just please let me spend some time with you. I promise to be on my best behavior. I would not do anything in this world to ever hurt you."

When the record stopped, he escorted her to the bar to buy her a drink.

"I don't drink a lot because it does not seem to agree with me."

Walter called his wife, Douglas's mom, and asked what she suggested for Carita to drink. She was a small woman with a southern accent. Her glasses fit her little face as her haircut with slight strips of gray enhanced it. She introduced herself as Lee Hilda.

"Most people just call me Lee, she explained smiling. "Lee Hilda is so much to say. What have you been drinking?" she asked.

"Well, screwdrivers, gin and squirt and sometimes rum and coke," Carita replied.

"You probably can't drink white liquor. Let's try VO and coke with lemon juice or E&J and water."

Carita decided to try the VO, coke and lemon juice. It sounded tasty. The drink was reasonably good. Douglas stood beside her as she took another sip.

"A bunch of the patrons often go to breakfast together," he said. "Would you consider going with me? I promise to be on my best behavior."

She decided it might be fun. After all, a bunch of people were going so how much trouble could he be? As they sat in a booth alone, he began to tell her how long he would be home on leave. They discussed other things such as where they went to school, worked, and hobbies. He reached for her hand as he was expressing his hopes and dreams; his eyes responded to the intense and profound appearance upon Carita's face leading her to believe he was as sensitive as he was sincere. She thought, at least he's not a dummy. He does have good sense after all.

While leaving the restaurant he asked, "How about going to the movies with me?"

"Only if you take me to see, *The Love Story*," Carita retorted.

"I should have known. That's what everybody is going to see these days. What about the *Great White Hope*?"

"We can see that the next time we go to the movies."

He smiled in such a way that she knew he would take her to see the movie she requested. They arranged for him to pick her up at five that evening.

In the theater, they got comfortable and Doug helped Carita remove her coat while placing the box of popcorn in her lap as he opened a candy bar to share. As the movie grew more intense Douglas saw tears coming from Carita's eyes. He placed his arm around her to let her know it was alright to express her passion, for he understood sentiment. After the movie the two decided to stop for a quick bite to eat. While waiting for their entree they chatted about the movie.

"What if that was me," questioned Carita, "and I had to tell you that I had cancer?"

"I hope that never happens," he responded. "I have no intention of losing you to anything ever."

Before she could reply Doug reached across the table and gently kissed her.

The week proved very interesting, with all of their activities. They played Spades and Bid Whist with some of his friends at Earl's house, an old school-mate. Doug stood behind Carita so he could help her play the hand of his favorite game. He enjoyed teaching her almost as much as she enjoyed learning. He had even tried to show her how to shoot pool. The gang had never seen Doug quite so taken with a girl before. They knew from past girlfriends, Carita had to be special for Doug to be so attentive to her. While playing cards at Earl's, another old school friend of Doug's came by. His name was Nate Jones. He acted as though he was a part of the group but Carita could sense something was not right with this young man. He did not seem to fit in like the others.

He sat on the arm of the couch and said to Carita, "I'm Nate and you are?"

"No, no, no," Doug exclaimed. "Nate, that's my girl. You need to park it somewhere else."

"Up to the same old tricks I see," said Earl. "Still can't get your own girl."

Everyone just laughed. Nate became angry and left. The group knew Nate only came around to keep turmoil present among the guys. It seemed that he actually did not have any friends of his own or even one he could truly call a partner. And, along with that, he didn't seem to be able to get a girl on his own. He was always trying to grab someone else's.

During the next couple of weeks, Douglas made plans with Carita almost every evening. He loved taking her to dinner, the movies, skating, and bowling. Of course, with the exception of dinner, most of the gang hung out with them. They were usually with Douglas' friends and their girls. Carita made Doug feel like a breath of fresh air. He knew in his heart he was falling in love with Carita. Her smile and the expression of her eyes let Douglas know she would forever be his. She was compassionate, kind-hearted and affectionate but most of all her understanding and her ability to communicate made her what he had always been searching for.

Douglas was from a larger family than Carita. She only had one sister. Her parents had been killed in an auto accident when she was four, leaving her maternal grandparents to care for them. Douglas had a brother and two sisters. Mike, his younger brother, had a crush on Carita. He actually thought Douglas brought her home for him to play with and discuss basketball. She was the coolest girl ever in his eyes. Carita got along with everyone. His sister, Whitley, had been married a short time and enjoyed Carita's willingness to teach her how to bake. Her favorite was German chocolate cake. Although the younger sister, Ronnie, was only eight, she and Carita did everything together. Carita helped her do the dishes, her homework, and they discussed sports. Mike was right in the midst because he did not want to be left out. Douglas' parents were always telling both of them that Carita did not want to be bothered and even though she looked like a kid, she was an adult. The children would just laugh and say, "But she might be our sister one day so we want to break her in!"

Soon Carita realized Doug's leave was almost over. Although friends and family had entertained them, they had not spent very much time alone. Douglas came up with a suggestion.

"We could go away for a few days, where it would be just the two of us. We can enjoy ourselves a lot better with what time we have left without everyone being around."

Douglas decided that they might be able to travel north and spend time on the lake. This time of the year, the rooms might be a little cold but a fireplace would provide the ambiance of a romantic weekend. Douglas arranged for them to rent a room at a lodge close to the lake, about two hours from town. They ate a succulent dinner of stuffed pork chops and wild rice. Douglas enjoyed watching Carita devour every morsel for most of the time she ate like a bird.

Douglas found some soft music on the radio as ReRe (his nickname for her) went to slip into something more comfortable.  She put on a new pink silk nightie then exited the bathroom and Douglas turned the lights to a soft glow.

He looked at Carita with passion that made his heart skip a beat. He walked toward her and just held her for a moment, swaying back and forth, to what had become their favorite song.  He gently carried her to the bed and laid her down.  He couldn't stop looking at her.  This was their first time being intimate, and he wanted to be gentle with her.  He smoothed her hair and then slipped his hand into hers. He knew he would never allow any harm to come to her. He would be her protector, her comfort, her everything. Her face was radiant and without speaking any words and he understood that she belonged to him and him alone. And Carita knew in that same instant that he was special and wonderful.  He had the grace and charm of a truly gentle man and her body ached for his touch. The tenderness of his voice saying her name made her blood rush hot through her veins and she felt secure in his love for her, a love she had never experienced before.  It was whole, complete, and she felt totally protected from all past hurts and fears.  She was sheltered from the storms and finally this had to be what true love meant.  He began to kiss her slowly on her forehead and then her cheeks.  He worked his way down to her lips and gently kissed them and she responded with a breathless sigh. She lost track of space and time, there was only her and Douglas in the world and nothing else mattered.  Her hands slowly touched his face, letting him know he belonged to her and she wanted so much to be a part of him.

Her whimpers of pleasure from the touch of his hands allowed him to understand the unspoken language of love. Her feelings for him were untainted and pure.  The softness of her eyes held warmth and understanding while her lips quivered with anticipation of ecstasy.

His hands slipped in and out of her garment until it slid off her body. The touch of his lips on her breasts with such tenderness and warmth soon lead to the compassion of ultimate desire, with affection for and a sense of belonging to each other.  They held on to one another as the passionate feeling of a romantic desire reached a level of ultimate sensitivity. Douglas held Carita for what seemed to be forever and she did the same. They drifted into a land of compassion. As Carita woke up the next morning, she found Douglas rekindling the fire to keep the room warm.

"Good morning, sleepy head. How did you rest?" he asked as he walked toward the bed and placed a soft kiss on her forehead.

"Fine." She answered smiling as she held his hand.

"Let's shower so we can go get some breakfast."

"You go first," she said. "I want to lie here for just a few moments."

He looked puzzled as he thought that he might have hurt her. Concerned he asked

"Oh Carita, I'm sorry I didn't mean to hurt you last night."

"No my love she said touching his face. You didn't. I just wanted to recapture last night."

After they showered, they walked to the lodge where Douglas had already ordered their breakfast. He had planned a surprise for Carita and insisted that she dress warmer than usual for the day. After finishing their breakfast, they stopped at the lodge's small quartermaster store to rent snowsuits and sleds.

Douglas thought that it would be fun for them to go sled riding. They met some more couples on the slope and spent several hours sliding and walking up and down the slopes while laughing and talking. They even managed to have a race and a snowball fight. Finally, Carita was too tired and cold to spend any more time in the great outdoors. They said goodbyes to their new friends and headed for their room.

While Carita showered, Douglas took the sled and snowsuits back. He decided to purchase some dinner and a bottle of wine. They ate and sat in front of the fire, enjoying its ardent glow as they discussed their hopes and plans for the future. Finally, Douglas suggested they turn in. He wanted to get an early start the next day. He kissed Carita on her check as he held her in his arms while finding their way to a passionate slumber.

As they drove from the cabin, Carita thought of the family.

Carita knew that, over the next couple of days, he would belong to them. He would be gone for a year and, for them as well as her, that seemed like a lifetime. After all they were very close and he was their big brother.

"What's wrong," Douglas asked Carita as her mind seemed to be anywhere but on him.

"I was just thinking. A year seems like a lifetime and although we have spent some quality time together, I will have to allow your siblings their time with you also."

Douglas smiled and said, "We still will have a couple of days together before I leave."

Before dropping Carita off, Douglas stopped by his mom's to let the family know they were back from the lake.

"Carita, Ms. Lee declared, we're having a special dinner for Douglas on Sunday. I expect for you to be here."

"Yes Ma'am, Carita replied. What would you like me to bring?"

"Bring whatever dish you like," replied Ms. Lee.

Whitley interjected. "Carita do you think you could bake a German chocolate cake. It's not Doug's favorite but it is mine." They all laughed. Whitley was definitely eating for two and seemed to be craving all types of pastries and baked goods.

Carita felt so special to be included. She knew Ms. Lee's menu would be to die for.

Most of the family members arrived after Sunday church service. Ms. Lee had planned a very special dinner since it would be Douglas's last home cooked meal for a year. Her menu included all of his favorites: juicy fried chicken, mouthwatering cornbread, macaroni and cheese, tender fried cabbage with onions and green peppers, green beans, and for dessert several tasty apple pies, pound cake and ice cream. Walter said grace and everyone sat down to enjoy the meal. Most of the men returned to the family room to watch the game while the women stayed in the dining room and kitchen to help Lee with the cleanup.

Ronnie looked at Carita with her big brown eyes and said sadly, "I've got to wash all of these dishes. Would you help me, Carita?"

"Certainly.

I'll help too," Mike said.

Lee chased the two younger children out of the kitchen and reminded Carita that she was a guest.  Once or twice, Douglas came to check on Carita. "Are you alright honey?" he asked.

"Douglas," his mother said sternly. "Carita is alright.  We are not going to let anything happen to her."

Some of the family members laughed. They had never seen Douglas so concerned about a girl.  Marilynn, in particular, thought that the ordeal was funny. She remembered how Carita didn't want to be bothered with Douglas.

Around six that evening, most of the family members began to leave. Douglas wanted to spend some time alone with Carita.  She was scheduled to work the next morning but had taken Tuesday off so she and Whitley could take Douglas to the airport.

"Mama," Douglas said. "I really like Carita and I want to spend some time alone with her.  I'll be back in enough time to spend the rest of the evening with Mike and Ronnie."

Carita rented a small apartment on the hill.  It really was just enough space for one person but Douglas felt so at home with her.  He placed their wraps in the closest while Carita got glasses for the wine.  Douglas put on the dimmer lights to the lamps so they might be a little more comfortable.

Carita moved her face away. She did not want him to see the tears.  He had come along and changed her whole life in just a matter of weeks.  Now in less than forty-eight hours he would be gone to a foreign land.

Douglas gently turned her face to his lips and began to kiss the tears away. He fed her the wine so she would calm down.

"I can't believe that day after tomorrow you will be gone. You had to come along and just take my breath away didn't you?"

"Are you angry?" he asked.

She looked at him and said, "Hell yes. Now what will I do while you're gone.  What do I do when I want to touch you, hold you, and kiss you?" Suddenly, she broke into uncontrollable tears to the point that she began shaking and Douglas had to hold her tight.

He said, while softly brushing her hair behind her ear, "You'll think of all the precious moments that we had together and know that God is our father.  I will forever remember that you did not want a relationship, but I am thankful to God that he changed your mind. Carita, I think I love you and I know you love me. You have your job and I'm sure you have enough friends and activities to keep you busy. I will remember the smell of your perfume, the softness of your lips, and how bright your eyes light up when you get excited.

They held one another with short kisses in between sips of wine before he had to leave.

Carita got off work, left the office, and planned to spend some time with her best friend Shelly Stewart. Shelly, a little older than Carita, had moved from out of state. She had married a native from the area. Rod worked afternoons and had very little time to show Shelly around the valley. Of course being a native, he thought nothing of the small town and assumed Shelly should not have a problem finding her way around. She and Carita met at work and became fast friends. Shelly was like the older sister Carita never had. Shelly depended on Carita to help her learn her way around town. A time or two, Carita had to pick her up and show her how to get back home. Shelly was glad to see Carita for they had missed a couple of shopping dates. She fixed coffee so that the two could catch up on what was going on.

"I am so happy for you, Carita. The last couple of guys you dated didn't work out, but Douglas seems to be a nice guy and knows what direction he wants his life to go in."

Shelly had met Douglas when he had lunch with Carita and some of the gang from the office. She was very impressed with his plan of action for the future. She was just sad that Douglas was leaving for overseas because he seemed to have Carita's best interest at heart and the two had connected in a way that appeared breathtaking. Shelly could tell Carita was slightly upset and she understood.

"I seem to find nothing but losers," Carita alleged. "Then, Douglas Langston comes along and sweeps me off my feet. Now he has to leave. Isn't that nothing! And to think, I didn't want to be bothered with him. He's really a decent guy. How am I ever going to get to know him better?"

"You two will be writing and even though he probably won't call, sometimes one can express themselves better when feelings are written."

Carita agreed and began to tell her about the wonderful dinner Ms. Lee prepared and the other family members she met on Sunday. She shared with her friend all of the feelings she had for Douglas. She was wondering if her feelings were true or was she just fantasizing. She realized while talking with Shelly, Douglas was really a good guy. God willing, they may have a very bright future together. She had always planned to complete college and acquire her degree. That was one of the things she thought of doing too busy herself during his deployment. By this time, Carita and Shelly drank a pot of coffee. Carita told her she had to go. She knew Douglas would be calling soon.

As she arrived at home, the phone rang. Douglas called as promised.

"Hi babe. How are you? Remember, Whitley is going with us tomorrow. We don't want you driving alone from the airport. This is her address so write it down. You can pick her up on the way to get me."

Summit Hills was known for all of its snow and the airport was two hours away. As much as she wanted to be with him, she could not bring herself to ask him to come over.

At the sound of her voice, he also wanted to hold her in his arms.

"Babe," he said, "I'm going to finish playing this game of pool then come up to your place. I want to spend a little more time with you."

"But what about your friends?" she asked.

"They'll be alright. I'm not in love with them. I'm going to finish this game and I'm sure that I can be there within the next hour."

Carita had just finished showering and putting on her pajamas when the doorbell rang. As she looked through the peep hole, there stood Doug with a grin on his face. She quickly opened the door. He walked in and picked her up while giving her a quick kiss on the cheek. She held him so tight around his neck, he could hardly breathe. He wanted to surprise her as well as spend a little time with her before his departure.

He looked and said, "Please smile. I like to see your eyes light up when you do."

She honored his request but at the same time, she touched his lips with a silky kiss. He returned the kiss and held her as they walked to the living room. The living room comfortable with modern art told him Carita was compassionate as well as affectionate. He gathered her in his arms as he carried her to the bedroom, telling of his love for her. He just wanted to lie beside her and hold her in his arms. To him this was better than sex. They caressed one another while their kisses were amorous to the solicitous call of their bodies. Although they were both anxious to the call, they wanted to be considerate of one another. They had serene insight of the sensitivity that each held for one another. They hugged, kissed, talked, and shared their inner most feelings with each other.

He placed his arm around her, letting her know he not only liked her but he whispered in her ear "You are my love for a lifetime."

"And you my love are my knight in shining armor in this lifetime and the next. You are good, faithful and dependable; and we are one."

The time came for Douglas to leave. He knew Lee and Walter would be waiting for him. He kissed Carita and coddled her as though holding on for dear life. He left reluctantly while tears fell softly from her eyes.

Carita picked Douglas and Whitley up at nine o'clock in the morning. His plane scheduled to leave at one o'clock, gave them time to eat some lunch and check the bags. They talked about many things on the ride to the airport. Whitley told almost all of Douglas's childhood secrets.

Just as they finished lunch, it was time to walk Douglas to his departure gate. Whitley allowed them have a few more moments of privacy. As Douglas saw her eyes swelling, he stepped over to his sister and told her to take care of Carita. He reminded her that Carita would be good company until her baby came. He held onto both of his girls for a brief moment and then made his way to the gate.

# Chapter 2

After they watched Douglas leave for his gate, Whitley took her Kleenex and wiped Carita's eyes. "Don't cry Whitley said and then hugged her. She really seemed to be a big sister. The year will be gone before you know it, and he'll be back at home."

"I know. That's what everyone has been telling me," Carita replied, sniffling.

She smiled at Whitley as they walked back to the car. There was a forecast for snow and they wanted to get home so Ms. Lee didn't worry.

"I made you girl's dinner," Lee announced upon their arrival. "We know Whitley can eat any and every thing, at any time. And you, Carita Smallwood, I'm making sure you put something in your stomach. I know you are worried about Douglas but he'll be alright."

Lee learned from Douglas that Carita's favorite was fried chicken wings, so she prepared a few along with fried potatoes, onions, and green peppers. Whitley was particularly hungry, blaming it on the baby. Ronnie and Mike looked forward to spending some time with Carita. As a matter of fact, Ronnie asked her mom if Carita could spend the weekend with them. Walter thought it would be a good idea. When she helped Marilynn, she could just come upstairs and go to bed if she did not feel like driving home.

"Yes," said Ronnie. "You can sleep in my room. I have bunk beds. You can even use one of my drawers."

The family laughed as they explained to her that Carita was not moving in. After some dessert and more enjoyable conversation, Carita excused herself. She needed to go home to prepare for work. Lee kissed Whitley on the forehead and gave Carita a soft hug. She told both of the girls to be careful and to call when they got home.

Carita dropped Whitley off at her apartment as it was on her way then went home.

Shelly called and said, "I see that you have gotten back safely."

"Yes," Carita replied. "Oh, Shell I miss him already."

"I know, but you'll have plenty to do to make the year go quickly."

They talked about the ceramics class they were to join. Shelly told Carita it would fill some of her time while Douglas was away. Carita also crocheted. It had become another one of her favorite pastimes. She would experiment with different patterns to see how they would come out. Since Shelly did not know some of the stitches, Carita was glad to teach her. Shelly had five children to care for and, oftentimes, was all over the place – figuratively and mentally – for dropping them off at all of their different activities. When their conversation ended, the two girls decided to go shopping for yarn and patterns over the weekend as well as other items they might need to complete their projects.

After they hung up, Carita began to think about Douglas. She missed him. The very thought of Douglas made her wish she had been a little more friendly to him in the beginning of their relationship. She knew it would be a couple of weeks before she heard from him and it was all she could do to hold the tears back. She amazed herself for she had not felt this way about anyone. It was good to know that they had a rapport that was warm and understanding. She really wanted to be there for him as well as being a friend to his family.

Douglas was headed to Guam. He wondered what it would be like since this was his first trip out of the states. He laid back and thought of Carita. What a good time he had while home on furlough. She was warm, friendly, and understanding. It seemed as though his family liked her. He could only hope that she would stay in touch while he was gone and through letters, they might become better friends. She had told him that she would write and if there was anything he wanted she would try to accommodate him. This was good news to him as he needed someone he could depend on. Carita so far had seemed like a dream come true.

Shelly and Carita went shopping as planned on Saturday. They also looked at living room furniture. Shelly wanted to decorate her living room.

"I'm really tired of an empty living room and would like to at least have an idea of how to furnish it. Right now, the children's needs comes first so I guess the living room will have to continue to wait," Shelly disclosed.

"Why don't you look around and put a set in lay-a-way. If this is the suit and accessories you really like why take the chance of it being gone when you are able to afford it?"

Shelly thought that Carita's suggestion made perfect sense and considered the option. They continued their shopping and returned to Shelly's for a quick bite to eat.

After saying goodbye to Shelly and the children, Carita stopped at Lee's just to see how they were all doing. No one had heard from Douglas. She asked Ronnie if she wanted to spend the night with her. Ronnie was ecstatic at the thought of being with Carita and feeling like a big girl.

"Yes, yes, yes," she screamed. "Can we stop at the grocers and pick up some snacks?"

They stopped and bought hamburger, buns, chips, and soda. Carita told Ronnie they could make their own chocolate chip cookies. As soon as they got home, they sat down to plan their evening.

"What are we going to do first," Ronnie questioned.

"Don't you think we need to eat a little something? After all, I don't need your mother thinking I haven't fed you?"

They made cheeseburgers and toasted the buns. Carita made her special bake beans, one of Ronnie's favorites. She had a variety of condiments because her new little girlfriend seemed to like everything. After cleaning the dishes, they sat down to watch *"Charlie's Angels"* and *"Star Trek."* Before she knew it, Ronnie fell asleep. Carita decided they would bake the cookies the next day, allowing her to share them with Mike.

After a cheerful afternoon, Carita called Lee to let her know she was dropping Ronnie off. Carita had a short conversation with Lee and returned home to start a new afghan pattern. She thought that she might work on this from time to time and give the finish product to Douglas once he returned home.

Finally, after waiting for six weeks, she received a letter from Douglas telling her all about Guam. Guam was a territory of the United Sates located in the western Pacific Ocean. The weather there was generally hot and very humid with little seasonal temperature variation. The dry season ran from December through June. The remaining months, July through November, were considered the rainy season. He told her, in the letter, it should be fun. They had maneuvers in the jungle, not just for a day but weekends and two to three days at a time. He gave her fair warning that she may not hear from him from time to time. He went on to talk about some of the guys in his unit and the different parts of the country they were from. He told her that he missed home in particular his family. He went on to state that he missed her also. He said it was beneficial to be able to share his thoughts and dreams with someone who felt the same way. He did admit that Carita in her own way was like the other half of the puzzle. He liked the fact that she worked and believed in making her own money. He encouraged her in the letter to start back to school. She would be that much further ahead once he came home. He told her not to worry about him, but to keep the letters coming.

As Shelly predicated they begin to experience a better relationship through their letters. Letters from one another conveyed each one's confidences and expectations. They communicated the potentials of living a productive but cheerful life together, raising a family and always helping others. Each one's letter always closed with forever my love.

Carita dropped in on Lee to let her know she heard from Douglas and that he stated she would get a letter soon.

"Oh by the way, Whitley wants you to stop by," Ms. Lee said.

"Yes ma'am. I will stop in on my way home."

First, Carita wanted to stop by the store to purchase cards of inspiration and encouragement for Douglas and some humorous ones as well. She thought perhaps these things would keep him going and he would not have to think so much about home.

She stopped by Whitley's, as she promised Lee. She had not seen her since they had taken Douglas to the airport. She had gained a couple more pounds.

"Carita, Keith has to work midnight and we were wondering if you could stay with me over the weekend? Keith does not want me to be alone. This is my last month and anything could happen. Mama helps dad with the bar and it would be too much for her."

"It would be my pleasure," Carita said. "It will allow your parents to continue with their weekend schedule."

Carita finished work on Friday and gathered some of her crocheted items to complete while at Whitley's. Once she arrived, Whitley and Carita decided to gather baby clothes and put them away. With Whitley, everything had to be perfect. They had gone through babies' names, both boy's and girl's, and still did not have a clue what to call the child. Needless to say, the two young women had a wonderful weekend and got to know each better.

"Carita, you can spend the weekend anytime because the meal you prepared was delicious," Keith complimented. "Whitley does not feel like cooking so sometimes I miss out on some really good meals. Thanks."

Douglas continued to write, keeping Carita abreast on his living situation in Guam. She wrote him once a week and sent a card on the weekend. Douglas told her that he liked the idea of the cards. They broke the monotony of the letters. He often thought of Carita and the relationship she was building with his family. He prayed that everything would work out for he knew that he loved Carita and was planning to include her in his life. He knew that she had already gained the respect and love of his family.

Lee and Walter thought Carita was a very nice young woman. They saw her as respectful and very productive. Sometimes, she stopped by the bar to give them a hand. Lee and Walter wanted to do a weekend getaway and decided to ask Carita to stay with the children. As Whitley's due date drew near, Lee did not want to take the chance of Whitley staying with her siblings. Carita was delighted that Douglas's parents put so much trust and confidence in her.

"Carita," Walter said. "Why don't you make a list of everything you want or need for yourself and the children for the weekend? This way, you will not be running out to purchase extra items unnecessarily."

"That's a good idea," Lee voiced.

Walter gave Carita the money so that she, Mike, and Ronnie could select what food and other items they needed.

While shopping for their goodies, Carita ran into Ms. Eve Allen. She was an older woman that Carita had known since she was a child. They greeted one another with hugs and kisses. Carita knew Ms. Allen was good at tatting and making other fancy dollies.

"Carita, Carita Smallwood, is that you? Oh my, how pretty you look. I have not seen you in ages. How have you been?"

"Fine, Ms. Eve. It is so good to see you. How is the family and how have you been? I know that you are still doing everything in the church."

"Girl, yes. But you know how church folk are. They keep stuff going. But that's not what I want to talk to you about. You know that I tat, but my eye sight is not what it used to be. I desperately need something to do in my spare time. I understand you crochet. I wondered if you could teach me. I would be willing to pay you."

Carita smiled at Ms. Allen and said, "I could never charge you. I'll give you my number and, when it's convenient for you, call. We'll set something up. I am tied up this weekend doing a favor for friends of mine."

They exchanged phone numbers and Carita continued her shopping, picking up everything that the children might want or enjoy.

Mike and Ronnie were so excited that Carita was spending the weekend with them. Mike thought at last he would have Carita all to himself.

"Carita, will you play monopoly with me," Mike asked?

"Sure, but don't you think that we need to include Ronnie?"

"Well, I wanted to do something where it would be just you and me."

"Mike, that's being selfish. I'm friends with the both of you."

"Well, I guess you're right."

"See, I told you so. I knew Carita was friends with both of us Mike," Ronnie voiced. "Boys are so dumb."

They played board games and watched TV. Carita prepared very good meals, both days. She made enough on Sunday that Lee and Walter would have something to eat once they returned. After the three cleaned the kitchen, the phone rang. Carita answered, hoping nothing happened to the children's parents. The connection on the phone was terrible.

"Hello..." she said. "Hello, Hello."

As she kept saying hello, she could hear an echo. Then she heard the other party respond and thought she recognized the voice but it was hard to tell.

"Hello, hello mama?"

As she listened closely, she realized Douglas was on the other end. Apparently, he tried to surprise his mother but cherished the opportunity to hear Carita's voice.

"Carita, is that you? How are you? Where is mama?"

"She and your dad went on a weekend trip. I'm staying with the children... Doug?"

"Carita?"

Their conversation, such as it was, lasted only a few minutes before he faded. Carita just grew sick, but considered it a blessing to hear his voice.

The Langston's returned and felt quite refreshed. Lee hated she missed Douglas's call but was glad Carita got a chance to hear his voice. She knew that the two were more than just fond of one another.

Whitley called Carita at work to remind her that she was to spend the weekend with her. She mentioned that she had a couple of pains but the baby was not yet due. Carita assured her she would be there.

After the office closed, Carita stopped off at her apartment. She collected enough items for the two days so she would not have to return. She knew what Whitley's favorite munchies were and stopped at the store to pick up a few of them. Whitley gave Carita a sisterly greeting once she arrived.

"Here," Carita said, handing the bag of goodies to Whitley.

"What's this," she replied while looking in the bag?'

"Got to feed you and the urchin."

She laughed for she had missed Carita. They had become the best of friends.

Keith thought Whitley chose a very good person to befriend and perhaps they could ask Carita to be godmother for the baby.

Carita fried chicken wings, seasoned potatoes, and made a tossed salad for their early meal. They laughed at stories Whitley told and watched some TV.  Keith ate with them then took a nap before going to work. He left, praying Whitley would not deliver.

Early in the morning, Whitley came into Carita's room.

"Carita," she whispered in a concerned voice. "I'm all wet."

"Why?"

"I don't know."

"Has your water broken?"

"Please girl, I don't even know what that is?"

"Me either. Maybe we should call Ms. Lee."

"No, the bar closed a couple of hours ago and I don't want to disturb her."

Carita just looked at her strangely, not knowing what to do. They just sat up for a while talking.  All of a sudden, Whitley gave a big moan and Carita knew she was in labor.

"You're in labor and we need to call your mother," Carita exclaimed.

Even though Whitley asked Carita to wait, she ignored her request and called Ms. Lee.  Walter and Lee were there in what seemed to be a flash and the foursome reached the hospital in no time.  After all, this was their first grandchild.

All of a sudden Whitley asked, "Has anyone called Keith?"

Carita attained Keith's employer's number and left a message for him to get to the hospital as soon as possible. Three hours later, Whitley gave birth to eight pound, six ounce baby boy.  Carita spent the rest of the night with Douglas's parents.

Carita and Shelly continued to crochet and share their patterns with friends. Soon, they were making Afghans for everyone. Although they could have sold them, they made enough for Shelly's children. Carita gave Afghans to Michael and Ronnie as well as items for Whitley's son. Most of the Afghans were large enough to use as bedspreads and the girls gave them as presents.

Carita ran into Marilynn. They had not seen much of each other since she had finally acquired a position at a counseling firm and continued to assist her mother. She had been a drug counselor for a company in LA and wanted to stay in the same field. They exchanged niceties and made arrangements to meet for dinner and drinks. Marilynn was grateful to her Uncle Walter for allowing her to run a small business while seeking employment.

The most popular restaurant in town had always been Chellos's Café so the girls made plans to meet there for dinner.

"Girl, I'm so glad I ran into you. I hated not calling you but between working and taking care of mama, sometimes I don't know who I am."

"Marilynn, we're friends. You don't have to explain. I understand."

While sharing their experiences, Marilyn looked toward the door when a handsome man walked in. He stood 5'8" and his skin appeared as smooth as dark chocolate. His shoulders were broad and looked as though they would carry the weight of the world. His eyes were brown and large enough to notice everything. His hair was straight but in a kinky sort of way. His outfit was very becoming and he was impeccably dressed for a man. He walked toward Carita with his hand held out. She thought to herself, "who he is and what does he think he's doing?" As he approached their table, she recognized Harry Allen, Ms. Allen's son. She had not seen him in a while and did not know he remained in the area. Carita grabbed his hand, as he placed his arms around her and they exchanged smiles.

"Harry, Harry Allen. How are you? It is so good to see you."

"Ms. Carita Smallwood. You're still the prettiest girl in town."

They both kind of laughed because when they were children, they participated in a Tom Thumb wedding at the church. His mom, Ms. Eve never forgot and even had a picture of them at the event. She asked him to have a seat. Then, all of a sudden, a voice said, "She is pretty isn't she? She has to be the prettiest girl in town. Still going with Douglas?"

When Carita looked up, she saw Nate Jones.  She just smiled and introduced her friend.

"Marilynn, this is Harry Allen and Nate Jones."

"Pleased to meet both of you."

Harry offered to buy the girls a glass of wine and, even though they declined, he bought it anyway.  Harry smiled as he looked at Carita.

"You're still the best looking girl on earth."

Carita laughed. "The restaurant is either too dark or you need glasses."

"I'll say," Nate agreed.  "Are you still going with Douglas Langston," he asked again with a smirk on his face.

"I didn't know that Douglas had gone overseas.  I was in that area when I was out of the country," Harry explained.  It can be a monster.  If you get worried because you haven't heard from him just let me know and I will fill you in."

Carita smiled, letting Harry know she accepted his offer.  After all, Douglas's phone call did not help matters any.

Meanwhile, Nate asked Marilynn to dance but kept his eye on Carita. He obviously found her attractive.  Douglas has not changed he thought to himself.  He always had good luck with the women.  By the time, Marilynn and Nate had finished their dance Harry's party arrived.  He kissed Carita on the cheek and told her how good it was to see her.

"How was your dance with Nate?"

"It would've been alright if he hadn't asked so many questions about you."

"Me?"

"Yes you," she said. "This dude has some type of fixation on you.  It's weird."

"Wow," Carita cried.

They both laughed since both thought he was not all of that.  He appeared to be different from Douglas and Harry.  Neither one of the girls could understand why he was with Harry.  The girls continued to enjoy their evening, watching the patrons and dancing when asked.  They promised to stay in touch and to get together whenever possible.

Carita had not seen the family since she and Ronnie had gone on a two week vacation to visit her Aunt Anne but continued to call and check in. She always let them know she was available whenever needed. No one had heard from Douglas but Carita had continued to send letters and cards.

Ms. Eve Allen finally called Carita. She had some projects at church that she wanted to complete before she got into doing her own thing. Ms. Eve was on the deaconess board, the missionary board, and was a church mother. She was a very busy woman. Harry and his sister Helen were both still at home. Helen had two more years of high school to complete. Ms. Eva treated them both like babies, honoring their every demand.

"Carita, I'm sorry that it took me so long to get in touch with you. Are you still available to teach me how to crochet?"

"Of course, Ms. Allen. When would you like to get started?"

"I thought if you come by on Thursday, you could have dinner with us since you will not let me pay you."

Carita agreed and Ms. Allen was glad they could get started with her lessons. Harry was happy to see Carita once again and asked how Douglas was doing. She explained that no one had heard from him in the last two weeks. "Well," Harry said, "there all types of maneuvers he may be on. His unit might be scheduled to deploy as part of contingency operations or to a hostile fire area. In order to be precise, they would have to have life surviving skill technique module agendas."

He went on to explain other programs but it all went over Carita's head.

After dinner, Carita showed Ms. Eve the simple step of the chain.

"Ms. Eve, this particular stitch is called a chain. This is how all of your crocheted items begin. Now, you try it."

She had Ms. Allen practice the chain stitch until she returned. Twice a week Carita would go by the Allen's to help Ms. Eve with her crocheting. Although she could not read patterns, she was an excellent student. The more Carita went to the Allen's, the better friends she and Harry became. He continued to explain the maneuvers Doug was on and how tired he might be.

Carita continued to teach Ms. Eve several crochet stitches. On one of Carita's visit, Ms. Eve mentioned that Harry's car stopped running and since his father did not drive, there was no need for him to own a car. That made going to the store and taking care of other household chores difficult for Ms. Allen.  Carita offered her car until his was repaired.

"Ms. Allen, Harry is welcome to use my car to get you around.  While I am at work, it sits in the parking lot anyway.  Since Harry works midnight, I would like to be able to help out.  If he picks me up after work on time, you all can use my car.  I hate waiting for a ride."

Carita picked Harry up in the morning so he could help his mother with completing the payments of monthly household finances and other items that needed attention.  Harry and Carita became the best of friends.  One evening while helping Ms. Eve with her crocheting, Harry came home from a date early.  Harry told Carita that the girls in town did not have anything going for themselves and he was tired of the same old same old.  Carita mentioned that she had a couple of girlfriends, who lived in Berkley, just across the county line.  She had attended the University of Ashford there and remained in touch with several of the girls.  She knew one of them was not dating anyone special and offered to introduce her.  Carita got in touch with her friend from college and made arrangements for her to meet Harry.

They met Harry at the café and the three enjoyed a light snack.  Carita made her excuses so the couple might be able to continue their rendezvous without a third party.

Marilynn called Carita and asked to meet at the café.  The girls were conversing and sipping on a glass of wine when Nate Jones entered.  He sat next to Carita and began to flirt.

"Oh yea," he said.  "You'll fit nicely.  You can be my woman.  What do you need with Douglas?  After all, he can't do for you like I can.  He's out of the country."

She just looked at him like he had lost his mind.  He went on to say other inappropriate things to Carita, which were uncalled for.  Her behavior did not warrant such dialogue.

"I don't know what rock you climb from underneath, but you need to go back, because I am not the one."

"Oh," he said, "you think you're all of that? Well, one day, you'll see."

Carita just waved her hand, and retorted, "Poof be gone!"

The other customers at the bar laughed at him.

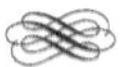

Carita continued to check with Douglas's family and visited as much as she could. The year flew by. Christmas was rapidly approaching.

"What would you like for Christmas, Ronnie?" Carita asked.

"There are a lot of things I would like."

"You can only choose one."

"And you, Mike?"

"I would like some trucks and cars."

Carita managed to find the items both children requested and picked up some things for the baby as well. She decided to bake cookies and send them to Douglas. She knew he liked board games so she picked up a couple of them. She also took her chances to find some summer items she could send. After completing the shopping for the Langston's and mailing Douglas's box, she began to shop for her family and friends.

About a week before Christmas, a special delivery package came for Carita. She had to claim it at the post office. Once she got home, she opened it. Douglas sent her a beautiful, white gold Seiko wristwatch accompanied with a beautiful card. It was simply gorgeous. His card explained with the watch she could now watch the hours, minutes and seconds for his return.

Carita saved all of the letters and cards from Douglas. From time to time, she read them all. She tried to imagine his voice. In the depths of the night and darkness, she tried to pretend he was near and his lips were next to hers melting her soul like wax on a candle in the heat of the night. Her eyes were teary. She missed Douglas so much. God knows it took all her energy just to stay busy because it was such a small town. She did not want anyone assuming that she was unfaithful. She knew in her heart that she loved this man. She put the letters away and snuggled down to a peaceful sleep.

*Chapter 3*

Christmas had come and gone. The holidays were enjoyable. Douglas wrote that he had received his box and was very thankful. She thought Douglas would have written a little more often but she always kept in mind what Harry told her. She didn't see Ms. Eve that much because the weather had been bad. Summit Hills was in the middle of the state's "Snow Belt" and it was no joke. You were lucky to get to work or anywhere for that matter.

She called Ms. Lee as often as she could to let her know she had heard from Douglas and he was doing well. Whenever possible, she stopped to see Whitley, Keith, and the baby. Carita was excited about Douglas's coming home within the upcoming months but the family did not seem to share her enthusiasm.

She arranged to meet Marilynn at the local bar to get her opinion on a surprise party for Douglas. The girls were having a drink when Carita noticed Nate Jones' presence. He came over to speak to them. He gave Carita a wink then spoke.

"You don't like me very much do you?"

"It's not that," Carita replied. "I go with Douglas and you know that. I don't understand why you keep insisting you and I get together."

"You don't know what you are missing," he said. "I'm just as good as Douglas. You think that he is all of that. You'll see when he gets home!" He then walked off in anger.

"He sure has a hell of a lot of issues about you and Douglas," Marylyn said. "I would not put anything pass him."

"I know," Carita said then quickly changed the subject. "What do you think about a surprise party for Douglas, when he gets home?"

"I don't know. You should ask my aunt to see if she has anything planned. She may want to do a family thing."

"You're right. I didn't think about that. It's just that the family has not been very receptive toward me lately and I don't know why. They're your family. Do you know something that I don't?"

"Stop it Carita. You're my best friend. If I knew something I would tell you. I think that it's your imagination. The family loves you. Maybe you're letting Nate get into your ear."

They both laughed and enjoyed the rest of their drink. The girls went their separate ways, promising to get together before Douglas got home.

Carita thought about asking Ms. Lee about a party for Douglas but, since she felt the family seemed to be so different toward her, she elected not to make bad matters worse. In any case, she pondered over the idea too long and before she realized it, two months had passed. Douglas's last letter indicated the day and approximate time of his arrival and even if he didn't call, she was first on his agenda and to be ready for a romantic evening.

The time had finally arrived for Douglas to come home. All day long at work, Carita kept thinking of his arrival and their romantic evening. She and Marilynn purchased several new outfits in preparation for the home-coming. Carita left work in a hurry. She didn't even say goodbye to Shelly. She wanted to shower and put on her very best before his arrival. She carefully groomed herself and put on his favorite perfume. She set the living room to hold passions in the air, as the red wine on the stand with crystal glasses awaited its amorous solution. Her last letter from Douglas carried love and passion, stating that he would be at her beck and call. He led Carita to believe an ardent evening would be in their favor. She imagined what he looked like and what he would say. She dreamed of his lips touching hers. Carita had sipped a small bit of wine while awaiting Douglas's arrival but he had not come or called. He devastated her. It was too late call Lee's house or Whitley for that matter. She put away the wine and made ready for bed as she had to go to work the next day.

Upon her arrival, Shelly waited for her in the break room. Shelly knew something had to be wrong. Carita's eyes appeared dark and swollen like she did not rest well.

"You okay?" Shelly questioned with the concern of a big sister.

Carita looked at her with tear-filled eyes and said, "He never came or called. I don't know what happened."

"Oh Carita," said Shelly. "I am so sorry. I just knew you all were together last night. That's why I didn't call."

"Come on," she said. "Let's get your face cleaned. We don't need everyone knowing your business."

They went to their respective areas for work and promised to meet for lunch.

Through the entire meal, Shelly and Carita could not come up with any reason that Douglas would not call or come over as promised. As they neared the end of the hour, Shelly suggested Carita call the house to see if she could talk with Douglas.

"Hi Ms. Lee. How are you?"

"Fine, Carita, and you?"

"I'm fine. Is Douglas around?"

"I'm sorry. You just missed him. He went to shoot a game of pool."

Carita hung the phone up feeling hurt and disappointed. She could not understand what was going on. She had been loyal and faithful yet Douglas and his family acted as though she was no longer a part of their lives.

She left work hoping to hear from him. The end of the week approached and she still had not heard from Douglas. She decided to call Marilynn.

"Hi Marilynn. How are you?"

"Fine, what's up?"

"Marilynn, I haven't heard or seen Douglas since he's been home."

"What! Are you serious?"

"I thought you might be able to give me some insight to what may be going on. The family has not exactly been cordial towards me."

"Oh Carita, I'm so sorry. I know that he is not dating or seeing anyone. I really don't know what's going on. Why don't you meet me at the bar and we can talk."

She left the apartment, drove up the main street in town and stopped at the neighborhood bar. Upon entering, she saw Marilynn and felt a little more comfortable. She looked around then spotted Douglas in the corner. He was talking to a group of guys. When he saw Carita, he walked over and kissed her.

"Hey babe. It's good to see you," he said with a smile.

"I can't tell," she replied with a blank look.

"Let me buy you two ladies a drink."

Despite having a drink in front of her, Marilynn quickly took him up on his offer. Carita politely refused. Douglas looked very surprised.

"Why don't you want me to buy you a drink?"

"Because I am capable of buying my own" she answered.

"Carita," he said, "Please don't be this way."

"What way is that?" she responded.

He knew he could not beat her at this game. Her vocabulary and clichés were absolutely exceptional. Instead, he bent down and kissed her again. "Let's get out of here."

Douglas and Carita drove to a small suburb of the city to have dinner. He told her about his experiences overseas and again thanked her for all of the trinkets she sent. She nodded her head.

"Why are you so quiet? What's wrong," he asked as he took her hand. He thought she would be thrilled to be with him.

She gently pulled away and responded, "Don't you think I should be asking you that question? After all, you were the one who wrote and told me how, when, and where we were going to be together. Now all of a sudden, I don't count. Why didn't you get your friends to write you and send the items you requested?"

It took him a moment to respond. "Please," he answered, "I don't want to argue. I just want to be with you and show you how much I missed you."

Although still hurt, she decided to let it go. The whole situation seemed to no avail.

Douglas felt upset himself. He never meant to hurt Carita and couldn't stand to see her in this state. It's just that, when a man comes home from being away for a year, everyone has so much to tell him about his girl. He was confused. He stopped at a small but quaint restaurant so they could order dinner. He calmed her down by telling stories of his experience over-seas and shared with her the places he had gotten a chance to see. He wanted to be with her but did not know how she would feel after their din-ner. She still did not have a big appetite and ate very little. He didn't know if she was still upset or not very hungry.

Since Carita seemed to be back to her old self, he said, "Carita, do you think we can spend some time together after we finish our dinner? I can stop and pick up a bottle of wine for us to enjoy."

He wanted to hold her in his arms, something he constantly thought about doing for an entire year. He knew she was good and kind and in his corner. He touched her arms as they drove. Her quietness bothered him. She smiled like she usually did when pleased. Somehow, he knew all was well. They stopped at a lodging house they stayed in before he left. Douglas helped Carita out of the car being careful not to drop the bottle of wine.

Carita noticed his awkwardness as he tried to guide her footsteps in the snow. It was all she could do to keep from laughing.

"I wish you could see yourself. You look like a cartoon trying to walk on ice."

They both laughed.

Once inside, she closed the drapes while Douglas hung up their wrap. He turned on the TV to break the tension between the two. Carita moved from the window to sit on the bed and he gently tugged at her arm then placed her on his lap as he sat in a chair. He poured a glass of wine for them to share. He took a sip then placed the glass to her lips. He pulled her face to his.

"You know I would never hurt you, don't you?" he softly said. "You mean too much to me."

"If you didn't want to hurt me, why didn't you call or come by when you returned home? Why did it take me going by a bar for you to acknowledge me?"

Douglas didn't know what to say. He thought he loved Carita and felt he could trust her. He couldn't let her know that Nate had poured out some negative venom about her as did other so called friends who co-signed Nate's statements. He didn't know how to respond. Everyone had so much to say to about her, most of it negative, when he returned that he really didn't know whom or what to believe.

He gave her a tender kiss while caressing her body.

"I don't know, Carita.  Everyone always has so much to say about your girl when you return home.  I've missed you, Carita, and I want to be with you."

He held her tightly, as though she would leave him.  Her hands begin roam through his hair.  He carried her to the bed and began to tell her again how much he missed her.

He blew her hair back from her eye with his warm breath.  How long it had gotten.  He gazed upon her as though she was a piece of chocolate.  He had longed for this moment.  Carita stroked his face and beheld what she had longed for the whole year.  She kissed his neck while unbuttoning his shirt and slid it onto the bed.  Her hands timidly loosened his belt as he slipped her top over her head.  He placed her on the bed and caressed her hips as his lips were smoothly brushing other parts of her body.  His mouth watered as he gazed upon her breasts.  She rubbed his chest and her hands massaged the most inner part of him. Their lips meet and drew the satisfaction of love while their bodies intertwined and received one another as the two lost souls they were.  Carita and Douglas embraced each other for what seemed like a lifetime.

While Carita slept, Douglas wondered about the things Nate Jones insinuated. Nate led Douglas to believe Carita had been somewhat promiscuous; leading him to believe she had slept with other men during his tour.  He wondered if Nate had been one of them.  Even though he looked to his sister and other family members for advice they could only give him accounts of town gossip.  The next morning, Douglas dropped Carita off at home so she could get ready for work.  He stopped at his mom's to let her know he was fine.  He kept the car as he had some errands to run.  He told Carita he would pick her up promptly when she got off.  They met the gang, went bowling, and ended the evening at Earl's playing Bid Whist.  Everyone chipped in for a couple of pizzas and other snack foods.

Carita really thought they were an item and assumed the relationship was back on track; for their expression of love and harmony left them both with an amorous disposition but to her surprise she did not see much of Douglas during his leave. There was always an excuse: the fellows, Lee, or his siblings. She had no choice but to let it go. She did have dinner with the family but felt odd. The eagerness she once received seemed absent.

"Ronnie and I will do the dishes," Carita volunteered.

"That's okay," Ms. Lee replied. "We'll get them later."

She picked the baby up and Whitley made an excuse that he needed to be changed. Carita offered but Whitley took the baby out of Carita's arms. She tried very hard to enjoy their company and eventually made her excuses to leave. She kissed Douglas and told him she would see him later.

She decided to drive out to Shelly's. She felt too disheartened to go home. Together she and Shelly tried once more to figure out why Douglas's change of heart but could not come up with any reason for his change of attitude. From that point on, Carita never saw Doug. If she called, he was never available. Two days before his deployment to western United States, Douglas phoned her as if there was nothing wrong. Carita listened to his dishonesties until he got to the real reason for his call. He wondered if she would take him to the airport. Again, she listened to his deceptions.

"You have been home for thirty days and for some reason, you found excuses not to spend quality time with me. I suggest that those people you spent time with assist you in catching your flight."

She politely hung up the phone, laid on her bed, and cried herself to sleep. She wanted to see him one more time but she just couldn't.

Douglas felt very badly, for he cared for Carita. But there had been so many rumors about her that he did not know what to believe. He thought about when he approached Harry, who admitted that Carita had been to his house more than once.

"Listen man, I don't know what you've heard," Harry said, "but Carita was teaching mama to crochet and came by a couple times a week. She and I became better friends and to my knowledge she has never done anything to disrespect her relationship with you. She and mama became closer friends and she has helped Helen better understand some of the things about life that mama is trying to teach her. She has been a good friend to my whole family."

When Douglas asked his mother for advice, she told him to just leave the situation alone, that it would all work out. She knew Douglas had been talking to Nate, so she questioned why he would lie on Harry or Carita for that matter. After all, he had all gone to school with Douglas and Harry and she didn't feel Nate was capable of telling a lie just to ruin someone's reputation.

Douglas left without any further communication to Carita. It absolutely devastated her. Her distress of losing Douglas, for whatever the reason, shattered her spirit. She ended up catching the flu and had to take a week off work to build her immune system back up. She tried to call Whitley and ask about Douglas but she was always busy with the baby. Lee remained very cordial over the phone but not very eager to share information. Shelly did what she could for her friend but her best was not enough. Carita did more crying than she did thinking.

As Douglas accepted post at his new base, he had a lot of time to think about Carita. He worked second shift and there was very little action. Why would Nate, his friend, just talk and talk about Carita. He could not figure that out. His negative opinions about her warranted no positive evidence. He found nothing to be true while home. Her helping Ms. Allen didn't prove anything. He thought for a minute. Douglas knew her birthday was coming and decided to give her a call to try and smooth things out. He felt in his heart that he loved her.

It was about midnight and he wanted to say "Happy Birthday" for the whole day so he decided to call her about one in the morning. She answered to phone in a soft groggy voice. He immediately felt badly, knowing he had awakened her.

"Hi Baby," he said. "Happy Birthday!"

"Doug," she said.

"Yes honey," he replied. "How are you?"

"Why do you care? To what do I owe this phone call?"

"It's your birthday and I wanted you to have a happy birthday."

"Really," she responded.

"Carita," he said, "are you mad at me?"

"What you do think," she said?

"Maybe I shouldn't have called."

"Maybe you shouldn't have," she replied and hung up the phone.

She felt so hurt that she had hung up on Douglas. But why call, if you didn't care, she thought. Carita got up, for there was no returning to sleep. She cried. She had prayed to hear from Douglas. She knew she loved him and now she had blown the only chance available to share her feelings.

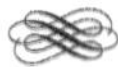

Carita, who was not herself at all, concerned Shelly. She decided to the call Marilynn to solicit her help. Marilynn told Shelly how Nate approached Carita a couple of times, making nasty statements about Douglas. She also conveyed the threat he had made. All of a sudden, Shelly figured it out. Nate Jones liked Carita and was jealous of her and Douglas. That was the reason for all of Douglas's misconception, she reasoned.

The girls got together for dinner to celebrate Carita's birthday, hoping Carita felt better. They talked about life and men.

Carita said, "Speaking of men… Doug called last night."

She shocked both of her friends. She went on to tell them about their conversation and how she hung up on him. Shelly looked at her in a way that she only could.

"Are you crazy! All of this crying over him and you hung up?"

Marilynn laughed. "Tell the truth, Carita. You were high off some wine."

Carita looked at the girls. "No, I just didn't know what to do or say to him. He spent very little time with me. His family isn't really talking to me, and I have missed my period."

"What!" Shelly and Marilyn exclaimed.

"Well," Shelly said, "with the flu that you had, and the depression, it's enough to send your body into that type of cycle that you would miss."

"No," Carita responded. "I have already checked with a doctor and the test came back positive. I'm pregnant."

"Well, you've got to tell him," Shelly exclaimed.

"How," Carita exclaimed. "I don't have a phone number or even an address?"

Marilynn, who paid close attention to the conversation, spoke up. "Wait a minute. You mean to tell me you hung up on this man without securing a number or an address, knowing you might be pregnant?"

"Dumb, hum," Carita said.

"I'll say," Marilynn replied.

"Let's just finish our dinner and sleep on this," Shelly suggested.

Carita left the café, saying to herself, "Well, this part is over with." She did not know how she was going to tell her two best friends about her stupid mistake. Now, she just had to worry about her family and Douglas. She knew her grandmother would look at her neck area in the front, see a second heart beat, and say, "She's pregnant." She was not really concerned about the rest of the family. Douglas, she just did not know how she would handle him. How could she get the name of the base? If she only knew the state? She pondered all night long over the situation. She finally decided that, if she went to a recruiter, they would have to know where all the bases are located. She worked a half a day to accomplish this task. The recruiter seemed very helpful. He secured an address for the base, through Douglas's serial number, as well as a telephone number. Now, she just had to think about how she planned to tell him. She called the number the recruiter gave her. The base operator on duty happened to be a friend of Douglas's. He remembered Douglas talking about Carita and mentioned that he did not know how he was going to apologize for all of mistakes he made during his leave. He took the liberty of introducing himself and told Carita he would be glad to help her get in touch with Douglas. They both worked second shift that week, so he called the tower.

Douglas happened to answer and the operator conveyed the message that Carita was on the other line. He smiled as he connected the lines so the couple could talk. He beamed as he felt good about helping a friend. Douglas was so glad to hear from Carita.

"Douglas, how are you?"

"Fine and you. Baby, I am sorry I upset you the last time we talked. Is it cold at home? Carita, I regret that I did not spend quality time with you.

I don't know what got into me. It's just that so many people had so much to say about you that I didn't know what to believe. How are you really?

"Yes, I know," she said. "I'll bet that one of the things said was that I was going with Harry."

Yes," Douglas said slowly.

"I was assisting Ms. Eve in learning how to crochet. Harry and I had become better friends as he would explain what maneuvers you might be on when I did not hear from you. I also lent him my car when his was being repaired so Ms. Eve could take care of the family business."

Douglas tried to apologize for all that happened while he was at home.

Carita just listened. She finally said, "I need to see you."

"Babe," he replied. "I can't come home. I was just there. I will have to build more leave and by that time, it will be time for me to be discharged."

Carita let him know she understood. Then she said, "What if I come to visit you?"

"Oh Re-Re, would you? That would be wonderful," he said.

"Can you do me a favor," she asked?"

"Anything, babe."

"Let's not tell anyone. Can we let it be our secret?"

He agreed.

Carita could not tell him over the phone.

She shared her conversation with Shelly and Marilynn. They were both happy to see her smile once again and thought it was a good idea that she did not mention the pregnancy over the phone. She was also advised by the two to avoid saying anything to anyone, not even her family.

Since the trip was in two weeks, Marilynn offered to help her pack and see if new clothing items needed to be purchased. Shelly offered to lend her any money.

After packing some things, the phone rang. It was Douglas. He seemed to be calling more often than Carita expected and she wondered why.

"Hey, babe. How are you? You'll be here soon. I'll be so glad to see you."

"I'll be glad to see you as well."

They talked a little about his job and he told her about the weather so she would bring the proper clothing. Douglas had called a couple of times just to check on her but Carita felt there was something he was not telling her. He told her how much he loved her and would be so glad to see her. It was then that she decided to tell him about the pregnancy. After he listened, he told her it was best for her to come west so they could talk.

Although he knew he loved Carita, after they ended the call, he worried about what people might think or say and chose to call his favorite girl, Lee, to get her opinion. His mom told him it was rumored that Carita was pregnant, and of course town speculation alleged the child to be Harry Allen's. She advised him to do what he thought was best.

Before you knew it, the two weeks had passed. Carita tried to be excited about her trip but was very apprehensive about Douglas's attitude. Her flight seemed to take forever. Douglas was on time and glad to see her. He hugged and kissed her and asked how she felt. Some of the guys he worked with had planned a picnic and wanted them to come. They stopped at the baggage claim only to find Carita's baggage had been lost and might not be in until the next evening. Carita became distressed. She had no clean clothes to change into, much less anything to sleep in. Douglas calmed her down and stated they would have to go shopping and purchase a few items.

The town was very small and dusty. After all, they were in the middle of the dessert. By the time they shopped and got to the hotel room, Carita was really too exhausted to participate at a party. She didn't want to disappoint Douglas so she put her best foot forward. She felt fortunate that she had her make up in a small carry on case. These days, it was difficult for her keep color in her face.

Everyone at the party was very kind and accommodating. Some of the women knew Douglas had to work and offered to pick Carita up from the hotel to keep her company until he got off. He had made arrangements to work days during her stay.

Douglas began to see Carita was somewhat tired and sleepy so he made their apologies in order to get her in the bed. Once they got back to the hotel room, he helped her remove her clothes. He could see her back seemed to be bothering her and offered to give her a massage. She had thrown a light robe on to maintain a little privacy. He rubbed her back ever so softly while kissing her neck and brushing her hair. He tried telling her how much he cared but he was now fighting feelings he never felt before. He had mistreated this woman and now she prepared to have his child. What did he tell her? What did he do? The feelings were there but he was not in the position to take care for a family and was afraid to face the rumors of paternity. He held her in his arms rocking her back and forth until she was sound asleep. He watched her tiny body as she moved in the bed toward him and again he gathered her in his arms for what might be the last time. "I wonder," he said to himself, "if it will be a boy or girl and who would it look like."

Somehow, it did not matter, for he had to share with her that marriage was out of the question.

# *Chapter 4*

Carita returned home wounded and upset. She never thought she would have a baby much less to have to raise one alone. For some reason, she did not fear the responsibility. She just wanted to be a good mother. Mama, as all of the grandchildren called their grandmother, had raised her and her sister in the church. Teaching the girls to pray and ask God was always the first order of business in mama's house. "He was the only true love that any of us should have and that we could always depend on him" her mama preached. Mama was always right and Carita believed in prayer and faith. She didn't even hate Douglas. She just hated what he had become. Shelly and Marilynn were still her best friends of course and were there for her.

"Carita, what really happened" asked Shelly? "Did you all have an argument or what?"

"No.  All I know is that he told me marriage was out of the question. He did not have the means to care for a wife and child.  He also mentioned that he was not at all sure about my feelings for him, particularly when he was gone."

"What is that supposed to mean," cried Marilynn.  "I wonder what that dam Nate Jones told Douglas."

"What in the world are you talking about, Marilynn?"

"Well," Marilynn conveyed, "Nate said some things in anger about you're not going out with him in the past that did not make sense at the time.  He appeared to have a jealousy for Douglas, like an obsession.  He said you would be sorry for not giving him the opportunity of dating him. Shelly just figured out that he was jealous of you and Doug."

"Oh my goodness Carita whimpered.  I think that you all are right. But you know what?  If Doug wants to believe someone that is nobody than there is nothing I can do about it.  If he didn't trust me when he was over-seas than he will never trust me."

Carita passed the time by crocheting baby Afghans and baby bunnies. From time to time-to-time, the girls got together at the café to catch up on things and suggest baby names.  Shelly even gave Carita a beautiful shower lun-cheon with their coworkers, Marilynn, and some members of Carita's family.

Carita was at the end of her time and the baby was due any day. Shelly could not style her hair for the office Christmas party and asked Carita to help her out.  Carita had a light supper with the family and began work-ing on Shelly.  When Carita completed her task, Shelly looked like she had stepped out of *"Vogue"* magazine.  Shelley's husband took Carita home but was somewhat nervous about doing it.

"Listen, Carita, when are you due?"

"I'm overdue," she exclaimed.

He shrieked, "Don't have that baby in my Mercedes Benz."

The three of them just laughed at his warning.

Once Carita arrived at her grandmother's, she sat in the rocking chair in her grandma's room. Shortly after, she felt wetness between her legs.  Not knowing her water broke, she continued to rock until she moaned.

"Are you in labor child," she asked?

"I think so," replied Carita.

Mama was quick to get on her feet.  She immediately called the other members of the family so they could get Carita to the hospital.  She went directly to delivery and the medical staff called her doctor. Carita slipped in and out of consciousness. She could not remember the day or much less the season.  She did however remember it was very early morning when the family got her to the hospital.  By eleven that morning, the baby still had not arrived. All of a sudden, she heard Nat King Cole singing *Chestnut Roasting over an Open Fire."*  It's the Christmas season but what day, she thought. The nurse checked on her periodically, maintaining she could not give her anything for pain.  She remained in labor twelve hours to no avail.  Carita, in excruciating pain, began to pray.

"Lord, if you help me out of this, I promise you will not have to worry about seeing me in another labor and delivery room again in life."

The doctor came in the late afternoon and told Carita she would be receiving a C-section as the baby did not want to come on its own. He was breach. "Thank you Jesus," she thought. Prayer does change things. The doctors delivered the baby at 5:03 p.m. He weighed seven pounds thirteen ounces. She named him Todd.

All of her family was there to congratulate her. She felt a little foreign as some of the family members, younger than she, already had children. Some of her friends' children were already going to day care, only proving she was still a late bloomer. Feeling pleased, she thought, "Douglas, you should be here too. You would be so proud of this baby," she said to herself. He looks just like you. He just has my nose and my mouth.

Mama had called Shelly, early in the morning, to let her know Carita was in the hospital. Marilynn and Shelly went to see their friend and Mama had given the family instructions to allow Carita and the girls their privacy.

Carita stayed with Mama for the next two months. Childbirth left her in no shape to care for the little one alone. She waited in anticipation for she knew that someone would call Douglas and or his family to tell about the baby and perhaps he would call. All of her wishing and loving Douglas, he never got in touch. She heard, through several friends, he was home. She went about her daily chores of taking care of Todd and cleaning the apartment. Twice a week, she took the baby to visit her grandparents.

After returning home from one of her visits, her phone rang.

"How are you doing" Douglas asked? After a long silent period, he said. "Carita, I would like to come see the baby. When will you be available?"

This shocked Carita but she was glad he took some interest in his child and asked about his schedule. Together they made arrangements for him to come to the apartment. His greeting felt strange, for the rapport they built had vanished. He gave her a warm "hi" while she took his coat. Timidly she brought Todd to him to hold. He fussed over him and even talked to him.

"Carita," he asked, "where's the diapers? The baby needs changed."

Carita took all the items he would need to the living room, while she prepared a small dinner and invited Douglas to stay. He politely declined.

She sensed he would not stay. She heard rumors he was dating Dena, a girl he dated before he met her.

"Before you go, Carita said nervously, we need to discuss your responsibility to this baby. I know you thought he wasn't yours and now you've seen him… I don't know, what you think?"

Douglas just looked at her in amazement. It wasn't like Carita to say very much. He gazed at her and said, "I don't know what to do, so you can do whatever you want."

"Please, Carita begged, this is something we should be able to work out together.

After all, Todd did not get here by himself."

Douglas agreed to meeting and making an arrangement for support. He is parents had an attorney and he would seeveneee visited the baby a couple of more times and Carita even dropped the baby off to Douglas so he could spend quality time with his father as well as his grandparents.

It was nice to be able to care for her son during the winter months. She only had to go out for a few groceries for the baby and household products. Carita had gone back to work and asked a cousin to babysit Todd. She had learned, through the grapevine, her job was being eliminated. She knew she would have to look for employment.

Over the next year, she gave the baby and her job most of her attention. Even though she heard less and less from Douglas, she still loved him. Eventually, she heard he planned to marry Dena. She felt crushed but wished him the best of luck, never telling him how much she cared for him.

Carita was planning a small birthday party for Todd. She could hardly believe a year had passed. She had not heard from Douglas in several months when he phoned and requested they get together to talk. They met at the café much to his disapproval. He kissed Carita on the cheek when she arrived.

He had taken the liberty of ordering sandwiches for the both of them. He knew from past experiences that Carita never ate much and if she was focused on other things she would skip meals. Carita thanked him but declined saying, she lacked an appetite. He looked very frustrated. He didn't quite know how to approach her. This was to have been the love of his life and once again he had to disappoint her.

"Carita," he said, "I'm getting married."

"I know," she replied.

He looked as though he did not know what to say next.

"Well, I'm hoping that we can still remain friends," he said.

She glared at him and said, "You hope we can remain friends? When were we ever friends? We had to end up in court in order for you to do the right thing and you call that being friends. You're marrying someone that you told me hurt you very deeply. Why? You don't have to worry about Todd because he has a mother who can be mother and father. And just so you know, the first thing Dena is going to do… that is her name isn't it… is have a baby for you just because I have Todd. I wish you happiness and the best of luck."

She left so abruptly that she almost ran into the waitress. She could hardly see how to get to her car. Douglas ran behind her because he knew he hurt her. He didn't want her driving that upset. She sped off in spite of his efforts to stop her.

The years went by quickly and Carita put forth great effort to be a good mother. She had moved to Somerset, a small suburb, and enlisted Todd into programs where he would learn to interact with other children as well as being exposed to different cultures and ideas. She helped him with his homework and read to him before bedtime. She was a hard worker and with her two years of college, managed to acquire positions that generated good salaries along with the responsibility of managing others. Each job Carita attained paid more than its predecessor, allowing her to move into better neighborhoods.

Tessa, Carita's younger cousin's daughter would sometimes spend the weekend with them. She and Todd became very close. They went skating together and sometimes Carita took them to the movies. They went to Sunday school and would join Carita for morning service when she arrived.

Carita only heard from Douglas through his support payments. She heard he was going to school and applauded him for it. It was the one thing she wanted to complete but had not quite gotten around to it.

Douglas, on the other hand, wondered about Carita. He knew, deep in his heart, he still carried feelings for her. He wanted so very much to call just to hear her voice. But since his marriage was not going as planned he thought better of the idea. He didn't want to hurt Carita any more than he had already. He decided to further his education which was easy for him financially with the GI bill but difficult since his wife was not a team player. He had heard Carita was doing fine and supported Todd in programs where he could intermingle with other kids. He always knew Carita would be a good mother. He changed his shift to nights because he thought he could get more accomplished. In the morning, he would fix the children breakfast and straighten the house a bit. Then, it was off to school. When he returned home, he would fix dinner. He would lie down to rest for his night shift, studying somewhere in between. Dena needed to pitch in. He understood that she worked too, but they were not a team. All of the burdens fell on Douglas: financial, emotional, and physical. Dena did not seem to care. He needed to talk to someone. Carita had always understood him and encouraged him to do more. He knew that she might be upset if he called for advice but he had to believe that she still carried some feelings for him as he did her. He had an old number but was not aware if it were still in effect. He tried it and to his surprise it worked.

"Carita," he said, "how are you? How's Todd?"

Carita was shocked. She had not heard from him in quite some time. What did he want she wondered?

"Todd's fine," she said. "To what I owe this phone call?"

"Carita, I needed someone to talk to. I'm going crazy with all I'm trying to do."

She listened to his woes and as much as she wanted to be nasty she couldn't. She knew she still loved him and he needed her help. She quickly wrote what he was trying to do on paper. She gathered a schedule for him and repeated it over the phone. She told him not to give up on his marriage but to pray and seek counseling. She hurriedly hung up the phone and ran to her room. All she could do is cry and cry some more.

He had not thought enough to marry her but she was good enough to give him marital advice.

She called Shelly for she was the only one she could depend on these days. Shelly reassured her that Douglas's call was sincere.

"Carita," she explained, "Douglas loved you. As a matter of fact, he still loves you and you love him. He learned while he was in the service to depend on you. He is probably sorry that things did not work out for the both of you. Your relationship with Douglas has to go full circle. I may not be here to see it but you all will get back together in time. Not your time or his time but God's time. If there were ever a relationship with true and pure love, yours and Douglas's is it. This relationship has to go full circle. Now stop crying because you did the right thing. You are a Christian and a good person."

Douglas took Carita's advice and tried to work on his marriage. They had two children who were very demanding. They loved their father. Dena had managed to get a job at the same plant as Douglas and he was grateful. For a while, things seemed to be getting better and they were getting ahead. Douglas came home one evening very frustrated. He had found that Dena reported to work only to quit and he did not know why. When he got home and tried to discuss it with Dena, she just stared angrily at him and screamed.

"I'm pregnant. I'm not going to stand on my feet, at that job, while I'm in this condition so I quit."

Douglas looked at her in amazement. "Did it occur to you to tell me first and we could have worked it out for you to get a job that might have been a little easier for you."

"I'm not working while I'm pregnant!" she screamed. Douglas walked out of the house. He needed a drink. Eight years of trials and tribulations. The situation had become absolutely redundant. All that they had done to get ahead was for not.

$$Chapter\ 5$$

Carita ran into Charlie Mack. He had been a good friend when she was pregnant. He would stop at her grandma's to see if there was anything she needed or wanted. Every now and then, when Charlie ran into money problems, Carita would make a budget for him. He never forgot all of the jams she got him out of. He was just delighted to see her and Gregory Todd as Charlie called him.

"Hey Carita what's up. How have you been? I see you have your little man with you. He has grown so much. Carita he looks just like his dad. How old is he now?"

"Ten. He's playing soccer and baseball. "

"Tell me something Carita. Does his dad come around? Does he know what a nice looking kid he has?"

"Funny you should ask. With all that I have gone through Douglas does call from time to time to ask about Todd. My only problem with that is, it's always when Todd is out. He never gets the opportunity to talk to his dad."

"Carita you are so silly. Can't you see?"

"See what, Charlie?"

"Douglas still loves you. He calls while the boy is gone so that he can talk to you."

"Charlie, I am just trying to do the right thing. I don't want my son seeing his parents going through changes with one another. He called the other day and wants to take Todd on trip with him to meet other family members."

"Let him go, Carita. He has a right to know his family. It has taken Douglas a minute but he is trying to build a relationship with you and his son. I, more than anyone, know how he has hurt you but let it go Carita for Todd's sake."

They stood outside the café for moment, talking, when Charlie invited them in. He wanted to buy Todd some ice cream. Charlie went on to tell Carita he had a friend who wanted to meet her.

"He's a nice guy," Charlie stated.

"What does he look like?"

"Why do women always have to know what a guy looks like?"

"No one wants someone that looks like Deputy Dog," Carita stated.

"He just hasn't met anyone decent. He drives a truck but it's local."

Carita respected Charlie's opinion and told him she would meet the both of them at the club later on in the evening. Carita was rather excited. It had been forever since she had a real date. A blind one seemed even more exciting. She was just hoping the guy was nice and liked children. Todd was her first love and her everything. She was going to protect him and he was always going to be first in her life.

She found some rather nice fitting slacks that complimented her petite figure and a blouse that brought color to her completion. Her auburn hair had grown long since she did not have the means to cut it. She usually twisted it on her head into a Ms. Grundy and pulled some bangs to the front. Her makeup was always perfect and her cooper skin complemented her eye shadow color scheme. At last, she was ready. She dropped Todd at a friend's who had twin boys his age. They enjoyed each other's company. She and their mother took turns watching the boys when an occasion to socialize would arise. As Carita exited her vehicle, she got many whistles, which made her uncomfortable, but at least she knew she looked decent. Charlie and his friend stood at the bar as she entered the café.

Charlie stepped forward to meet her and introduced the two.

"Carita this is my friend Anthony Lomax. Tony, this is Carita Smallwood."

He greeted Carita with warmth, offered to buy her a drink then suggested they sit at a table. He was a short man, red in the color of his complexion, with reddish brown hair that flattered his pretty gray and green eyes. His lips curved when he talked and his laugh was the most unique Carita had ever heard. Charlie excused himself so that the two of them could get better acquainted. They talked about their jobs and finally he asked if she had any children.

"Yes," Carita proudly stated. "I have a son. His name is Todd."

She showed him a picture of Todd in his soccer uniform.

He smiled for he admired young women who participated in sports and other activities with their children. They conversed a little more. "May I call you from time to time? I would like to get to know you better and I don't think that a bar is appropriate for a lady of your stature."

"Certainly," she replied. "I'll be looking forward to your phone call."

He escorted her to the car and watched her drive off.

Carita tried not to be excited for she didn't think she could stand another disappointment in life. She had not really dated since Douglas. It seemed like everyone was about themselves or trying to get over. Very few people had morals or principles anymore.

She stopped to get Todd and the twins asked to spend the night. She prepared her famous hot dogs with chili and fries for the trio. After supper, they all played Monopoly. She put the boys to bed leaving the radio on and returned to the living room to finish some crocheting while watching TV.

Saturdays were always a good day for her and the boys. The twins usually went with her to Todd's soccer or baseball games. Today was the baseball game and Tessa asked to go along. She dropped Todd off at the field and ran to pick up Tessa. Carita's Aunt Lois was glad to see her because she had a union meeting to attend and did not want to take Tessa with her. Such things were so boring for children, she explained. Carita planned for Tessa to spend the night and would bring her back after Sunday service. As usual the kids had a good time and the twins did not want to go home.

Carita had fixed popcorn for Tessa and Todd so that they could watch Fright Night. They both enjoyed Frankenstein and the mummy movies. After getting herself situated to enjoy the movie with the kids, the phone rang.

"May I speak to Carita?"

"This is Carita."

"Hi. It's me Tony, Charlie's friend."

"Hi Tony. It's good to hear from you."

"Will it be an imposition if I dropped by?"

"No, if you don't care about two kids watching movies than you're welcome."

Carita gave him the directions to her home and told him she would be looking forward to his visit. Within an hour, he arrived with pizza. She introduced him to Todd and Tessa. He handed the pizza to Tessa since she was the older of the two. The children were elated to have a pizza while they watched television. Carita offered Tony a seat and told him to make himself at home. After the movies were over, Carita put the children to bed and returned to the living room.

Tony took her hand as she sat on the couch and said, "I had been thinking about you and I wanted to give you a call."

"I'm glad you did. It gave you a chance to meet my son."

"Although I am an only child I do like children. I wish I had siblings. Your son seems to be very active. Maybe when we're better friends he and I can do some things together."

"Carita laughed, don't tell Todd just yet. He'll drive you crazy until he gets his special time with you."

They both chuckled and he politely kissed her on the cheek, expressing to her that he enjoyed the evening. He left with the promise to call some time during the next day and told her to take care.

Sunday service was fulfilling as usual and Carita prepared a good meal. She had enough to take to her aunt so she would not have to cook. Todd and Tessa hugged one another for they truly missed each. They would talk a couple of times on the phone during the week to make their plans for their next weekend together.

Tony called as promised. He and Carita had a polite conversation. He told her he would have to drive over the road the next day and may not get back until late but would be thinking of her.

As time went on, Tony called almost every day. He liked Carita because she was different. She was independent, worked, kept a clean house, took very good care of her son, and participated in his activities. She was sympathetic and compassionate to others but above all she had faith. She loved children and had an extra one to care for on the weekends. Carita begin to view Tony as a hard worker; he was considerate and very understanding towards her although he seemed to be somewhat jealous. He was very supportive to what needs she and Todd had.  On Friday's, Tony always picked Todd up to take him to McDonald's or where ever he wanted to go.  He drove a pickup truck, brown and beige in color, with silver running boards and matching pipes on the side.  Todd liked to hear the air horn and Tony enjoyed blowing it for him.  After one of their trips to Mickey D's, Tony told Carita they needed to talk.

So far their relationship had been a real courtship with morals and respect with most dates ending in a kiss. Carita herself wondered what was wrong with this man because he never approached her.  He asked her if there was any possibility that they could spend a whole evening together. He was willing to pay a babysitter whatever they charged.

He wanted to take her for a special dinner at a new restaurant.  Carita made the arrangements with her aunt and called Marilynn whom she had not seen for months.  She needed a new outfit and Marilynn seemed to know where to go.  They selected a pink two piece suit.  The pink brought out her eyes and complemented other facial features.

When Tony called for her, he thought she looked very stunning.  He took his time driving. He did not want the evening ending too quickly, wishing it could last forever.  They drove about thirty miles out of town to a restaurant called the Native New Yorker.  The club was just beautiful.  A crystal vase containing a piece of green ivy decorated each marble table. Glass tile covered the floors. White Roman columns stood throughout the room.  Each chair was white rod iron with seats padded in Marona Latte polyester. They were escorted to a table and presented a menu.  The maître d' asked if they wanted wine.  Tony took the liberty of ordering a steak, baked potato, and a salad for both of them. They enjoyed their glass of wine and discussed their families.

Their backgrounds were similar; both were raised by their grandmothers. Carita had one sister. Tony was an only child.  They continued to talk until the live band began to play one of Carita's favorites and Tony asked her to dance.  Carita felt nervous. It had been such a long time since being in a man's arms, but Tony held her close and told her to relax.

With a smile, he said, "I don't bite."

She smiled back. "I know."

By the time they returned to their table, their meal had arrived. The amount of food served astonished Carita. She knew she would not be able to eat it all.

Tony saw the look on her face and grinned. "I know just what you're thinking. I'm not going to be able to eat all of my food either."

They both laughed.

He said, "We'll just eat what we can."

After the main entrée, they both declined dessert. Tony then took her to the Chateau Capri Night Club, well known for its mixed drinks and wine. He saw a few people from his job and introduced them to Carita, then sat next to her. As she sipped her wine, her lips became so inviting that Tony could not help but to enfold them if only for a moment. He stroked her hand as he apologized. She softly told him that it was alright. He gently took her hand and led her to the car. The club started to fill up and he did not want to share Carita with anyone.

He drove until he found a hotel that would meet the standards of lady. That's how he felt about Carita. He looked at her and said, "We don't have to…"

She nodded, approvingly.

He returned to the car and escorted her to the room. He sat her on the bed then gently kissed her. "How did you become a wine drinker?"

She smiled. "I don't do whiskey to well."

They both laughed.

It broke the ice somewhat. Tony turned on the TV and helped Carita out of her jacket. They watched a little TV and talked. Tony moved over so that he might be able to taste the softness of her lips. He held her tight, wanting to show her how much he cared for her.

Carita did not know what to expect. This man showed her affection and gentleness that she had not experience in such a very long time. He began to slide her clothes away from her body while slipping out of his. He took the pins out of her hair, allowing it to adorn her shoulders. He gently touched her face. His lips caressed hers. His hands gently slide around her body until they rested upon her breasts. He fondled them until they peaked. His lips touched one than the other. She touched his inner being, stroking until her tiny fingers could no longer handle the task. As she gently placed her hands around his waist as he entered her and they joined together in the art of passion, thriving on their appetites of romantic desire.

As he held Carita in his arms, a tear dropped from her eye. He felt it hit his face and, oddly enough, kissed it away. Presuming he hurt her, Tony held her body and embraced her as though she were a new born. And she was; for he had not known such a beautiful obsession.

They slept the rest of the night in one another's arms. It was clear that, after years of pursuing a virtuous love, they had found such in one another.

Tony had practically become a part of the family. He had meet Carita's aunts, uncles and some of the cousins. He and Todd had become fast friends and Tony tried to do as much with Todd as he could. Tony had Todd's bike put together and, while the bike was bigger than Todd, he assisted him in getting a grip on it. Tony even liked the cat although he was not too fond of animals.

Carita worked at the consortium in Somerset when Tony told her of a better position in Berkley. He was from the area and knew the director of the program. The responsibilities seemed similar to her present position but paid substantially more than her present salary. Carita thought that this would be a good move since they had dated for two years and started to talk about a life together. It would give her a better access to save for Todd's future.

She moved with the principle of a brighter future in mind. Carita found Tony to be a good provider and a good worker even though he had a few issues. Tony had a temper and could be extremely jealous of Carita. He drank more wine than the average person. That coupled with his refer smoking made him very unreasonable some of the time. And although he knew her job took her many places around the county as well as the state, he could not help thinking who else may be approaching her.

Carita, a very bright young woman with lots of ideas on how to better to conduct human resources for the benefit of humanity, felt that she and Tony could work on them.

Tony soon asked Carita to marry him. Carita did not accept right away because she thought they needed some counseling first and was not at all sure she wanted to deal with his obsessive jealousy. She did not want to go into a marriage with existing problems.

Another issue with Tony, he remained very jealous of the rapport between Carita and Douglas. Although he knew Douglas was Todd's father, he did not like him and this fact became the worst scenario. His continued fixation of trying to control Carita and the relationship between her and Douglas became a dangerous obsession. Tony hated Douglas for whatever reason and was constantly accusing Carita of sneaking around with him. He refused to believe Carita and Douglas had a rapport only for the best interest of their son. Carita didn't know if this was truly Tony, the reefer, the wine or if all red men were just crazy.

Marilynn, whom she had not seen in months, called to tell her Douglas wanted to get in touch with her. He knew she was going with Tony and, given his reputation for his temper, did not want to place Carita in a predicament, Marilyn explained to Carita. Carita had never asked for his number and, since he never volunteered, she assumed he was not listed. Her move to the new area constituted a new number for her which she chose not to list. Carita heard he was going through a divorce and she felt a little sadness for him. Marilynn gave her a number where she could reach him. Carita pondered over the number for a couple of days, wondering whether she should call or not. It had been awhile since she heard from Douglas. She accepted that his marriage was going just fine and so was he.

She broke down and called Douglas. He answered the phone and immediately recognized her voice. He asked how she and Todd were doing and if they could get together to talk. She arranged to meet him at a restaurant downtown in Summit Hills. She felt that it was better since it was quaint, out of the way, and did not have as much traffic as the café. Douglas kissed her in the mouth. She wondered what this was all about.

Knowing she liked wine, he ordered her a glass. He decided to have a glass of E&J. She had never really seen Douglas drink like this before. Once they were both comfortable, Douglas spoke.

"I suppose you know I'm getting a divorce," he said.

"Yes," Carita stated.

"Carita, I am sorry for all the things I have done to you and Todd. I thought… after my divorce is over, we could try to make a life together."

Carita looked at him in amazement, too stunned to speak. Douglas went on to explain he always cared for her and they were so much alike. He knew she was a good woman and their life together would be successful. Carita began to speak. She wanted so badly to accept his offer for she was still in love with him. If only he had tried a month ago to get in touch with her.

"I have and will always love you. But I can't honor your request because there is more at stake here than just our love. Our lives depend on us moving ahead." I have already committed myself to someone. Our relationship would not work because rebounds usually don't. They're only good for the moment. I don't want to be your rebound."

He looked at her very sadly. "Carita, I love you. I suppose I have always loved you and I made a mistake by listening to other people."

"And I love you," she said. "I want you to be happy and I want to be happy. If only you had gotten in touch with me sooner."

She knew that he was regretful for everything that had happened but she could not take the chance that harm might come to him. She looked at Douglas after she had made the statement and placed her hand on his glass of bourbon.

"Don't do this," she said, referring to his drink. "This is not you. You will only get yourself in trouble if you continue. I know that it's hard but you are better than this. Do something positive with your degree. I know that it hurts but it will only hurt a little while. Move forward with your life. It is not the end of the world."

She got up to leave and Douglas grabbed her hand. She kissed him for what she felt would be the last time in life and ran to her car.

Carita started dinner for the threesome when Tony spoke. "So, your baby's daddy is getting rid of his wife, unh?"

"What are you talking about, Tony?"

"You know what I'm talking about and don't pretend that you don't. After all, you're the one who said you and your baby's daddy was cool. Did you think that I wouldn't find out?"

Carita just waved her hand and said, "Get serious while walking away."

He grabbed her arm and pulled her back. "You can try to leave if you want but nobody leaves me and gets away with it. You'll both wake up and find yourselves dead."

She knew within her heart he would try to harm Douglas and perhaps her. But she did not fear for herself. She didn't want him to harm Douglas. She snapped back to reality, pulled her arm away and looked at Tony. Carefully choosing her words she stated, "Douglas is my son's father and there is a certain amount of love that will always be there. You've given me more than ample opportunity had I wanted to be with him. I love you but you do not seem to understand that. You've had other relationships before me and never have I accused you of being unfaithful. So I suggest you get real or we can end this relationship here and now."

As much as she wanted to be with Douglas, she knew Tony's threat was real. She loved Douglas with all her heart and his happiness meant the world to her. She also had her son to consider. If something happened to either one of his parents, what would happen to him? There wasn't anywhere to go and no one to tell. She felt she only had God in her corner and had to have faith. Perhaps, God would bestow blessings upon her and the marriage would work.

Tony stepped back surprised at Carita's response. He knew, within his heart, she had not been unfaithful but the closeness of two made him wonder.

Two weeks after meeting Douglas, she stopped at the café to purchase sandwiches she ordered. She had driven to Summit Hills to pick up Tessa, who was spending the weekend with Todd. The sandwiches were her way of an easy meal and she would not have to rush with preparing dinner. As she prepared to leave the café, Lee came in.

"Hi Carita," she said. "Sit down. Let me talk with you a minute," she commanded. "You know he's getting a divorce," she said then nodded toward Douglas, who was shooting pool and had not seen either one of them. "I've heard you're getting married."

"Yes," Carita replied.

Lee said, "Carita, just wait and see what happens. I know Douglas loves you and I know that you love him."

"But, Carita replied, I don't want to be a rebound and right now he's very vulnerable. We've both been through so much I just don't think it would work."

Carita's heart ached. She knew Douglas was her true love but she had committed herself to Tony. She had to think of his feelings. He had been there for her with loyalty and obligation. And although that was true, she feared Tony's jealousy might lead him to do harm to Douglas. She was not willing to take that chance. Carita lied and promised Lee that she would think about the proposal but she knew it would not work and she did not have a choice. Tony was already outraged because of Douglas's divorcing and always questioning Carita's intent when he came to the house. He even frightened Todd. She really was tired of defending herself and feared that he might harm Douglas with his sick jealousy or perhaps the both of them. She felt that Tony was a good person but needed to understand that Douglas was Todd's father and the two of them would always have a rapport. She could only explain this by using his children and their mother as an example. Tony would do anything not to lose Carita since he wanted their relationship to work; he agreed to go to counseling. He knew his temper would only keep him in trouble and cost him the woman he loved. That would be a loss he could never replace.

# *Chapter 6*

As Carita sat at the kitchen table preparing for her spring wedding ceremony, she wondered if she was doing the right thing. She loved Tony in her own way but knew she still had feelings for Douglas. She was thirty-five and this was her first marriage. It had already been fourteen years between her and Douglas but the feelings had not vanished. Tony was a good person yet he maintained a bad temper as well other habits Carita considered distasteful. Although you cannot change a person overnight, Carita believed with prayer and God's watchful eye Tony would change in time.

She wanted so badly to talk Douglas. She knew he understood her. But, she could not bear to see him unhappy and therefore elected to not see him at all. She would have to go on without him. She sat down and placed her hands over her face.

"Oh," she responded, as she wiped her face with her hand.

"What's wrong hon," Tony asked as he entered the kitchen, returning from the store.

"It's just these wedding plans," she lied.

"They're beginning to get to you, unh?"

"Yes, in a way. It just seems to be so much to do when I thought that everything was ready. Spring is just around the corner you know."

"Baby, we'll be fine. Everything will turn out just the way you want it."

Carita and Tony married in April. They invited family and close friends. After the ceremony, a photographer took pictures then they gathered at the restaurant for a small sit down dinner. Carita looked stunning in her off-white dress. Tony wore a black suit. This day had been a long time coming and the couple was glad it was over. They enjoyed the meal along with the family and soon departed for their short honeymoon. Carita stopped at a table and hugged and kissed Todd, who planned to spend the night with his best friend, Steve.

"Mom, I'm so glad you're happy. You deserve it. Things will be better now you'll see."

"Thank you, son. You behave while I'm gone."

Todd, almost teenager by now, was glad to see his mom happy. He watched her make sacrifices for him, through the years, as well as other people she cared for. He and Tessa always thought Carita would marry Douglas, a least that was their wish. They did not have a problem with Tony, just suspected Carita was still in love with Todd's dad. Todd knew from Douglas's visits that his mom always seemed sad when he left, like a part of her was missing. He knew his mom loved his dad and his dad loved her but he was afraid to discuss it with either one of them. Douglas would call Carita from time to time to check on Todd. At one point, he took Todd on vacation with him for week. Carita was glad because it gave them the chance to bond and him the opportunity meet more family members on his dad's side.

Tony continued to drive a truck; and while he did bring his money home, drinking with his friends, and partying were his first priory. Carita referred to his friends as his rug rats. Most of them she couldn't stand because they had no purpose in life. This was a big issue between her and Tony. The drinking, smoking, and womanizing had begun to get on Carita's last nerve. She thought, after their marriage, he would somehow curtail these habits. Six months passed and his habits, coupled with his friends, become quite excessive. He was not able to see that they were not an asset to either one of them, much less to their marriage.

One day as Carita entered the house, she could smell refer.

"Tony what are you doing?"

"What does it look like?"

"You need to stop smoking that refer and drinking. It's going to cause you problems later on in your life."

"You don't tell me what to do. I'm grown. Ain't no woman ever gonna tell me what to do. If I can't smoke and drink in my own house, I know where I can go."

Tony did not understand that you could not always take your friends with you when you married; and to that point, some of them would begrudge you the opportunity of having more or doing better. This did not set a good example for Todd and while Carita wanted him to understand phases of life, she did not necessarily want him exposed to life's entrapments. This scenario continued, causing a big distraction in their marriage. After a year of marriage, Tony moved out with an old girlfriend, leaving Carita to endure on her own.

She continued encouraging Todd in school while looking for better employment as well as housing. After about six months, Tony returned home and seemed to want a better life for a little while.

Of course old habits die hard and Tony continued to stress Carita with his unnecessary habits and friends. She continued to pray and ask God for strength and wisdom. For the next six years, Carita kept Todd encouraged and focused on continuing his education and life as well. She participated in most of his school activities as well as attending his games when she did not have to work. They worked together on applying to different colleges. Carita knew, from her son's record of accomplishments, he might be able to acquire a scholarship.

"Well, ma, graduation will soon be here."

"I know, son. Where did those six years go?" It just seemed like yesterday you entered junior high school. Now you're eighteen and almost a grown man."

Todd told his mom about several get-together parties for the seniors and that he might be pass his curfew. One evening, Todd entered the house at one in the morning. Tony had just moved back home from one of his escapades.

"Is that Todd just coming in? It's one o'clock. Listen, this boy can't come in my house this time of night. He'll have to go stay with his daddy."

Carita, awake and patiently waiting on Todd's arrival said, "First of all, he told me he was going to be late. Second of all, you just got back into this house and have not paid a dimes worth of rent. Third of all, he can go stay with his daddy but where he goes I go."

Tony decided to lie down and shut up. For all the years he had put Carita through bullshit it had only made her stronger.

Graduation finally arrived and Carita prepared all of Todd's favorite foods. She scheduled a party the day after graduation and expected a considerable amount of friends and family. Todd had just come in and stopped to grab one of the cookies Carita had taken out of the oven.

"It's here," Carita said, referring to the graduation.

"I know, ma. Steve is going to go on to college and I have decided to go the service. This way, I can serve my country and get an education at the same time."

"That's a good choice but I thought we could apply for some more grants."

"I know, ma, but you have done enough. Dad has helped me with some of my senior expenses and so has my God mom, Shelly. We didn't want you worrying about all of my senior activities."

For mother and son, they had become very close. It seemed like they only had each other.

"Ma, now that I am an adult, can I ask you a question?"

"Sure son."

"Why have you stayed with Tony all of these years? You have carried the load ever sense I can remember. He has humiliated you by leaving home I can't even count the times, and yet you allowed him to come back and kept it moving. Why didn't you marry my dad? God knows that he loved you and, even though he has married for the second time, he still loves you and I know, with all my heart, you love him?"

"I don't know, son. All I can say is vows and commitment."

Todd shook his head but hugged his mother. He knew, without her positive attitude, he would not have been the person he was.

Douglas arrived early so that he might be able to spend some time with Carita and Todd. He kissed her on the cheek and just smiled.

"Carita, you've done a wonderful job with our son.  He turned out to be a good looking young man too.  Of course he got his looks from me.  His brains are all you," he said.  "Really, Carita, how have you been?"

"Fine," she said with a smile.

Although he knew Carita never complained, he worried about her.  He had always been concerned about her.  He knew Tony had a temper and he felt Tony should have respected Carita more than he did.  The whole town knew of his escapades with other women.  Douglas just could never understand why Carita stayed.

Later that evening, Tony tried to make an issue out of Douglas's participating at the graduation party.

"So, you're man was here?"

"What are you talking about?"

"Douglas, that's what I'm talking about."

"Listen, that's the boy's father.  He deserved to participate with his son.  After all, he paid his dues.  What did you do for yours?"

Tony turned and walked away since he realized he could not upset Carita.  He always suspected something between the two since they had a child together.

Todd spent the summer working a job and going to other open houses.  He assisted Carita with refinishing the birch tables in the living room while thinking of what his life would be like in the service.  He planned to send Carita an allotment but she would not hear of it.  She wanted Todd to live his life stress free and not worry about her.  She had made her choice in life and although things were not as she wanted, she knew within herself that God would eventually prevail.

$$\mathcal{C}hapter\ 7$$

Carita's prayers were answered. Little by little, Tony began to change and better understand what Carita's purpose to a better life was all about. Although he still had issues about Todd's father, he tried to let it go.

"Tony, I'm just really tired of this job. I work second shift and all I do is direct phone calls and messages to doctors. It's boring and unfulfilling."

"Honey, use your time to try and find what it is you want. I'm working steady now and you can even go back and finish school if you want. I know you wanted to buy a home but maybe it's not in the cards right now."

Carita continued to seek more people orientated employment. She was getting older and needed a position with more benefits.

Tony started to see what Carita told him all of these years about his friends. She often told him, when you get married, you could not bring all of your friends with you. Most of Tony's friends were still single and into meaningless relationships. As he began to better understand Carita's assessment of life, he wanted her to be content. He knew she dreamed of owning a home and together it could be accomplished. It appeared that Tony worked harder than ever to make Carita's dream come true.

"Tony, I spotted a two story house around the corner. It looks kind of big but I would like to check it out."

"Okay. See if you can't get in touch with a real estate agent so we can get in to see it.

Carita found the Daily Living Real Estate Company in the phone book. She called and they assigned an agent. She was a younger woman who had been with the company for several years. She knew most of the finical institutions rules and regulations and had a good reputation for selling homes. They made an appointment to meet at the house at five in the evening.

"Mrs. Lomax, I'm Theresa Simmons your real estate agent.  It's so nice to meet you."

"Likewise.  This is my husband, Tony."

"Shall we go in?"

The couple looked around and agreed that the house would make a terrific home.  Although it had a large frame, the rooms were average size.  It had three bedrooms, a kitchen, dining room, living room, bath, basement, and a two car garage. Theresa went to work on the financial end for Tony and Carita, and soon their prayers were answered.

God continued to pour blessings upon them when Carita secured a job with benefits as well as a very good wage. Todd called home when he could. He was elated that his mom was able to secure a home. He knew it had been a lifetime dream.

Shelly and Marilyn stopped to see Carita's new home.

"Carita, I'm giving you an open house."

"That's not necessary, Shelly.  I'm just so glad we're still friends and that you like my new home."

"Carita, all this time we've been the three musketeers and we want you to know that we're happy for you.  Let me and Shelly do something for you."

Douglas continued to work at the plant. Out of the blue, he called Carita to check on Todd, who had been in the service for five years now.

"Carita, how is our son?"

"Todd is fine.  He's working hard and attending college.  He doesn't know when he'll be able to come home."

"That's good.  He's at least doing something with his life.  Speaking of life, I've heard you had a dream come true."

"Yes.  We were able to buy a home.  It's just wonderful."

"I'm glad for you, Carita.  You deserve it."

After some continued conversation and Douglas's securing Carita's new address, they said their good-byes.  Carita wondered, after their conversation, why Douglas needed the address.  While preparing for dinner the doorbell rang. Carita opened the door and Todd stood on the porch with the biggest smile. His father stood beside him.

"Hi mom. I wanted to surprise you. On our last conversation, I knew you were waiting on the approval for the house but I never called back. I called Tessa and she told me you all had moved but did not know the address."

Carita just smiled and hugged her son with tears in her eyes.

"How long will you be home?"

"About a month."

Douglas kissed Carita on the cheek and told her he would talk with her later. He smiled to himself. He enjoyed seeing Carita happy and although he still felt it should be the two of them in a new home, he prayed Tony would not cause any problems during Todd's leave.

Todd visited friends and family. He assisted Carita in completing two projects she planned for their new home. He also spent quality time with his dad and visited his grandmother Lee, who prepared some special dishes for her grandson. Having enjoyed his leave, the time had come for him to deploy to Greece for the next eighteen months.

As Carita began to enjoy the fruits of her labor, Tony took ill. His employer called and asked her to meet them at a local hospital.

"I think he's had a stroke," said one of the owners of AMI Trucking Company. "He brought the truck back, loaded. And when he got out, his face was twisted. He appeared to be intoxicated but we knew he wasn't. I have called an ambulance. What hospital do you want him taken to?"

"I'll meet you at Bell View. I am on my way out the door now."

Carita was so nervous that she arrived before the ambulance. She did not know what to do. She called Douglas. He calmed her down and told her what signs to look for and the questions to ask. He made her promise to call and keep him posted. When Tony arrived, he appeared in better condition than she expected.

The doctors in the ER wanted to keep Tony overnight. Tests were completed, determining Tony had a stroke.

Tony, who never complained about any numbness before the suffering the stoke, definitely grumbled about it afterwards. Dr. Rea, the couple's primary care physician for several years, took a series of tests that provided evidence of a possible blood clot at the base of the brain. Tony was sent to Cleveland Clinic for a complete scan of his brain. The tests confirmed that a blood clot did exist and he was scheduled for surgery.

Carita took time from work to care for her husband as any wife would. It had already been determined that he would not be able to return to his job because his medication was in such high doses that he might be a danger to himself as well as others. He was advised to seek some type of disability. Watching Carita take on the responsibility of the house, bills, his care, and sometimes working overtime for the extra money concerned Tony. She always seemed to have so much to bear.

"Carita, since I am not working, I will clean the house and take care of the kitchen."

"Really," she said.

"I'll make your coffee in the morning. I'm up anyway. Just show me how. I'll make sure both vehicles have their oil changed and what other maintenance they may need. The only thing you have to do, Honey, is cook and wash clothes."

It was a very generous offer but it came just as Carita fell ill with pneumonia. She was already an asthmatic. Carita and Tony nursed themselves back to better health but the stress Carita was under caused more and more asthma attacks.

"Carita, we have been here in this house for nine years. The going up and down the steps really isn't good for you. The going up and down the cellar steps when you're doing laundry is a big chore. You're working overtime every chance you get so that we'll have enough money for our medication. Girl, I have got to get you out of this house."

"I don't know, Tony. We've been here so long. I had always hoped that this was just a starter home, but our illnesses have put us behind."

"Carita, let's try to find something on one floor. Do you still have a phone number for the agent that helped us get this house?"

"Yes.  I'll look on the computer at real estate sites and call Theresa."

Finally, they located a home in a small suburb beyond Somerset called Marlboro Heights.  Everything was on one floor with a finished basement. Carita fell in love with it because she had the fireplace she always wanted in a home.  It also had two bedrooms, two baths, living room, dining room and open kitchen dinette area with an adjoining family room and an entrance to an enclosed patio and a two car garage.  There was enough lawn to keep Tony busy winter and summer.  This home was truly a dream come true.

The day arrived where Tony and Carita could move and they proclaimed this to be their last move.

"Baby, I love this house.  It is so quiet and peaceful.  I know that I am going to spend the rest of my days here at peace."

He continued to keep his promise. He did more in this house than he ever did in the two-story dwelling.  He totally took over the care of both vehicles as well as kept the house clean.  He got up early, every morning, to make Carita's coffee before she departed for work. He ran the vacuum, washed down the kitchen, scrubbed floors, and washed windows inside and out twice a year.

Carita smiled. Tony was finally happy at home.  She just looked up and said, "Thank you Jesus."

*Chapter 8*

God continued to blow blessings upon Carita and Douglas as well. By this time, both had purchased second homes as well as excelled in their positions at work. Five more years had passed and Tony and Carita had become the best of friends. Although Tony's medication left Carita celibate, she did not mind. God had answered her prayers. They were a couple. Tony was now able to understand what Carita's objective had been. She planned to retire in a couple of years so they may be able enjoy life together. They did everything as a couple. Carita returned to school after all these years, and acquired her degree in graphic design. Tony applauded and supported her as well.

Todd served his country, acquired a degree in security, and worked as a specialist for a large firm. He married a real southern bell, Alexis, who the family just adored. They had a daughter Aeleta, the apple of both her granddads' eyes. Although Todd was a married adult, Douglas and Carita maintained their rapport. Tony, still somewhat jealous, learned somehow to accept it. With this, out of the blue, Douglas called Carita to let her know he planned to retire sometime during the year. Douglas also discussed some personal problems he had and, of course, Carita listened with interest and gave him the best advice possible.

Just as things were going well for both families, the devil decided to have his way. Douglas called again and told Carita he needed to see her. They met in the park by the pond. They embraced one another as usual while they sat on the bench. Douglas took Carita's hand. He looked at her with a smile yet sadness in his eyes.

"Carita," he said, "I'm getting a divorce. After all of these years another divorce."

"No," she screamed. "You can't. You just retired so that you can enjoy life. Divorce and do what," she exclaimed. "Doug, you can't. What will you do? I know you believe in God and you can work this out. Have you thought about counseling?"

"Yes," he said, "but she is emphatic about this divorce. Re, when you're told there is no longer any love, there is nothing to do but walk away."

"Oh Doug," she said. "I am so sorry. What can I do to help?"

"Be my friend," he said.

"I have always been your friend," she replied, half smiling. "Doug, I'll always be there for you."

"I know," he said. "Oh, Carita." He moved to embrace her and they hugged.

She hugged him as hard as she could and told him things would work out for she knew God had a plan. They smiled at each other and kissed on the cheek and parted. Carita ached inside. She knew how Douglas felt. He was more than a friend and she could not stand to see him hurting.

She checked on him from time to time through Ms. Lee, gaining her promise not to tell. Douglas, of course, went through a state of depression. He rented a small apartment and put some of his things in storage. The divorce took longer than he anticipated. Every time he thought the divorce was over, a new scenario appeared. He still shot pool almost every day. It seemed to take his mind off his present situation.

Geraldine, a girl Douglas had gone to school with, stopped in the bar for a cold beer one evening with a friend. Geri, as they called her in high school, introduced Douglas to her friend Suzie. Suzie, who was not from the area, lived in the valley just short time. She was tall with long legs, light in completion, and had a fairly good grade of hair. She used all of those possessions and more to her advantage. She greeted Douglas with enthusiasm. Geri had already informed her Douglas was a good catch but going through a divorce.

He offered to buy the girls another drink while he finished his game of pool. Geri begin to talk to other folks she knew from high school and the area. Suzie sat at bar just looking and watched Douglas shooting pool. Douglas noticed her interest but kept on playing. When the game ended, he offered to buy her another drink. She accepted. They chatted for a few minutes then he made his excuses and departed.

Suzie was slightly disappointed for she could usually hold a man's attention longer than five minutes. She stepped over to where Geri chatted to meet more of the guys. After a while, the girls left to compare notes on their way home

"Why didn't you get Douglas's attention?" Geri asked.

"I tried," said Suzie, "but he some excuse about a meeting and left."

"Listen," Geri said, "You don't want to let that one get away. Besides going through a divorce and he is retired from the plant. He had more than thirty years in. He has big house but of course his wife is still in it. You don't know how this will go."

Suzie gave thought to everything Geri said. Douglas, in short, was a good catch. Although she had a small income, it would be nice to have a man around to help, she thought. She knew from experience and life most people who were going through this type of situation would be vulnerable; and this would be an excellent opportunity for her to establish a relationship. She had not forgotten all of her lessons as a young woman. Now older, she played the game very well. She and her husband had been separated for quite some time, years, maybe, because she had forgotten. But she figured, as long as she kept him in the mix, giving her finances, she could surely convince a younger man to do the same.

The next evening, she went to the bar alone and saw Douglas. She bought herself a drink and sipped on the straw while switching around the table to get his attention.

He smiled at her and said, "What's up?"

"You." She smiled back.

He laughed then sat with her at the bar. He ordered himself a ginger ale and Suzie another drink. She knew there was going to be a gathering at her friend's house over the weekend and desperately needed to be accompanied. She thought Douglas might be the man to take.

"Do you have plans for the weekend?"

"No."

"My friend is having a small set and I thought you might like to go with me."

Douglas was not sure about this. He had not gone out with a woman since the separation from his wife.

"Let me think about it and I will be in touch."

She wrote her number down and he left for yet another meeting. Suzie could not get over these meetings he attended. What were they and where were they? She thought.

Douglas was not ready to get into a relationship. He did not know anything about this woman and was not really willing to learn. The only women he trusted at this point and time were his mom and Carita. He trusted Carita because he believed she had always been his friend first and his confidant. He missed Carita. He had not called her in sometime. He knew she was still married and trying to go to school to complete her degree. He missed her voice and her advice. He missed her. If he had not been so stubborn all of those years ago, listening to other people and trusted her he thought, he may not be in the predicament.

Douglas called Suzie to get the address of the set. He told her he would meet her there. He was not to cool about parties, as he did not drink, but felt that it was a way for him to kind of get away from his usual routine.

Once he arrived, he saw a lot of old friends and listened to a lot of conversations. Suzie showed up and tried to play the role of them being a couple. Douglas backed up for he was not into this. He was just coming out of something and did not want get caught up into anything just yet. While watching people talk and play cards, Suzie brought him a ginger ale. She remembered someone telling her Douglas didn't drink. She stood by him and smiled with what small talk she could find to interest him. She managed to get closer and closer to him as the rooms begin to get crowded with other friends. He finally suggested they step outside to get some fresh air. They talked about little things such as the area and how many children they had. Suzie told a few jokes and Douglas managed to laugh. He appeared nervous to her.

"Crowds make me nervous too," she said. "I know how it is when you're going through a divorce. I have kind of sort of been there myself."

Douglas looked at her in awe. He did not think anyone understood how he felt. She proposed that they leave. There were so many people that her friend would not miss her anyway.

"Where are we going?"

"I have my own place," she responded.

He followed her home.

She fixed a glass of soda for him and found a can of beer for herself. They started watching TV and she made a few comments about the show. She sat next to Douglas and kissed him on his lips. Douglas, surprised, didn't know what to do so he kissed her back. She slid her tongue down his throat to meet his while she glided onto his lap. She rubbed his head while her tongue floated back and forth meeting his. Her wet lips touched his outer ear where she blew warm air into the ear to meet the bliss delight of sensuality. She busied her hands to unfasten his belt buckle so she might be able to touch his most inner part to make it ready to receive her. Her mouth watered as she slid off her blouse as well as his shirt to be able to touch and pull the taste from his chest. She placed her breast into his mouth so that he might be able to flavor the taste of a real woman. They rolled off the couch onto the floor and she began to place her body on top of him so she could enter him while she held his head with his tongue between her breasts. She slid her hand up and down to make his penis wet and slippery so that once he entered her she could flawlessly capture him into her world of fantasy. She worked with him until there was nothing left but blood, sweat, and tears. She kissed him on his lips and down his throat to keep his emotions rising, to bring about what sheer pleasure she could to make him believe she was his ecstasy. She held him tight to let him know there should be no doubt in his mind that she was the only partner he needed sexually or otherwise.

He began to visit her almost every day and, while she didn't cook, he took delight in taking her out to eat. She explained to him about her past, leaving pertinent parts out so that he would cater to her needs.

Although not entirely happy, entertaining her seemed better than going through this phase of his life alone. He thought she understood, about the divorce and him. He needed to get a grip on life to figure out if this is what he really wanted. He was not quite out of the marriage and did not want to get into another relationship just yet. He needed some time to think. He wanted to call Carita but what would she think? He could not have her thinking any less of him than he did himself. He knew within his heart that he should not have gotten involved with Suzie but it was too late.

Not too long after Douglas retired, some friends from the executive division of the plant where he had worked were going to Europe for business and pleasure. Owning a home in Florida and needing someone to house sit, they asked Douglas if he would be interested in staying there for a year or perhaps longer until they returned. The couple always admired Douglas for his knowledge and fortitude. They had become very good friends over the years and understood his situation. Once Douglas thought about it, it seemed ideal. He discussed it with Suzie, who objected to high heaven. Douglas could not understand her attitude. Florida was a good idea. He could become a better person once the divorce concluded and would clear up some of his issues as well.

Suzie called Geri and they went to the bar to have a drink. Suzie went on telling Geri about Douglas's plans to leave the area and live in Florida for a while.

Geri, not fully understanding Suzie's uneasiness, didn't see anything wrong with it.

"Are you crazy?" Suzie exclaimed. What about me? Do you think I have gone through all of these changes to get this man for him just to leave me with bills I will have to pay? He is supposed to be my help."

Geri looked at her and said, "You dummy, all you have to do is move to Florida with him. Get your check direct deposited so you can get it out of any bank. Have your old man send your money by Western Union. Douglas does not have to know all your business."

Once Suzie got all her lies together, she went home and talked to Douglas. She explained how much she would miss him and asked why he didn't invite her. He smiled then hugged her.

"Because, babe, I want to get myself together. I can't do that here. I need a new and clear area where I can think."

He went on to explain he would not forget her. He planned to drive or fly back every couple of months.

Suzie tried once more to get Douglas to see things her way. It caused some aggravation and a raised voice from him. She thought it best to leave things alone for the moment.

Douglas called Carita to get her opinion. She was glad to hear from him. She had been busy taking care of the house and Tony as well and working full time. Douglas explained some of the things he was going through but did not mention Suzie. Carita thought it might be a good idea for him to move away for a while to bring closure to his divorce and other issues going on in his life.

They chatted about their son and other topics they generally discussed. He promised to keep in touch with her.

'Doug, will you do something for me?" Carita asked, sadly.

"Carita, you know I will do anything for you."

"Don't get involved with any of those Florida women. Wait for me."

He asked her to repeat herself and Carita, being Carita, did.

"What will we do with Tony?" he asked.

"I don't know," she replied.

They hung up on a sad note and he promised to let her know before he left.

Douglas flew to Florida to see the house and to figure out what he needed to bring with him. It was located in a development with new homes. The little community had its own club house as well as tennis court and other amenities.

After he returned home, he took Suzie out to dinner and tried to have a pleasant evening but she remained too upset. He continued to tell her he would travel back and forth but she still refused to accept his departure. He tried to made love to Suzie but she remained angry. Neither party was happy. The following morning, he packed what he needed in his SUV.

Before hitting the road, he stopped to say goodbye to Lee. To his surprise, she had a whole breakfast spread ready for him. He ate and talked to her and his dad for a while then decided it was time to get on the road.

Douglas continued to participate with the mentally challenged children. He was so dedicated that the organization certified him in several areas. He kept his promised to Suzie and drove back in forth whenever he could. He was so grateful to Carita to suggest he do something with his degree. Although a volunteer position, it was his way of giving back to the community and God.

As he watched his team in the relay, he realized he had been in Florida a year. He often thought of Carita. He had not called or heard from her. However, he learned from his mom that Carita was well.

Adhering to his fall cleaning schedule, Tony washed the outside of the windows. He had washed windows for Carita, for years after becoming disabled. When she attempted to assist him, he sent her away because she smeared the windows so badly he would have to redo them. They ate a very appetizing dinner later that evening. Carita was still a good cook. She noticed Tony had a slight cough and seemed to have difficult time breathing. When she questioned him about it but he said, he was fine. During the night, he woke Carita up at least twice. She tried to do what she could to make him comfortable so he could go back to sleep. Tony slept on and off, without getting any rest. He continued to cough and had difficulty breathing. Carita, thinking he caught the flu, purchased items to suppress the cough and clear his breathing. During the next two nights, Tony's condition worsened. When Carita got in from work, she told Tony was taking him to the doctor or ER. She could not endure another restless night.

Later that evening, they went to ER. She figured they would see him, medicate him, and send him home. Instead, they admitted him. His breathing had become very much labored. Carita continued to go to work but Tony was her first priority thereafter. She visited him after work and later in the evening before going to bed. She worried about him and didn't get much sleep. Dr. Rea had a team of doctors from several different fields checking Tony but no one came up with a diagnosis. He just seemed to not be doing well at all but would not complain to Carita.

Carita went to work in spite of all she carried. Her supervisor, Michelle, stopped at the site to see how things were going. She could sense Carita's nervousness. Carita had to tell her but she had not even shared Tony's illness with Renee, her best friend on the job. Carita busted into tears.

"Get it all out, Carita. You'll feel better."

Michelle let Carita get it all out, as she began to talk.

"Carita, I know that work is essential. But, right now, the most important thing for you is to take care of your husband. If you need to take, off then do so."

She told Carita things were going to be alright and the doctors would find the cause and effect of Tony's illness. She also told her, as her supervisor, she would do whatever she could to assist. Carita thanked her and finished the day's work going immediately to the hospital.

She freshen her make up before going into Tony's room at the hospital. She didn't want him to know she had been crying.

He hadn't had a good day himself. He wasn't eating as well as the nurses would have liked.

He smiled at her. "Hi honey. How was your day?"

"Okay," she lied.

She waited for the next sentence to come out of his mouth. She knew Tony. After all, they had been together for almost thirty years.

"Hon," he said, "they don't seem to be doing anything for me. I am still on oxygen and it's not helping. Doctors have been in and out and have not said a word. Carita, I think we should go somewhere else and get other opinions."

"I agree," she said. "The team of doctors Dr. Rea has assisting her with your diagnosis are not accommodating to you. We don't even have a prognosis, much less a diagnosis."

"I've been watching and nobody is telling us anything," Tony said.

"Where would you like to go?" asked Carita.

"Cleveland Clinic," he said.

"I will call Dr. Rea as soon as I get home."

They kissed one another affectionately and Carita rushed home to catch the doctor before the office closed. As she entered her home, the phone rang. Dr. Rea called with her diagnosis. She said Tony had cancer, leukemia as a matter of fact. Carita told her about the discussion with Tony and requested to transfer him to Cleveland. Dr. Rea agreed and hurried to make life flight arrangements for Tony.

Renee called concerned about Carita and Tony after Michelle told the entire staff. Michelle reminded everyone how Carita had been there for several of them and it was their turn to return the kindness. Renee would do anything for Carita. She even drove Carita to Cleveland the next morning. They arrived to find Tony in ICU. The doctors had already determined Tony had leukemia. He was heavily medicated, sedated and did not know Carita was there. She and Renee stayed for the afternoon and decided to leave for home.

Carita reported off work that evening so she could travel back to the hospital in the morning. Upon entering his room the next morning, a team of doctors were already discussing a plan of treatment with him. Tony gladly introduced his wife and told them they would need time to consider the factors. Carita asked Dr. Anjali to report the causes, effects, and the treatments. After listening and careful consideration, Carita saw no reason to wait. She requested the chemotherapy to start as soon as possible. The staff was very encouraging, pleasant, and helpful. The nurses took Carita's work number and the supervisor's name in case of an emergency.

Her co-workers kept Carita in prayer. The assistant supervisor always requested blessings for all. Most of the time, Carita made the drive back and forth alone; praying that God kept Tony until she arrived. Her phone rang. Thinking it was her aunt, she answered.

"Hi auntie."

The voice said, "This is not your aunt."

To her surprise, it was Douglas. Their son told him about Tony's illness and his mom was a little down.

"Oh hi," she said.

"How are you," Douglas asked.

"I'm fine," she replied.

"Really," he answered. "Todd called to let me know what you are going through. Why didn't you call?" he asked.

"I didn't want to worry you," she replied.

"Re," he said. He had not called her that in very long time. It seemed like ages. "We are better than that."

"I know."

"Will you promise me one thing?"

"It depends on what it is," she replied.

"Don't hesitate to call if you need me for anything," he said. "To talk, money, or whatever. I am here for you just as you have been for me."

"Okay," she said, silently.

"Promise," he said, sternly.

"I promise," she said.

On that note, they hung up with Douglas promising to keep her and Tony in prayer.

*Chapter 9*

Funerals are so final and calling hours was a formality Carita could do without. She knew, in the months to come, Tony's absence would be astronomical. His illness had done one thing if nothing else. It allowed him to experience true love and laugher. Although absent from his children's lives, his death brought them closer to one another.

Why didn't I listen to Tony, Carita thought, when he told me he felt like he would not make it? She remembered him sitting on the couch, early one morning in February, waiting for Carita to complete his breakfast.

"Carita," Tony said. "We need to talk. Honey, I am so sick. I fear the end is near. But it's going to be alright."

"Yes, it is," she said, happily. "We are not going to entertain any negativity. You must have faith. If you have faith as small as a mustard seed you will be fine."

"Carita, I have made my peace with God. Nothing can change that. I need to know what type of insurances you have on me and how much."

"Tony, we are not going to discuss that. You will be here for a long time. You will probably outlive me."

"Listen, Clyde," he responded, referring to his nickname for Carita when she was being abstinent. "We have to be serious please."

Carita gave in to Tony, which she usually did. She began to explain the insurance policies and their values.

"Carita," Tony said softly. "This is what I want. Do not put all of your money in the ground. Put me away decently. You only need one funeral car. As a matter of fact, you don't even need that. You can drive your SUV to the church or wherever you decide to have my service. Do not let my family tell you about cousins or other family members who want to attend the services and hold you up.  If we have not met them and you know that I don't know them, forget them.  Go through with your plans.  Now, Carita, I want to say thank you."

She looked at him with tears in her eyes.

"For what," she asked?

"You have been my best friend, the best wife a man could ever ask for. You have helped me to have a good life.  You have exposed me to things and people I would have never met had I stayed in the streets.  If I had stayed in the streets and continued to do the things that I was doing, I would have been dead a long time ago.  So, Clyde, I thank you.  You will never know how much I truly love you."

He put his arms around Carita as she began to cry.

He whispered in her ear.  "It will be alright because I am free.  Let's eat the breakfast you prepared."

Carita, as usual, depended on God and knew that taking him to Cleveland Clinic had been the best and right choice.  She convinced him that everything would be alright with the assistance of a good doctor and God in control.  She continued to tell him to have faith.

Tony counseled with Rev. Carter, who had married the couple, after being admitted to the hospital for the second time.  Tony told Carita he spoke to Uncle George, who had passed just two weeks prior. Remembering her grandmother always said, "When the living are ill and speak of communicating with someone who is dead, they are soon to join them; she had to accept the end for Tony might be near.

Carita's mind snapped back to the situation at hand. Just as she excused herself from Tessa and Todd, to retrieve a credit card so she could make hotel accommodations for out of state family members, her phone rang.

Tessa, seeing Douglas's name on the display of Carita's cell phone, thought her aunt wouldn't mind if she answered.  For years Tessa, Todd, and Ruth, a niece in Florida knew Carita and Douglas loved one another. Tessa spoke briefly to Douglas.

Douglas was glad to learn their son and Tessa were by Carita's side.  He called periodically, over the months while in Florida, to check on Carita. Tessa however told Douglas that she and Todd were relatively concerned about Carita.  She told him how the doctors said there was no hope, how Carita rushed home from Cleveland and packed a bag then returned. When Tessa and Todd arrived on Saturday morning, Tony had slipped into a comma.

Carita, as strong as she was, had not cried and appeared to be in control, Tessa revealed. "Of course," she said. "That's Carita. She will maintain her composure until she's alone."

Carita returned and Tessa handed her the phone. Douglas's voice soothed her. She knew he was genuinely concerned. After all, they've been the best of friends and in love for forty years.

"Carita, I'm sorry to hear about Tony. Is there anything I can do for you?"

"Thank you," she replied. "But I'm okay. Your call means so much to me."

"I'm here for you. Whatever you need I am only a phone call away. Don't hesitate to call," Douglas said before they ended the call.

She promised but he knew her pride would not let her. He called Lee tell her of Carita's misfortune.

"Mama, I need a favor," Douglas said. "Could you drive to Carita's just to see her face? She says she's fine, but I don't believe her. Our son is there but I need for you to go and look at her then I'll feel better."

Lee, now a little up in age, honored Douglas's request. She phoned Carita the next day and offered to bring all of Carita's favorite food but insisted on coming at a time when she might have Carita's undivided attention. Arrangements were made for Lee to visit after Tony's burial.

A gentle tap on the window brought her back to reality. The wind brushed softly in her hair and the tears rolled down her face when assisted out of the family car at the cemetery. She attempted to walk behind her husband's casket as the pallbearers moved it to its final place of

interment but the funeral attendant held her back.

"Please Mrs. Lomax," he said, gently. "You don't want to go over there. I'm afraid that it will be a little too much for you."

After all the years, she thought, of good times, bad times, ups, downs, and now they were gone. "How am I going to go on without him?" Carita quietly said to herself. Although a strong person, probably the stronger of the two, her heart felt void and she began to think back on their courtship and how they met.

Lee and Walter came the day after the services to offer their condolences. They spent quality time with her, letting Carita know they considered her family. And anything she needed, they were only a phone call away.

The following days became lonely and unfulfilling. The house appeared empty but, somehow, Carita could still feel Tony's spirit. Because sitting around only caused more depression, she decided to return to work a little early. Dr. Rea had already prescribed medication to help her sleep at night.

The job became Carita's "*Calgon.*" As long as she worked, she did not have time to think about Tony or the emptiness in her heart. She even accepted some overtime. Shelly felt Carita tried to do too much and knew all too well what she was going through. She talked with Carita to make sure she felt up to the extra work. Carita was an asthmatic and, during this period of time, had become a borderline diabetic with high blood pressure.

Carita designed graphics for a few customers to break the boredom at home. Receiving her degree in graphics the year prior, had become her soul source of energy. Tony was so proud of her that he turned the basement into a computer lab. Carita had also taught him some basics of the computer as well as Microsoft office. They became a team when a project was in demand.

Lee called every day to let Carita know the family was there if she needed them. Douglas called Carita from time to time also. He did not want to overwhelm her. He was very concerned. He had never stopped caring for her. He felt guilty for not being able to be there with her. When talking with her, it seemed she tried to make her voice sound strong but in essence she was disguising it so he would not worry. She did this a lot in the past. It was just her way. She never wanted to cause her friends and family concern.

The later part of June, Douglas called to check on Carita. He let her know he would be flying home to take care of some personal business and wanted to stop and see her. He had put off coming home, unsure of his feelings. Although he was in a situation with someone, he often wondered what it was all about. He thought he cared for Suzie but, since Carita had become single again, old feelings aroused. He did not know what to make of them. Suzie had been there for him during his divorce but, unlike Caritas's character, he could not seem to bring himself to be open with her in discussing all his problems. Carita had always been there for him, since day one. He couldn't understand what took him so long to realize it. She had been his best friend.

She greeted him at the door with a smile and a hug. He hugged her back. She looked better than he expected and that made him a little more relaxed. Her home was beautiful and really reflected her character. She suggested they sit on the enclosed patio and drink iced tea. She remembered, he thought. She remembered that I liked tea. She asked if he would like to look around her home and he accepted. He loved it although the wall paper to in the dining room was not to his taste. He asked her why she went back to work so early. She explained and Douglas got upset at her thought process.

"You should have taken some type of vacation," he cried. "You needed to go somewhere to rest. God knows you've been through a lot."

She looked at him in a sad manner. "Where would you have suggested I go? I don't have a lot of money to fly around the country just because you feel that's what I needed to do."

As much as he wanted to tell her to come to Florida, he didn't. She appeared to be in a disturbed condition and God knows he did not want to upset her any more than what she seemed to be. He took her by the hand and led her back to the patio. They finished their conversation, talking about their son and his other children. Soon it was time for him to go. He told her he would try to see her again before he left. As he exited the door, he gave her a quick kiss on the cheek.

Carita regrouped, thinking how pleasant their visit was and how well Douglas looked. She could not help but to think Douglas was hiding something from her. He didn't seem happy. She tidied the patio and locked the house, for it was time to retire.

The summer days rolled on with Carita missing Tony every day and twice on the holidays. She purchased flowers to decorate his grave. His children called to make sure she was doing well and offered their assistance. She begin to settle down and became regrettably use to the silence and loneness of the house. It had become easier for her to stop and pick up her dinner rather than cook. All of her aunts called her every day. They were all widows and understood her pain. Shelly called every evening before bedtime. Lee called often as well. Lee had even come to spend a weekend with Carita to keep her company. Much to Carita's surprise, Douglas started calling once a week to chat and to keep her spirits up. They discussed the weather, world events, their children, grandchildren and other subjects of interest.

On Saturday, as she entered the family room, her cell phone rang. She was not able to answer. Her hands were full. She went about her chores, putting away the items she purchased. After folding the bags, she sat to take a load of her feet. She checked her phone for messages. She saw Douglas had called and left a message for her return the phone call. She did so as hurriedly as she could. Douglas did not usually call on a Saturday. She figured something might be wrong with one of the children. Upon answering the phone, he sounded calm. His voice always sounded pleasant and friendly.

He was glad to hear from her and told her of all the events happening in Miami. He continued to mention that American airlines had tickets on sale for the next month.

"Why do you keep telling me about airline tickets being on sale?"

"In case you may want to fly somewhere."

"Listen," she replied, "I don't know anyone that is far enough away for me to fly and visit. After all, that costs money and I'm a widow. I don't have that kind of cash."

"You could come to visit me," he replied.

Carita laughed. "Don't temp me. I may be knocking on your back door in the next few minutes."

"And you would be welcome," he said. "When are you coming?"

Carita, at a loss for words, asked him to give her a chance to check her hours on the book from work. He suggested she choose a time when they could enjoy the city and all it had to offer.

When they completed their conversation and hung up, Douglas began to think. He had known for years that he had feelings for Carita. He just did not know how deeply. He did not want her to be hurt or unhappy even though losing a spouse was tough. He wanted to make up for not being there when she needed him the most. He tried to imagine how the vacation would be once she arrived. They had maintained a rapport but had not been alone together for over forty years. He just wanted to be near her and comfort her. After all, she had always been there for him and neither one of them had even realized it until now.

He busied himself with a few household chores, thinking of places he could take Carita that she might enjoy. In a way, he felt nervous about some of his thoughts. His second marriage ended in a disaster. He believed Carita was a different type person and would never do anything to hurt him or anyone for that matter. He wondered if fate had decided to be kind to him after all. He realized there were things did that he would have to answer to God about, Carita being one of them.

Carita shared the Florida invitation with Lee. They had become better friends than ever. Lee seemed just as excited as Carita. She obviously thought the two would eventually get back together. She, like everyone, knew they always loved one another.

"You could have been in Florida before now."

"What do you mean?"

"When he told you that you needed a vacation, what did you think he was talking about?"

They both laughed. Carita always let things go over her head.

A few days later, Carita told Shelly about Douglas's invitation, as well, and mentioned her uncertainty about going.

"Listen," Shelly said in a big sister scolding manner. "What's the matter with you? No one cares what other people think. They are not paying your bills. Tony is gone and he is not coming back. You know and I know you have always loved Douglas. Maybe nothing will come of it but, if not, you will have had a nice vacation. If he did not have your best interest at heart, he would have not extended the invitation. So what do I need to do to help you? I am so excited for you."

Carita checked her time at work. She had more than enough hours to take some time off, and therefore proceeded to submit the necessary paperwork. Once she received approval, she called Douglas to let him know.

"What would you like for breakfast when you come?"

"If you just have coffee and toast, I will be fine."

He laughed and said, "I drink tea. Will that be alright?"

"No, I drink coffee."

"I don't own a coffee pot, but there's some instant here."

"I don't do instant," she retorted. "Just wait until I get there. I'll buy a coffee pot and the coffee."

He finally agreed.

"We've planned breakfast but I haven't told you when I'm coming," she said with laughter before giving him her itinerary."

"Carita, this is only five days, five days… really?"

She explained to him that it was just a short holiday. "I'm not trying to move in."

He understood but had to wonder if she was just being a gracious lady or afraid of discovering that they both genuinely loved one another all of these years.

Excited about taking the trip, Carita contacted Tannie, her beautician. She needed her to come up with a style that would last for the week. Douglas told her Florida gets very humid. Carita, knowing the softness of her hair, figured it would not last long in that type of environment. Tannie came up with an awesome style requiring very little upkeep.

The only thing left for Carita to do was tell their son. She really did not know how he would take the news. When she reached Todd, they exchanged their niceties as usual then she explained that she was going on a short vacation. He became ecstatic. He remembered that she had not taken a vacation since he was nine years old.

"Where are you going, mom?"

"To Florida," she replied.

"Florida," he exclaimed. "Who the hell do you know in Florida?"

"You forgot your cousin Ruth."

"Oh yes, I did forget about her."

"But I am not going to see her," she said. "I am going to see your dad."
There was complete silence.

"Dad?" he asked. "Mom, I never dreamed that you and dad…"

"Your father and I have always been friends. I know you know that."

"Yes ma'am," he said.

He had always known, even though he had nothing against his step-father, there were times he wished his parents were together. He, with his cousins Ruth and Tessa, knew the two were always in love. Their eyes told a story that would make the gods jealous. He just didn't want his mother to get hurt.

Carita could hardly sleep. Although the flight did not leave until ten in the morning, she woke up at three. That's the time she usually rose for work. She checked and double checked to make sure she packed all the necessary items. Shelly called to make sure Carita was alright and to give her the best. She also told her to just call if she needed anything. Lee called to make sure she was alright and to encourage her.

She still had some doubts about going even though she and Douglas had always been good friends.

The plane arrived on time in Miami and she had her luggage carried to the outside arrival door. Since she did not see Douglas at the gate, she knew he would just pull the SUV up to the curb. Her cell rang. Her Aunt Anne called to make sure she landed safely. Aunt Anne seemed disturbed that he had not picked up her up yet, but Carita assured her Douglas would be there soon.

Just as they finished their conversation, he arrived. He gave her a quick kiss on the cheek and put her luggage in the truck. Carita noticed a real estate sign on his truck and thought that it would make good conversation. He reminded her that he held a real estate license for years and, when he was not doing real estate, he assisted mentally challenged children.  Often times, there were meetings regarding new techniques.  This way he was utilizing his degree as Carita had suggested years ago.  It made him better appreciate the gifts he received from God.

After leaving the airport, they stopped at the store to pick up a coffee pot and the coffee.  While there, Carita wanted to purchase a few more items. She planned to prepare at least one good meal for her friend. When they arrived at the house, Douglas escorted Carita to a huge bedroom. A bathroom with a Jacuzzi tub was attached.

Douglas showed her to the walk in closet where she could hang her clothes and, once she put her belongings down, he showed her the rest of the house.

Two bedrooms appeared about 13x16 in size and a third had been turned into an office.  The computer and printer sat on a beautiful desk covered with a glass top. Carita could see Douglas did his laundry in this room. The ironing board was up and jeans hung on hangers.  The dining room and living rooms joined together. Beautiful hardwood floors adorned both while an imitation fireplace sat in the left corner of the living room.

As Carita entered the kitchen, Douglas asked her if she was alright.

"Of course." She smiled.

As much as he wanted to just hold her in his arms, he refrained.  While putting away the few items they purchased, he asked what she wanted for dinner.  He planned to make her steaks. She agreed, only if he allowed her to prepare a salad.  He showed Carita how to use the remote for the TV and explained that he did not have cable.  Carita looked at him. She knew he could be conservative with money.  He saw her look and explained when he got home, from meetings it was often times late and he usually went to bed.

She smiled. As long as he had a computer, she would be fine.

While Douglas prepared the steaks, Carita mixed the ingredients for the salad. Since neither one of them wanted bread, she decided to bake garlic potatoes.  Douglas observed her in amazement.  Neither one of his wives could cook or even wanted to try.  It was one of Carita's favorite pastimes, even during her present condition.  He was just so surprised at her con-centration and composure.  She tried to set the table but he reminded her that she was on vacation and completed the chore himself.  He marveled over the tasty salad. The garlic potatoes tasted so delicious, one might have believed that they were prepared at a five star restaurant. Together the cleared the table and cleaned the dishes. Carita was ready to watch a little TV but Douglas reminded her that she had an early and long day, and suggested they both turn in.

Douglas slept in the bedroom at the end of the hall. He had been up early, worrying if the flight would be on time, what Carita was really like as a full grown woman, how to keep her entertained, and just making her happy so she would enjoy her vacation. About to nod off, he remembered that the nights in Miami got somewhat chilly. He did not want Carita to get cold. He found a blanket that would keep her warm since he couldn't. He knocked at the door and called her name but did not receive a response. He quietly opened it and placed the blanket over her. She looked so peaceful. Her skin, smooth as silk, didn't reveal her age. She slept quietly and peacefully. He admired the gentleness of her body. He wanted to touch and hold her. He did not want hurt or harm to come to her ever. She had been through enough, even with him. He kissed her tenderly on the forehead and silently left the room.

Three o'clock came early. For a moment, Carita did not remember where she was until she collected her thoughts. She tossed and turned. She didn't want to wake Douglas. She remained in bed as long as she could. The rhythm and custom of her body that typically woke her for work would didn't stop just because she was on vacation. Finally, she had to answer to the usual routine and get up. She quickly took a sponge bath before going to the kitchen to put on a pot of coffee. She was reflecting upon the beautiful home when she felt a hand on her shoulder. She turned and he gazed at her.

"Why are you up? It's four o'clock in the morning."

"I'm sorry," she said. "I didn't mean to wake you. It's just that I am usually on my way to work by now and my body does not know I am on vacation."

He shook his head. "I am going back to bed. I have a nine a.m. meeting but have to leave at eight. I have to pick someone up. I probably won't get back here until eleven or so. Will you be alright while I'm gone?"

"Sure," she said with confidence. "I will probably just check out your computer."

After two cups of coffee, Carita decided to lie down for just a little while. Douglas knocked on her door to let her know he was leaving.

"Just call if you need anything," he said.

Carita fell off to sleep for about forty-five minutes. She showered and elected to prepare brunch with the previous night's leftovers. She cut the steak away from the bone and reheated it with onions and peppers. The leftover potatoes were diced and placed into the pan with the meat. She poured the orange juice when she heard the truck pull into the garage. The water had already been in the microwave for his tea. She only had to add napkins to the table setting.

The aroma of the food met him as he got out of the truck. What's she up to he wondered? When he opened the door, he smiled.

"Lady, what are you doing? You're supposed to be on vacation."

She beamed and replied, "My grandma and your mom didn't believe in throwing away food. They raised us the same way. So I just the thought I would make us a grand buffet with lasts night's leftovers."

He pinched her arm as he walked by to let her know he approved. The meal hit the spot and he was very appreciative. He volunteered to do the dishes for her and, again, reminded Carita that she was on vacation. As he did the dishes, he bent over and smiled at Carita as though he wanted to kiss her.

"Re, whatever happened to the twelve kids you wanted?"

"What twelve kids?" she replied.

"You know," he continued. "When I met you, you said you wanted twelve kids. I was just thinking, if we had gotten together, I would have given you all twelve of them too."

She just glared at him as though he were ill.

He continued, "They would have been good looking kids. After all, look at how handsome Todd turned out. He looks just like me."

Carita just looked at him. "I think you have lost your mind. I need to check and see what seasoning I used in our entrée."

The both laughed uncontrollably. Her cell rang. Tessa called to make sure she arrived safely. Tessa went on, asking personal questions just to get Carita's goat. She asked to speak to Douglas. He laughed.

"We're too old to have sex, much less make a baby."

Again, they both had a good laugh.

Tessa always looked out for Carita. Carita was the one who always seemed to understand her at the most difficult of times. She had grown to love Douglas because he was Todd's dad and someone she could look up to.

After the phone call, Douglas shared some old pictures of the children and some of his old classmates. He asked Carita if there was any way to preserve them. Carita told him that they could be scanned into the computer and she could save them to a flash drive. Knowing he did not have a lot of computer knowledge, she suggested they go to Wal-Mart so they could purchase some of the products needed for the projects.

While Carita worked on a project for him that evening, he told her how proud he was of her for going back to school and completing her degree.

"I never asked, Carita, what did your receive your degree in?" he asked while ironing some jeans.

"Computers and graphics," she replied.

They both laughed. He, now, understood her excitement to complete the projects he requested. While ironing, Douglas confided in Carita about just how difficult his divorce had been. He discussed the financial changes he been through as well as several other emotions. Carita listened attentively then gave him encouragement, letting him know that everyone has been through their own private hell. She told him that, although she had never been through a divorce, to continue to pray. She reiterated the biblical cliché that when prayers go up, blessings come down.

"You are blessed. Douglas, you may not think you are but I know you are a child of God," she voiced.

"Re, he said with affection, you have been better to me than either one of the wives I've had. You have always been there for me. I could call you day or night. You have given me good advice, which I did not always follow. You have been my best friend. You know when you disrespect people and you know that you're wrong, God has a way of making you pay."

She immediately knew he referred to the situation with her and Todd.

"Doug, it's alright," she said, quietly. "It is what it is and I do not hold any hard feelings. In life, sometimes, fate deals us bad cards. Let's let the past be past and move forward with whatever God gives us."

Still busying himself with his jeans, he asked, "Carita, Why you did stay married to Tony. Why didn't you leave?"

Her marriage in the early years to her husband had been pure hell. The area being just a small town made it worse than Payton Place because everyone knew your business.

She smiled then said, "Vows and commitment."

He looked at her and replied "That's bull. Look at how many people divorce every year. Look at me."

"I am not everyone," she stated. "I am very old fashion. I was always taught you make your bed, you lie in it. Vows and commitments are made to God as well as the person. That's why they shouldn't be broken."

He sensed she was upset by the tone of her voice and decided not to push. He knew Carita well enough to know she gave any situation her very best. Carita told him she was all talked out and would see him in the morning. She kissed him on his cheek and said good night.

She got up at six, which was a little better. She got her coffee and moved to the office, excited about completing some of the projects for Douglas. Soon after, she felt a hand on her shoulder. He made her a smoothie and wanted her to guess what fruits it contained. She guessed all but two. Little later, he returned with breakfast. She smiled as she decided to eat at the kitchen table with him. He mentioned that he wanted to show her the town. She excused herself so to get ready.

After her final preparation, she found Douglas patiently waiting in the living room. He made a comment about women being slow.

She glared at him and said, "I couldn't go looking like, dammit I'll bite you."

He laughed while opening the door for her. In the car, Douglas brought up the twelve children again.

"Why Carita," he asked, "why didn't you have more children?"

"Doug," she said, sadly. "When I was delivering Todd, I could not remember what day it was, the month, the year, or the season. I could only remember Nate King Cole singing "*Chestnuts Roasting over an Open Fire.*" Then, I knew it was Christmas. I was passing in and out. The pain was horrible. After giving me the opportunity to deliver the baby on my own, the doctor decided to do a C-section. I had been in labor 17 hours. I asked

God to subside the pain. He if could do so he would never have to worry about me being in a labor/delivery room ever again in life. I ended with the surgery as well as clamps and stitches."

"I'm sorry," Douglas said. "You never told me you had such a hard delivery."

Carita replied, "You never asked."

Douglas took her to the most scenic places in town. Knowing she was a history buff, they elected to find a few statues downtown by the wharf. They ran into a man who was making roses out of reeves. Douglas had one made for Carita and kissed her when he handed to her. They took the ferry across the river much to Carita's disapproval. Douglas just wanted to show her everything. On the return ferry trip, he suggested they eat at the one of the restaurants at the wharf while watching the boats go by. Carita asked if he had lost his mind.

"Look at those birds," she said. "They are walking just like people. I know that they are trying to find a table just like us. I would like to eat when we get home."

Douglas just laughed and laughed. He gave her some tokens as a souvenir. She asked if they were to remember him.

"No," he said, smiling, "when you look at our son, you should remember me. Those are to remember your trip to Florida."

On the way home, Douglas stopped by a quaint restaurant and they ate a delicious meal. He questioned Carita about her degree in computers and inquired about the different skills she had obtained. He found out, she could help him with websites and other graphics for his real estate business. He told her about a real estate seminar the following day. He wanted them to go.

After returning from the real estate seminar, Douglas asked Carita why she stayed with her husband again. Carita's answer remained the same.

"Come on, ReRe. We both know better," Douglas said.

"Okay," she replied. "I have loved you for forty years. No forty one. Todd's going to be forty this year. I learned how to love Tony for the thirty years we were together."

Douglas, not expecting this answer, found himself at a loss for words. "Oh my God," he said to himself. "All of this time, I thought she was being kind to me because of our son." On that note, he pecked Carita on the cheek then squeezed her hand and went off to bed.

The next day, Carita wanted to go to the beach and naturally naturally Douglas made all of the accommodations. He got up early to do his yogi exercise and made a picnic lunch. Carita enjoyed the beach with the coolness of the wind and water smashing against her face. She walked on the sand like a little princess, making Douglas look at her a little differently. How strong she is, he thought, and how naturally she saw worthiness in other people. She was forever trying to unequivocal unequivocally solve blameless situations.

For an instant, she looked lost as she dug her toes in the sand like a little girl. Douglas came up behind her and she vanished into his arms. Wanting to provide a sense of safety, he pressed his lips to hers and the sun made them feel like a piece of melted sweet chocolate. He embraced her affectionately. He wanted her to know his feelings for her were more than just a reaction of the moment. He cuddled her hand into to his as they walk back to the truck.

Douglas had something planned every day for Carita. They went to his favorite store, Dollar Tree. Carita teased him about being cheap. He replied, "You are too." She did not like to spend money any more than he did. She claimed to be thrifty. While in the store, they found a dictionary. Douglas looked up cheap and Carita looked up thrifty. They both laughed. The definitions were so similar.

Douglas purchased some Dixie ice cream cups and other items. Carita had no idea what he was doing. They stopped at a couple of other stores to round out some of the things for their Sunday dinner. He had wanted to take her to dinner and the movies on Saturday but she elected to stay home and watch Tyler Perry movies. After dinner, when Douglas put on the first tape, they just held hands. Douglas told Carita how special their relationship had been over the years. She just smiled and said, not everyone got a chance to have what they had.

Douglas went to the kitchen and came back with a spoon and a Dixie cup of ice cream. He placed Carita on his lap and began to feed her. He kissed her on the nose and told her to enjoy it. It was something he always wanted to do.

On Sunday, after Douglas's mental health meeting, they complemented each other in the kitchen as each one completed entrée entrée a variety of entrées. They discussed occurrences of the past as well as matters of concern for the future. Douglas helped Carita pack some of her clothes. She decided to leave the newly purchased items. Douglas would bring them later, to keep her bag from being overweight. They cleaned the kitchen together, laughing about never having the twelve children.

Carita saw the evening winding down. It was her last night with Douglas. She did not know what to expect. He had not approached her, exactly. She kissed him goodnight and retired to her room. Teary eyed she lay on top of the covers. She knew she would not sleep.

Douglas sat in the living room, wondering if he should expose his emotions to her. He did not want to frighten her or have her think their relationship was cheap. He could never have that. Who has a relationship, clean and pure, that lasts for forty years, he thought as he stood by her door for a brief second? He saw her light still on but decided that he loved her enough to forgo anything that might make her feel uncomfortable.

Carita showered around four in the morning and finished her packing. She went to Douglas's room to wake him so they would be on time for her flight. The airport was almost a two hour drive. In the car, Douglas noticed Carita's quietness.

"What's wrong? What are you thinking about?"

"Nothing," she replied, politely.

He said, "Ump. You just sit over and think I believe that."

She tried to talk but nothing would come out. They soon arrived at the terminal and Douglas placed her luggage on a cart, hugged, and kissed her. He reminded her to call as soon as she got home.

On his way home, he thought of how much he would miss her. His missed the smell of her cologne and let's not forget her coffee. He asked her to teach him how to make it for her but she emphatically said no. Once home, he went to her room. He could not believe that week had gone so quickly. He hugged her pillow so that he might be able to dream of her smell, her laughter, the gentleness of her voice, her smile, and just her. Oh my, what are these feelings?

*Chapter 10*

As she boarded the plane, she could not believe how fast the week had gone. Douglas had done everything she wanted and had been the perfect gentleman. A lady could not have requested better accommodations from a five star hotel. She felt so very blessed to have a great rapport and friendship with the man she loved for forty years. She felt sad not realizing the trip would go so quickly. Had she known, she would maybe have planned for a little longer than five days. She was going to miss him. Maybe they still had a chance to be as one, she hoped. She prayed that God showed them favor.

After catching her breath and bringing in her luggage, she made her phone call to Douglas.

"Doug, it's me. I'm just calling to let you know I'm home."

"I didn't expect for you to be home this quickly. Wow, the flight didn't take long at all."

"Yes, I know."

"You're completely in the house?"

"Yes."

"Get some rest and I will be in touch with you later."

"Okay. Thanks Doug, for everything. I had a good time and a restful vacation."

She called Shelly to let her know she had arrived home safely. She unpacked her suitcase, hung clothes up, and placed soiled items in the hamper. She called Lee as well. Lee offered to take her to dinner so would not have to cook. Lee picked her up about 4 p.m. and they went to their favorite restaurant. She wanted Carita to have enough time to tell her all about her vacation and still get her home for a good night's rest.

"So how was your visit with my son?"

"It was wonderful."

"Really?"

"Yes.  He was a perfect gentleman.  I could not have gotten better accommodations at a five star hotel."

"And you all?"

"I really don't know.  I didn't realize I had all of these feelings for him. I always thought, as I got older and since I got married, they would vanish. I dared not tell him for he may look at me like a fool."

"I don't think he would, but at least you know and are willing to admit you are still in  love with my son.  We have all known that you all loved one another. It was just getting the both of you to see and admit it.

Lee smiled and gave a special pat on her hand.  They enjoyed their meal and talked about family and other topics of interest.  She recapped Carita the offer of staying with her and Walter if her home got too big and lonely. The girls made plans for later in the month to take their first shopping trip together.  She also reminded Carita that Doug would be home soon.  All of the kids came home this time of year to spend a month with Lee.

Having had an enjoyable afternoon, Lee and Carita parted so they could get home.  Once Carita walked through her door, she began to think about Douglas.  She thought, "what if we had made love."  She questioned why they hadn't and, more importantly, how he felt about her. She questioned to herself, wondering if he still, possibly loved her.  After forty years, people usually feel differently about things as well as each other.

Douglas came in from a meeting.  The house seemed so empty.  He had gotten use to Carita's smile and enjoyed their camaraderie in the kitchen. He missed her clowning and just the way she would say, 'Is that right." She said it in the funniest way. He also liked how she said "Have you lost your mind?"  Now, he had to get use to an empty house all over again.  Carita had been a breath of fresh air.  As much as he wanted to hold her and to let her know things were going to be alright, he couldn't.  He wasn't sure how he felt or how she felt for that matter about their relationship. It may have been too soon after her husband's death. He knew he still had very deep feelings for Carita but did know what to do with Suzie. He had not told Carita anything about this relationship. He knew, if he did, she would not have come to Florida and he so desperately needed to see her. He needed to be with her so he would know how he really felt. He went to bed thinking of Carita and what they had and what they possibly could still have. The only problem was Suzie.

Douglas continued to call Carita from time to time to check on her and she loved it. She would call him in the morning on her way to work and leave an inspiring Bible verse for him on his voice mail. He thought how nice. But he especially loved when she called on a Sunday morning to let him know she was on her way to church. Most men want a Christian woman or at least one who attends Sunday service.

Douglas called to let Carita know he was on his way home. He needed to know where she put the bag that contained the items purchased when they went shopping. Her heart skipped beats. She thought he would surely forget the bag.

When he arrived, he called to let her know he was home and would see her the next day. Thrilled, she did not get any sleep; not that she slept well anyway. Sleep was something of her past, since Tony's demise. She reported off work and spent the day buying items Douglas might enjoy eating.

Douglas called at six to let Carita know he was on his way and had a surprise for her.

Carita looked very nice in her skinny girl jeans with a vibrant yet conservative sweater. Lavenders and mauves had become her favorite colors and they did wonders for her complexion. Every strain of pixie haircut was in place and her make-up was impeccable as usual.

The doorbell rang and Carita hastened to answer it. Douglas gave her a long kiss then pecked her on the check. The man behind him grinned. She looked a second time and saw Mike.

"Oh my goodness," she exclaimed. "Mike, I am so glad to see you."

He just smiled and said, "You know, all of those years ago, I thought Doug brought you home to be my girl."

"Oh yea," said Douglas in a joking voice. "Have you lost your mind"

They all laughed. Douglas gave Carita the bag and she quickly placed it in the spare bedroom. Mike complimented her home and Carita gave him a quick tour. Carita asked Douglas if he would make smoothies.

"Make smoothies," he said and laughed.

"When I move back home, I will not be here to make you smoothies all the time. I have a girl," he said very emphatically. "I'm not coming all the way over here to do that for you."

He kind of laughed because he thought it was funny. Then he went on tell Mike he had spoiled Carita while she was on vacation with him.

Carita could not believe her ears. She knew he was seeing someone but she did not know the depth of the relationship, nor did he tell her of any plans to move back to the area. She felt hurt, crushed, embarrassed, and like a fool. How could he do this to her? He invited her to Florida and now humiliating her in front of his brother. Carita looked at him with a look that could kill.

"Yes you do and I'm the damn girlfriend."

Mike just laughed and laughed. Ordinarily, she would have told him off in no uncertain terms but this was the first time Mike had visited her and it was not polite to go off when entertaining company, especially on their first visit. Carita did not have much to say after this incident. As a matter of fact, she knew that a request for smoothies prepared by him would never come from her lips again. Carita was the type of person that, if she requested something of someone and it seemed to be a chore or the person did not want to honor it, you would not have to worry about her asking you to do anything for her again.

The threesome went on with small talk with Carita hardly saying anything. Douglas had the nerve to say "What's wrong babe?"

Carita just glared and said nothing.

Mike asked, "Are you sure?" He felt a little coldness coming from Carita.

She smiled at Mike and said, "I'm okay."

Mike suggested they leave so Carita could prepare for work in the morning. They were on vacation. Douglas promised to come over the next day and needed to know what time she would be home.

Carita's friends were all ears the next day at work but Carita didn't really have anything to tell. Both women suggested different outfits for Carita to wear. Both of them wanted her to have a companion but, most of all, they wanted her to be happy. As Carita drove home from work, Douglas called to see if they were still on for the afternoon. Carita made excuses. She was still not over the previous night and suggested he wait until the following day. Hurt she didn't know how Douglas could have said those things like she was nothing, knowing he never told her anything about another woman. This was something she vowed to never forgive him for. She would never expose him to cruelty or hurt from anyone and she certainly would never do anything to hurt him.

When Carita arrived from work the next day, Douglas was waiting in the driveway. Her hand automatically cupped her mouth. She thought he must have felt some of her coldness from the previous two nights. He jumped out of his truck and bent down to kiss her on the cheek after she pulled into the garage. He aided her with her items from work as she took them out of her truck. She invited him to make himself at home while she changed her clothes. She made some hot tea for Douglas while she took on a cup of cappuccino. They sat on the love set and looked out the patio door.

"How did you feel when you left Florida," he asked?

"I had a great time. I rested, got a chance to see the city, and I had a wonderful host who was the perfect gentleman. How did you feel?"

"You left me in shock," he stated.

"Shock," she said. "What are you talking about?"

"When you told me you had loved me for forty years, I did not know what to say. I always assumed that you were kind to me because we had a child together."

"Douglas," she whispered in a soft spoken voice, looking innocent. "Children do not keep people together. Where did you get that nonsense?"

"Carita, I just didn't know what to say. Why didn't you ever tell me?"

"Doug, only a promiscuous woman would have done that. You were married and I was married. How and why would I tell you that? Besides, I thought you were happy and I would never do anything to ruin your happiness. I have always loved you. I will love you until God calls me home."

"Oh, Carita I wish you had told me," he said in a slight whisper. "What else have you not told me?"

"I have several things I need to tell you. First and far most, I told you half truths about having additional children other than Todd. It's true that I was in pain from hell and asked God for help. After his birth, I found I still loved you but I knew I had to go on with my life. I only heard from you through your support checks, most of the time. I felt than that we didn't have chance. If I couldn't have any more children with you, I didn't want any. I was not going to have a baby here and a baby there. I elected to have my tubes clipped, burnt, and tied."

Douglas shouted, "What! Back in the day, the doctors didn't do that. How old were you when you had this done?"

"Yes they did. If you knew how to be articulate and were loquacious enough you could get anything you wanted. We all know I have the gift to gab. And besides what did age have to do with it?"

"Oh Carita," he said, sadly, as he hugged her. "I'm so sorry."

"It's alright. I have Todd and he is my life and my life is full. We have a beautiful granddaughter and one day we'll have great grandchildren." She smiled and kissed the tear on his face.

"Why, Carita? Why? Why didn't you tell me?"

"Like I said," she answered, "only a promiscuous woman would do something like that."

"I would not have thought that about you," he said.

"Oh yes, you would have, because you were married; and it would have cheapened our relationship."

This made Douglas hold onto Carita much tighter, for he knew now that it had been as she said. She loved him for forty one years as he had her, but had never admitted it.

"And the other," he said.

"The other," she repeated in a gentle voice. "I don't really know how to say this, but please don't laugh at me." He held her face between his hands and she looked down embarrassed. "I have been celibate for ten years."

"What!" he shouted. "Now, that, you didn't have to do!"

"Yes I did," she said. "I believe in vows and commitment. And who knows what one can catch just to satisfy an emotion at the time."

Douglas could not answer her. He just grabbed her and hugged her as hard as he could, still asking why.

"Anything else," he said.

"Yes," answered Carita. "I am the world's biggest cry baby. I'll cry at the drop of a hat."

At that point, tears rolled down her cheeks as big as gumdrops. Douglas tried to kiss all of the tears but they fell too fast. He placed her head on his shoulder and tried to dry her tears with his handkerchief. He lifted up her face to his and softly kissed her lips.

"We have got to talk," he said. "I just want you to listen."

"I am with someone. I'm in a relationship. I did not know how you felt about me. You should have told me."

"But I did, Doug. You didn't listen. Why didn't you tell me this before I came to Florida," she asked in between the tears.

He could not answer her. "What do I do?" he asked. "I just can't just kick her to the curb. She was there for me at a time in my life when I needed her."

"Be honest," she said. "Whatever we do, we must be honest." Carita continued, through the tears, "I have loved you forty Doug years. I cannot give you forty more years because I don't believe God has forty more for me. At best I may have twenty, only because there is a long lifeline on both sides of my family. Tomorrow is not promised to any of us. I need what time God may have for me, for me, if there is not going to be any us. If you decide that we do not have a future, I will walk away."

"Walk away!" he screamed. "And what will you do? And why are you putting this on me?"

"You're the one in the relationship," she said.

He could not argue with that. She was right. But he was still angry about her keeping this secret all of these years.

"I have kept this to myself for forty one years and no one knew. Please know that I love you and I would never put you in an uncompromising position. Before I would bring any harm or unhappiness to you, I would walk away."

Completely filled, Douglas decided it was time to go. Carita seemed upset and he had done his best to calm her down. He thought the two of them were not ready for any more surprises from their past. They needed to focus on the elements at hand. He held Carita for what seemed to be a lifetime. He rocked her back and forth until he brought her head to his lips. He chanted.

"Oh, babe. Oh, babe."

Carita tried to maintain her composure. She did not want Douglas to worry. She walked him to the door and told him they both should pray on the situation.

"Prayer changes things," Carita said. Douglas agreed. They kissed again and he promised to be in touch before the week was out.

Carita became so upset over Douglas's disclosure she decided to report off. She had to think. Why did Tony have to die? Was her life over? What now? There were just so many questions and the tears just rolled downed. Finally, she nestled down to try and get a good night's rest. She looked forward to another day and perhaps an answer.

Carita went about the next couple of days without really talking or seeing anyone. Her heart ached but she did not know how to handle this kind of rejection. She just did her daily routine and worked on some graphics. While in deep concentration, Douglas called requesting they meet for lunch. Carita was not much for going out to eat and decided to surprise him with some of her homemade chili.

When Douglas arrived, a heavenly aroma filled the house. He only smelled home cooking at Lee's. Suzie did not cook. It was too important to her to impress her friends about her man, so she and Douglas always went out to eat. As Carita opened the door, Douglas held onto her for dear life. He knew what she had gone through the last couple of days. He bent down and gave her a soft kiss on the lips.

He smiled and said, "It smells good in here."

She beamed and replied, "I remembered that you liked beans. Since it is a little chilly out, I thought I would surprise you."

A fall arrangement completed the table setting. Douglas was pleased by Carita's thoughtfulness. He always knew she liked to cook, and was surprised she still held the passion while being alone. They ate and talked about Carita's job. She told him some of the events occurring over the last couple of days. She turned on the TV so he could watch his favorite program. She began to clear the table as Douglas approached her to assist. She kissed him gently on the cheek and sent him back to the rocker, which had become his favorite chair for relaxing. Talking to her while she completed the chore of cleaning up, he said his parents were elated that everyone was home and doing well. Lee was in seventh heaven, cooking and taking care of her little chicks.

When Carita's task of cleaning the kitchen ended, she sat on the couch, commenting on the program Douglas watched.

Douglas looked at her, strangely, and asked, "Why are you sitting way over there?

"Where do you suggest I sit?"

He slapped his lap quickly. "Here"

Carita smiled. "Don't you think it would be a lot of weight for the chair?"

"I've been sitting here for a while and it hasn't broken, so if it breaks you did it."

They both laughed and Carita promptly honored his request.

Douglas placed Carita's head on his shoulder while rocking them back and forth. He whispered, "Carita, what are we going to do?" He touched her lips with his.

Her small hands touched his face so that she might be able to express how she felt. She kissed his cheek and then his nose. She continued until she reached his neck and returned to caress his lips.

"Pray and try to reunite. Let's see what God has for us. I know that this is difficult for us both and I don't know what else to say."

Douglas continued kissing her while turning her body toward his and gently stroking her breasts through her blouse. She held onto him as tightly as she could and, as the moment of ecstasy arrived, his phone rang. He gathered his composure and answered. Carita excused herself. When he completed the call, he apologized to Carita. He had to leave but told her he would call very soon. He kissed Carita then left, looking discouraged but knowing they would be able to bond soon.

Douglas was glad he could answer Suzie's call without Carita knowing it was her. Somehow he had to find a way to tell her about Carita but decided it was not the time even though he remembered Carita saying they should always be truthful.

Once he arrived, he became depressed. Suzie didn't want anything; she was just checking his whereabouts. Suzie was going through her changes and having issues with Douglas socializing with friends and family. She wanted him to spend more time with her. After all, she was there when he needed her and felt he should be subjective to her woes.

"Where have you been?" she asked with an attitude. "I have been calling you for almost two hours!"

Douglas glared at her. "How many times have I told you that it is not necessary for you to check on me? Sit down," he commanded. "I have something I want to tell you." He paused. "Earlier this month I invited Carita to Florida, to get way." He felt remorseful.

Suzie looked at him with hostility.

"What," she screamed. "Why?"

She knew Carita was the mother of his first child and their relationship went far deeper than just being parents of the boy. She always viewed Carita as a threat until she met her at Lee's, the year before, during the holidays. Dealing with her ill husband gave Suzie the confidence to believe she would be able to keep Douglas. From his description of their relationship, she knew Carita was special to him and their bond was not because of their child, but a love that lasted a lifetime. She knew he had been loyal but could not figure out why he would do such a thing.

"Carita lost her husband and needed to get away. She had not been on a vacation for years," he explained.

"Well!" Suzie exclaimed. "I'm you're woman. This is something that you should have discussed with me first. What did you think? That you could bring him back? We should have been together when she came."

Douglas looked at her as though she lost her mind. "Listen," he said loudly as though he had to get his point across in no uncertain terms. "Carita and I have had a rapport for forty years. We have a son together and a granddaughter. One day we will have great grandchildren. We have had forty years of occurrences that needed to be discussed and none of them concerned you!"

"Oh," she yelled. "It's like that!"

"Yes," he stated. " "It's like that!"

He abruptly walked out of their small apartment and jumped in this truck. Times like these, he wanted a drink but remembered when Carita told him it just was not him. That served as a source of stability and he was not willing to risk his promise to God or himself. Suzie refused to understand his relationship with his son's mother. During times like this, he needed Carita. She always seemed to understand his frustrations even when he didn't. He decided to let it go. He would talk with Carita later. He did not want to burden her with his problems. Her plate seemed full enough.

The next day, Douglas called Carita. The phone went to voicemail. He left a message. He then went to Lee's to pick up Mike so they could visit with some of the fellows they went to school with.

Douglas remembered, later in the afternoon, Carita had not returned his phone call. This upset him somewhat. He also noticed that, the last few times they were together, she appeared somewhat despondent. He called again and Carita answered.

"Hi," he said in a happy voice. "I was going to come over to get some more of that chili. I called earlier but you didn't answer."

"I worked over for a couple of hours. As usual, young people don't like to come to work particularly when they're on second shift."

'Is it alright if I come over and get some more of that chili? I can be there in twenty minutes."

"I'll see you in a few," replied Carita.

Carita pulled up to her driveway and saw Douglas's truck. They exited their vehicles at the same time and Douglas casually kissed Carita on the cheek. This time, he seemed to be more at ease. He seemed glad to see her. She changed her clothes and asked him if he would like to go out to eat, her treat. He felt slightly disappointed. He had his heart set on the chili. But she convinced him they could have that another day.

The restaurant was not far from Carita's. On the way, Douglas noticed a pet shop and stopped. He didn't like the idea of Carita being alone. Their son lived out of state and could only come every so often to check on her. They looked at all of the dogs and cats too.

"Why did we stop here?"

He said, "I thought you might be lonely in that big house so I was going to buy you a dog."

"Really," she replied. "Do I have to feed it?"

"Of course, silly," he said.

"Then I don't need it."

They both laughed and left to continue their dinner date. Afterwards, they stopped to get some ice cream and returned to the house. As they sat on the couch, they discussed some of the past. Again Douglas noticed Carita became despondent.

"Carita what's wrong?"

"I haven't slept well at all since my husband's death," she answered. "Although Dr. Rea prescribed pills for me, I don't want to become addicted."

"Oh babe I am so sorry. How long has this been going on?"

"At least six months"

"What can I do to help you?"

"Oh Doug I don't know. I guess it's just the way it is."

He turned Carita's head toward his. He touched her eyes. They had become very seductive to him. He pushed back her hair, as he leaned her body on the pillow from the couch, and began to kiss her. Her nose had always been a delight to him so he pecked it and smiled at her.

She was not sure what to do at this point for it had been so long. His body started to relax. He slid toward her. His hands caressed her hips as her breasts begin to fill with delight and her hands begin to fill him with pleasure. He gathered her up and took her to the bedroom, where he laid her gently on the bed.

He softly said, "If I lie down with you, do you think you'll be able to sleep tonight?"

"I don't know," she said.

"Let's try," he offered.

As they lay on the bed, he began to touch her with contentment. He had never known such devotion from any woman. They begin to remove one another's clothing. Douglas reached to pull the covers as Carita shivered. He gently laid her on top of his body so the he could keep her warm and feel the taste of her succulent breasts. He glided her body up and down his so his tongue could savor the thrill of her body.  Her nipples stood at attention as he gently drew the taste from them with his lips exulting in sheer delight.  Her fingers slithered like melting butter from hot biscuits to touch him while he eased her body onto him and placed his tongue wherever he could to sample the virginity of his love.  He placed his hands on her hips then rolled her gradually beneath him. He pushed himself into her so that he might sample the pleasant ecstasy from the thrill of reuniting with his lost love.  His arms coupled around her body as the reptile does his prey so he could feel the inside of all that was his and all that he had regained. Their bodies intertwined and begin to rapture in the years of pleasure they had missed.  The loss of self-control had an intensity of serenity that dominated all that was to be theirs once again.

Carita closed her eyes. She had not known this kind of sensuality for a very long time. Douglas noticing her quietness held her close. "What's wrong babe? Did I hurt you?"

"No," she responded.  "I'm okay."

Douglas softly brushed her face with his fingers. He did not want to leave her. He'd found the missing link in his life.  He felt more confused than ever.  He knew he only had a few more days before leaving for Florida, and he wanted to spend as much time as he could with Carita.  He held her tight and told her he had to leave.

She knew this moment would come. She clutched his waist.

"Doug," she said, I hope you know I would never put you in a precarious position."

He looked at her and said, "Why hon? Why would you say that?"

"I just know that you have a lot of things on your mind and that your plate is full.  I just want you to know I care about you and would never do anything to hurt you."

"I know that, babe," he said. "Now get some rest."

She attempted to leave the bed and he gently pushed her down. "You need to get some sleep.  I can find my way out."

When Douglas arrived at home, Suzie became livid.  She had been calling him all afternoon and even went to all the places he frequented plus Lee's.  She screamed and yelled to no avail.  Douglas just wanted to be left alone. He had Carita on his mind.  He did not want to lose what he just recaptured after all these years.  Suzie marched upstairs, hollering and screaming.

Douglas seemed smitten with Carita.  He sat in a chair, reminiscing about the fulfillment of their passion.  He drifted off with only thoughts of a happier life.

<h1 style="text-align:center">Chapter 11</h1>

Douglas could hardly contain himself the next day. Happy and relaxed, he found what he thought to be the missing link in his life. He worried because he did not know how this love triangle would affect those involved. He decided to let things go on as there were for a while. After all, Tony had only been dead a few months and he was not sure of Carita's feelings for him. All he knew was she had treated him better than either woman he had married.

He went to Lee's. He and his siblings were taking their parents out for dinner. Suzie became upset because, according their annual tradition, only birth family members participated. Later, Douglas called Carita to make sure she was alright. They had a pleasant conversation and he promised to stop by the following night. He wanted to do something special for Carita but could not think of what. He had not actually courted or dated in a long time and had forgotten how. Then he remembered she liked stuffed animals and proceeded to buy her one. He founded the cutest little bear with a Hershey's Kisses around his neck. The brown bear wore a blue jacket, one of Carita's favorite colors.

She arrived from work and took a quick shower. She freshened, her makeup and combed her hair. Ready to replace her lipstick, the doorbell rang. Douglas arrived on time. He kissed her and they sat down for a moment. He glanced around looking for the smell of chili. Carita laughed and went to the kitchen to prepare his meal. As he watched TV from the rocker, she sat the table. He was always pleased at the table setting. It made him feel like a special guest. He contemplated if he should tell her, now or later, about leaving for Florida in the next day and a half. He hated to lose her smile. She had been so happy the last few times he spent the day with her.

"Babe," he said softly.

She knew what followed. After all, in their own way, they had been soul mates for most of these years. She knew him almost as well as he knew himself.

"I'm leaving on Sunday morning to go back home."

She looked at him with tears in her eyes. The end of their long awaited rendezvous approached while both Carita and Douglas did not know if they could withstand.

"It will be alright," he stated as he squeezed her hand.

She allowed her lips to curve in approval but she really did not want him to know how sad she felt. They ate the delicious meal. Chili is always better the day or two afterwards. He insisted on helping her to clean the table as well as the dishes. She tried to be positive and get him to talk about his vacation with his siblings. She had not seen very much of his mother or Mike and the girls because she did not want to run into Suzie or put him in a position. She could not stand for him to be in any predicaments. While Carita loaded the dishwasher, he went to the truck. Not really paying attention when he returned, she finished up in the kitchen then entered the family room.

"Come sit with us," he said.

The statement confused her. She looked closer and saw a teddy bear in his lap. He moved the teddy over so Carita would have room to sit. "And who is this little fellow?" She beamed. "Now, what do I do when you leave?"

"You will have teddy when you need to hold on tight. He will be there for you just as I will."

She grabbed his neck to hide her tears.

But he knew. He knew her as well as she did him. He stood and took her by the hand, leading her to what had become their retreat. He placed on her stomach, knowing her back bothered her. He slipped the snaps lose on her bra so he might be able to have access to her complete back area. His hands were ever so gentle and soothing.

She soon felt his breath on her neck. "Baby I'm so sorry," he said.

"Quietly," she asked, "Why, what's wrong?"

"I really don't want to leave. We have just found one another again and I don't want to lose what we have. But now, I don't have a choice."

She knew he indirectly referred to Suzie. She figured Suzie made things so very difficult for him. She rolled from her stomach to her back to catch his face in an agonizing state. She pulled his face to hers and kissed his lips and his nose. She loosened the buttons on his shirt and he assisted her with his belt buckle. He always said he did not want her to break her nails. He thought she has such pretty petite hands. He slipped out of his pants. She did the same. They held on to each other, fondling their favorite parts of one another's bodies. The majestic fragment of their desire seemed only clandestine for those who not willing to accept love whole heartily. The aspirations of the two began when she massaged him, tickling the cup of his loin. He groaned as he slowly entered her. The calling of his tongue as she caught it stroking her lips sealed their whimpers of delight. They pleasured one another in exultation. Their bodies eagerly climaxed in the moisture sealed like honey from the affection of their passion as their love-making came to a gratifying cease. She kissed his nose while he kissed her forehead. They showered together, enchanting each other with stokes of love, then return to their bed. They lay in the arms of warmth next to one another.

Douglas moved quietly after he saw Carita drifted off into a peaceful sleep. He would call her the next day and try to get by to see her. When Carita woke up, she thought he left all alone. However, Douglas had placed Teddy in her arms.

Once he arrived at the apartment, he found Suzie had packed some bags.

"What are those packed for?"

"I'm going to Florida when you leave," she said.

He looked at her. "Really! And, how are you going."

"If you think I'm going to give you the opportunity to invite that bitch to stay with you and I'm your woman, you are sadly mistaken. I'll be going with you."

"No you aren't! When I leave, I will be alone." The purpose for me being in Florida is to get myself together."

Suzie went on to say, "We'll see about that. I don't give a shit if the bitch is your son's mammy! What did the two of you do for a week?"

"That doesn't come before you," Douglas emphatically stated.

She wasn't as concerned with the love Carita and Douglas shared for one another as opposed to how it might interfere with her finances.

The quarrelling between Douglas and Suzie continued until Sunday morning. She insisted on going and had her bags ready. Douglas, thinking she might pull a stunt, put his bags in the truck the previous night. As he got up and tried to be polite to Suzie, he could see it wasn't working. He exited the door and Suzie followed with her luggage. He hurried to the truck, hopped in, and left her standing in the parking lot in tears. He became so upset that he could hardly drive and decided not to go by his mom's house. The last thing he wanted was an incident there. He continued to drive for at least one hundred miles before he called Carita. He apologized for not seeing before he left and, as usual, she understood. He also told her would call to check on her more than ever.

Although she appreciated his gesture, she could tell something was wrong. His voice denoted that he was upset.

"Are you alright?"

"Yes."

"Hon, I don't like you talking and driving on the road. Please call me when you reach your half way mark. Always remember, I will keep you in prayer."

Douglas was so thankful Carita did not ask any more questions. It was not her demeanor. She had not changed over the years, he thought. She always been a genuine person and he felt lucky to have her.

Suzie feeling humiliated, could not believe Douglas would treat her this way. She knew he cared for her but what happened? "If this is the way he wanted to be," she felt, "we'll just see about that." Torn and embarrassed, she returned to her apartment and prepared to go see Geri.

When she arrived, Geri knew things had not gone as planned. Like Suzie, Geri had been something else back in her hay day. With dark brown skin and a short haircut, she was not a bad looking woman. Her dark brown eyes complimented her round face. Her height along with her long legs suggested she could've been a model back in the day, but the streets took all that could have fared in living the good life. Now limited to funds as well as living arrangements, she did not have much and always tried to find a way to unjustly take from someone less fortunate than she.

"What happen," she asked Suzie.

"He's gone," she replied.

"See I told you," announced Geri. "When you told me the bastard had his baby's mammy with him for a week, I knew there was more to it than that. So what are going to do about it?"

Suzie looked at her. "We have to come up with something."

"I told you need to keep something on the side."

Suzie never replied but contemplated on how to make sure Carita did not return to Florida.

The next two weeks were heavenly for Carita and Douglas. They called one another and chatted daily. They seem to be getting reacquainted. The forty years committed to other people left them at odds of really not knowing one another. They talked about their children, education, and the wealth of the nation, politics, and other interests they both shared. They even discussed their pensions and Carita's retirement.

Douglas knew he would not see Carita until the first of the year when he return to the area. He wondered if Carita would be able to fly in for one of the holidays. He contemplated asking her to come at the end of Christmas and ride back with him after the first of the year. This way, they could start the New Year off together and perhaps fate would deal them a favorable hand.

Suzie knew she had to do something before Carita messed up her plan. Although she cared something for Douglas, it became more evident to her that he loved Carita. She had to play all the hands she could to keep him in tack. Her husband's condition did not present any signs of him leaving this earth anytime soon so she decided to attach herself to someone who afforded her fewer struggles than she would encounter if on her own. Geri gave her good advice and she had not dismissed it, for she was not new to the game.

She called Douglas to see if he would apologize for such a rude departure.

"Hey baby, how are you?"

"Hi Suzie, how are you?"

"Are you still upset with me?"

"I was never upset with you, just disappointed."

"You had some nerve entertaining some woman while I was not there. I just want to know what's really going on."

"I told you about Carita because I was trying to be honest. Yes, I care for her and I always will. You didn't have to do or say any of the things that you did," he said. "I thought that you were more woman than that."

"You made me so upset," she cried.

"We'll talk later," he said. "I have to run."

He was really disappointed with Suzie. She had been very kind to him while going through his divorce. She was understanding and available to his every whim. She told him bits and pieces of her past but never the complete truth. She convinced him to be with her while painting a façade of what their life could be together and her willingness to be at his side. She talked about all the places they might be able to travel. Although she found cooking distasteful, she led him to believe she was the next *Julia Childs*. She allowed him to think his family, in particular his mom, were her top priority. She told him she would always be there for him. Now, he thought, if their relationship was truly secure what was the problem?

Suzie called her man on the side. He was glad to hear from her. He had not spent quality time with her since Douglas arrived back in town. They only held quick telephone conversations. Missing her and her body, he embraced her once he arrived at her apartment.

"How was your time with your man," he asked.

"It was alright," she said.

"I thought you would be going back to Florida with him."

"We thought we'd wait until later."

"Really," he replied. "I know Douglas and he was not ready for you to come. Besides he has always been in love with Carita, even when I put the doubt in his mind about his son being some else's and not his."

"Listen Nate," she said, "cut the bull shit. I have to get to Florida to keep Carita from going."

"No," Nate answered, "you have to get to Florida to keep your money thing going."

She glared at Nate.

"Come on baby. Don't be mad. It's been so long since I've had you," he said.

She smiled and slithered toward him like a snake winding around its victim. She grasped his hand. They skulked and kissed up the steps. Once in the bedroom, he slipped his pants off while she hurriedly stripped herself. She found her lips were hot with passion. Nate made her feel as though she was all that love could conquer as they lay in each other's arms. She slid around the bed with him, touching his body with her breasts, fingers, and tongue. She slithered up his front to taste his ears than placed her tongue in his mouth while her body groped his growing. He grabbed her with both hands and placed his steaming mouth on her, first one breast then the other. He licked her down her front until he heard a shrill from her. She enjoyed his sex for it made her feel young. He placed his watering mouth upon her chest while pulling her body toward his, licking to her entry then gliding her so she could enter on top of him. He sucked her breasts like child extracting milk from his mother. Her fingers begin to force themselves up and down his chest, stopping at the perked parts of his chest swooping them with her drenching lips. She rolled over. He entered her as far as he could. She accepted it, biting where she enjoyed the rapture of him pushing all he had into her. They shrilled together as her wide mouth and pink lips continued to cream the dampness of their pleasure. They remained in each other's arms and enjoyed what each of them had missed.

"So," she said. "Are you going to help me do what I need to do?"

"What do you need to do," he said, "is go to Florida?

"Do you think that will help?"

"If you intend keeping your relationship in tack.  Like I said, he has always loved her."

"I need money.  You know my funds are limited," she said.

"I knew that was coming." He smiled. "I don't know why you just can't leave him and be with me."

"We discussed that," she said with an attitude.  "And you know the answer."

He just nodded his head and asked her how much.

Carita and Douglas continued to enjoy their telephone conversations, acquiring information of what they may do together in the future.  With the interest they both had in real-estate and graphics, there was extra money to be made. Between their interests and their pensions, they viewed the sky as the limit.

Friday finally arrived and Carita was ready for a weekend of rest and recuperation. Checking her phone, she saw Douglas had called. It frightened her. He never called during this time of the day.  He knew she was working. Perhaps something was wrong with one of the children, she thought, as started listening to the message. Come to find out, he was checking on her. She returned the call. He answered.  His voice sounded strange for some reason, not at all jovial.

"What's wrong," she asked,

"My friend is here," he said strangely.

"What!" Carita screamed.  "Did you know she was coming?"

"No," he answered her.

Carita calmed down, figuring he could hear her tears and disappointment.

"She is just here because you came, and to stop you from coming back. She plans to stay through the holiday and visit family."

"And you're going to allow that to happen?" Carita said.

"I have no choice," he whispered.  "You know the games you woman play."

Carita said, "You just wait a minute. I don't play games. For one thing, life is too short. For another thing, how could you have been making plans and not know what she was doing? Number three, if you think that I am hurt… yes, I am. And oh, yes, I am crying. I told you I'm the world's biggest cry baby. Am I angry? You're damn right I am. So I'll tell you what you can do for me, Mr. Douglas. You can leave me the hell alone and don't bother to call me ever again in life."

After she abruptly hung up the phone, Douglas walked outside upset at himself for being honest. He knew that sometimes you just have to wait to see what happens in a situation before you tried to control it, but he had not expected this. He did not know what to do. Carita had enough on her plate and now he had upset her. He knew she was hurt because, within himself, he knew Carita truly loved him and he was hurting as well. He could not call Lee. She would burst a gasket. He ached inside. He had done something he never intended to do, hurt Carita again.

Douglas went to his meeting for the mentally challenged participants to get the procedure for a new technique. He listened to the speaker and tried to apply the situations to his life. He thought of Carita because of their past and decided to put a time limit on the situation with Suzie. She had some issues to clear. Even though he knew Carita loved him, he didn't know how deep. He was not sure at all where Suzie was coming from. In his eyes, she had swayed from how she initially portrayed herself.

Carita could hardly see how to drive. Her eyes filled from sobbing. She could not believe she went off like that when Douglas just tried to be sensitive and honest. Now what? She hurt so badly and had nowhere to turn. She called Lee and asked to come over. She met Carita at the door. Carita immediately burst into tears all over, trying to tell Lee what had happened. Lee placed her arms around Carita and told her to get all of her tears out. Lee then convinced her that Douglas was just trying to be honest and would call.

Time went by and Douglas didn't call. Carita feared the worst. He seemed just as through with her as she with him. She signed up to work on Christmas day, giving some of the younger folks the opportunity to be with their children. Lee and Walter invited her over but Carita excused herself. Working the day after Christmas offered the usual holiday cleanup. Tired when she arrived home, she decided to turn in early. As she prepared for bed, her phone rang. She answered.

"Hi baby," Douglas said.

Surprised but elated, she responded.

"How are you and how have you been?"

"Good. I have missed you," she continued.

"No. I have missed you. I didn't know whether to call you or not. I just decided to take a chance."

She remained very still while listening.

"Are you still there," he asked.

"Yes," she spoke slightly above a whisper.

"Baby," he said. "Are you angry with me?"

"No… I would just like to apologize for going off. I don't know what happened to me."

"It's okay. We'll fix that."

He talked a little longer to make sure Carita was calm. "I need to see you."

"Okay," she responded. "When are you coming home," she asked.

"I am home."

"Okay," she said.

"Then come and open the door."

"Oh my God," she screamed as she jumped up.

He stood, smiling on the porch, waiting patiently to get in. He gave her an unbelievable hug while almost picking her up off the floor. She squeezed his neck so hard that he almost could not catch his breath.

"I have missed you," he said.

"And, I you," she responded.

She fixed a light supper, knowing he was hungry. They talked a little about their situation with Douglas wanting to explain.

Carita just looked at him. "I know. She was there for you when you really needed someone. But was she there really," she asked. "What about your parents, and your siblings, the people from your community service you told me that we're so kind to you? Maybe while we're calm, it would be better if we made a decision."

"What are you talking about?" he said.

"I have loved you for forty years," she stated. "I cannot do this. I would rather walk away."

"You want to walk away," he said. "You're willing to walk away with forty years of history. We have a baby," he exclaimed.

She looked at him despondently. "Doug, the baby is forty years old. All we have is a history. This situation is just as hard for me as well as you. Before, I could let things go because I thought you were happily married. Now, I don't know. This woman is not your wife but you will tell me things like, you are not able to answer the phone or you promised to take her to the movies. Or you're going to a party with her friends and then there is the scenario like earlier this month, you were not aware she was coming to Florida. I really don't know what to do or believe."

"Don't you see what's she's doing. She's got us at odds, and no..." he said in an empathic manner. "I will not lose you a second time around. You cannot walk way."

He pulled her to him his lips, savored in condensation from the affection they maintained for one another, and kissed her. And their love was once again sealed. He sat her on his lap in the rocker and pecked at her nose, telling how much he loved her while his hands gently massaged her hips. His nose glided up and down her neck. She softly placed her lips to his. Her hands caressed his head as she turned her face to pat his check. He lifted her into his arms and his body ambled toward the bedroom. They disrobed each other while accepting warm but welcomed embraces of affection. They melted into a rhapsody of eagerness while rediscovering the pleasure each gave to one another. They remained and each other's arm while taking note of their happiness, Carita stroked his chest as he held her close.

Once in the door, Suzie called Nate to let him know she returned and things had not gone to badly in Florida.  She felt that she had gotten her relationship back on track.  He was glad that she was happy and needed to know when they could see each other.  She made arrangement to him the next day at their favorite place.

The first of January rapidly approached and Douglas wanted it to be his year.  He tried to move on with his life so he could get some goals accomplished.  He also knew Carita's birthday would be coming soon and wanted to give her something very special.  He told Carita about his plan to move back to the area. His friends were returning from Europe.

Carita did not ask.  She knew he and Suzie would be an item.  She was afraid of where it might leave them.  Would they really have a second chance at life?

Douglas knew he loved Carita but felt a sense of obligation to Suzie. He thought about the best move for him as he traveled back and forth for Florida retrieving the rest of his possessions. While at home, Douglas stopped in the bar to shoot a quick game of pool and ran into Nate.

"Hey man! What's up," Nate asked?

"Oh just trying to get my thoughts together for this move."

"What move?"

"I coming back to the area and thinking about the long drive alone," responded Douglas.

"Man, you know I'm retired.  I can help you drive if you want," replied Nate.

"That's good to know," Douglas answered.  "I'll keep the offer in mind."

While driving down the highway to Florida, Douglas's mind begun to wonder. He anticipated getting his own place. He realized that he allowed Suzie to sway him into living together permanently.  She told him of all the things they could do together. She had all of the finances worked out as well as their daily routine. His only problem was Carita. He loved her and she deserved better than the short visits he gave her but he didn't know how to explain his dilemma.

"Hey," Nate hollered as Douglas dosed off. Douglas tuned back in.

"Thanks man," Douglas said.

"Hey man," said Nate. "Maybe you should let me take the wheel."

Nate was rather glad Douglas asked him to drive with him to Florida. It gave him the opportunity to find out how Douglas really felt about Suzie. Douglas's response might afford him the opportunity to appeal to Suzie for a more stable relationship with him. He knew Suzie was elated to see him travel with Douglas because it left no chance of Carita going.

While Nate drove, Douglas wondered why Nate wanted to be so close to him. Always at the pool room and always wanting to ride with him. Even though they went to school together, Douglas never quite trusted Nate. But Douglas being Douglas, he could not mistreat anyone.

They finally arrived at the house. Nate suggested it would make a nice second home for Douglas and Suzie. Douglas ignored his comment.

When Douglas got the opportunity he called Carita to let her know he arrived safely. She sounded wonderful and could not wait for him to hurry back. He phoned Suzie and, as usual, she was out and about but glad he got there safely.

While Douglas attended a meeting, Nate elected to stay at the house and get some rest. He, of course, called Suzie to update her.

Suzie sounded very disappointed behind Nate's inability to get any information but remained hopeful. They still had a couple of days in Florida in addition to the ride home. Packing and cleaning the house, took less time than Douglas anticipated. He told Nate they would leave on Wednesday since he wanted to be home no later than Friday.

"That Suzie must be something else. You want to get home that quickly."

Douglas didn't comment but Nate's questions and comments concerned him. As long as he did not brooch the subject of Carita, Douglas would be fine.

Driving back home, Nate questioned Douglas about his son, Todd.

"Where is he at now? He's probably doing drugs like everybody else's kid," Nate said. "Yea man, whatever happened to that bitch that had the baby for you?"

"First of all, Nate," Douglas said, "that is none of your business but, since you asked, my son is doing very well. He has a master's degree and is working on his doctorate. He's the head security for the largest security firm in the U.S. As for the bitch, as you put it, you have a mother and sisters, so why would you refer to someone's mother and sister as a bitch?"

"Aw man," he said. "You know how it is."

"No, I don't," said Douglas. "And this conversation is finished."

They arrived back home on Friday evening and Douglas was glad the trip ended. He took Nate home then stopped by Lee's to drop a package off. He then grabbed a quick bite to eat before driving to Carita's. He knew he should have called Suzie but was not up for twenty questions. He hoped Carita would be home because she did a lot of volunteer work at the church.

As the garage door lifted, a smile came across his face when he saw her truck. He would be able to surprise her. He was grateful that she had given him a key to the front door and a remote to the garage during his last visit. Carita was nowhere to be found as he entered the house. He called and found her in the bedroom. She had retired early, having a long day at work. When she heard his voice, she reached for her robe but he had entered the bedroom by that time. She grabbed him around his neck and hugged him as tight as she could. He smiled and said, "I need to go away more often." They both laughed. He apologized for getting her up but she did not care. She prepared him a cup of tea while she drank a glass of cranberry juice.

His eyes suggested he had a surprise for her. She clapped her hands and begged for it. Douglas purchased a dozen of roses made by the man on the wharf. Supposedly, they would turn white in a year. He could not have made her any happier.

"Babe, I have to get going"

"I know Carita whispered softly."

"I'll be back in a couple of days."

They kissed and Douglas reluctantly left.

Douglas entered and Suzie hung up the phone. He just stood at the door.

"What?" he said. "No hug or kiss?"

"Why yes," she responded. "You have to give me a chance. I was not expecting you until much later."

"Oh," he replied with a slight smile.

He kissed her on the lips and then her check.

Suzie contemplated getting him in the bed. She knew he had been to see Carita. After she helped him bring in most of his belongings, they both went to bed. She rolled over to him then told him how much she missed and cared for him. She touched his groin to make sure it was at attention then rolled over to kiss his lips. She placed her fingers in his ears while he kissed her face. Soon he was within her entry wall and she began to sway back and forth, bringing all of what he held back to the surface. He kissed her on the cheek and rolled over for a night's rest.

The winter passed quickly. Carita and Douglas celebrated his birthday at his favorite place then returned to the house to open his present as well as partake of the special apple pie she prepared for him. Douglas appreciated of all she did for him. During the day when she returned from work, she shared her computer skills with him. He had wanted to start a business but needed to be a little more computer literate.

Carita's birthday approached and Douglas wanted so much to do something special for her. They usually went bowling and participated in other things they both enjoyed. He knew of an upcoming jazz concert but wanted Carita all to himself. They had gone to plays, symphony concerts, museums, and other cultural events in and around the area but this was a special birthday.

Finally, he engaged the idea of going to the lodge where they spent the weekend before he left for the service so many years ago. The place was still around and more beautiful than ever. When he asked Carita what she wanted for her birthday, she said to spend the weekend with him. He told her to have a small bag packed and ready to go on Friday.

As she completed her packing, Douglas had arrived. He kissed her and smiled but would not tell her where they were going. As they neared the lodge, Douglas had Carita close her eyes and put her hands over her face. She just giggled like a little girl and asked why. His stern look told her this was not a laughing matter. A few moments later, the truck came to a complete stop. Douglas insisted on her keeping her eyes closed. He opened her car door and carried her to the lodge then told her to open her eyes. She was flabbergasted. He kissed her and said, "Happy birthday."

He returned to the truck to get their bags. When he finished, he lit the fire in the room so it would be toasty when they returned. They walked to the main building where he had made reservations for their dinner. They walked hand in hand back to their room, enjoying natures as well as the conversation. Douglas wanted to surprise Carita with just one more gift but did not tell her about it.

Carita put special night attire in the bag so she would be comfortable while lying in Douglas's arms. She slipped into the bathroom to put it on. When she returned, she saw a package wrapped in her favorite color on the bed.

"What's this?"

"Open it and see," he replied.

Carita opened the package to see a necklace and earrings to match, fashioned in her birthstone.

"Oh my goodness," she exclaimed.

She looked at Douglas and kissed him with all the love and affection she carried in her heart over the years. He laid her gently on the pillow while moving the present to the stand. He kissed her, telling her how beautiful she looked. He rocked her back and forth and remembered that forty years ago, during his last tour of duty in the service, did not afford him this opportunity. He slipped her attire off and covered her with blankets while the fire danced to the tune of the music. His body felt the elation of a man who had finally fulfilled a love and desire that long awaited his affection of a special kind of love.

# Chapter 12

Carita stood quietly and looked out her kitchen window at the buds on the trees as spring approached. A continued pain in her back persisted and she began to wonder if her job was getting next to her. The floor at work was concrete and since employees worked eight hours straight, they were entitled to breaks but not a lunch hour according to the union contract.

Douglas noticed her quietness. "What was wrong?"

The pain became so prevalent she never heard his question. Her facial expression suggested she was in pain. It concerned Douglas that she would not share her discomfort with him. As soon as he stepped near her, she leaned back but he caught her in his arms. His lips touched hers. He carried her to the couch and waited for her to regain her composure.

"Babe, take a warm bath. I think you may feel better," Douglas suggested. "I'll give you a back massage."

Carita, worried about their meal, suggested they eat first.

As usual, Douglas enjoyed the meal. Carita was still a very good cook and presented him with all the amenities that his counterpart did not.

She slipped into the shower while Douglas cleaned the kitchen. Dr. Rea told her, long before Tony's death, she needed to lose weight. Although she managed to decrease the pounds requested, Carita thought it was coming off too fast. She was not trying to lose any more weight than necessary. The doctor only wanted her to get down to one hundred forty pounds but, since she seemed to be losing weight at a rapid rate, she had not told Douglas she had a doctor's appointment to check for the back pain as well as the weight loss. Actually, she did not know how to tell him. He was so concerned about her prior appointment. She had a cat scan done the week before and unknowingly was allergic to the dye concentrate used in the scan. Carita was sick for 24 hours.

As she slipped into something more comfortable, Douglas exited the kitchen and gently put his arms around her before she lay on the open bed. The lotion felt cool and soothing. The touch of his hands and fingers demonstrated his gentleness and that his heart was her heart. He rolled her over from her back and brushed her hair. He kissed her forehead, nose, and cheeks until he reached her lips. He caressed her body and she fell hopelessly into his arms as they begin to feel a part of one another.

As she lay safely in his arms, she gained enough courage to tell him about her next doctor's appointment and revealed the results of her test. It showed a mass behind the liver.

"Hon, the results of the cat scan came back. It showed a mass behind my liver."

He became slightly upset. He liked going to doctor's appointments with her so he could understand all the procedures and ask questions she may forget. He had not been a part of so many things with Carita, including their son's birth. And now that life gave them a second chance, he wanted to leave nothing to fate.

"Why are you just now telling me?"

"I didn't want to worry you."

"You're not a worry babe. I've told you that before. I love you."

They chatted a little more about some of her health issues before Carita drifted off to sleep. She promised to tell him the date for the biopsy.

He eased out of bed as best he could without disturbing Carita. She was still not sleeping well at night and, if he could leave while she lay quietly under the covers, she might have a good day. Even though he tried to be quiet when walking to the bathroom and closing the door, his absence aroused Carita.

His leaving was the part of their relationship she hated. He left her home, only to return to a place that in reality was just a place to lay his head. She knocked at the bathroom door softly.

He opened it reluctantly, knowing tears would be in her eyes.

"Carita," he spoke sternly. "I want to know when you are scheduled for your next appointment."

"'Hon, I won't know that until I receive the results of my biopsy."

"Nevertheless I want to know. I don't want you to be alone when you go for tests."

"I will," she promised.

She walked to the refrigerator to retrieve a bottle of water so Douglas would not be parched on the road. They kissed and he tugged at her nose, letting her know he loved and would miss her.

He hated leaving Carita all of the time but it is what he felt he had to do until he could resolve this relationship with Suzie. In his own way, he felt obligated to Suzie since she had been there for him during a difficult time in his life. He wanted so badly to stay and hold Carita in his arms and tell all but it was not feasible at the time. He felt sadness as he drove away from what would eventually become their home. He loved Carita for over forty years, as she loved him. He just never had the courage to mention it, not even to himself until now. He could only dream of the happiness they could have because they were both deserving of such.

Carita had been a patient of Dr. Rea for some years. She and her husband were among her first patients. As a matter of fact, she and Carita had become the best of friends. Dr. Rea entered the exam room ready with a hug and kiss for Carita. She had not said anything to Carita but did not like the weight loss either and was quite concerned. She already scheduled a biopsy for Tuesday, hoping she would come to some conclusion. She gave Carita the same instructions the hospital would, nothing by mouth after 6 p.m. and someone must be present to drive her home. An anesthetic would be involved in this procedure.

The morning of the biopsy, Douglas arrived early so he could ease any concerns Carita may harbor. They left early to compensate for the heavy traffic. While Carita prepped for the procedure, the nurses insisted she remove her cross. Extremely reluctant to do so, she gave them somewhat of an argument. Douglas, being very observant, wondered why she was so hesitant. He thought it might have been the last piece of jewelry her husband gave her. Although he understood, he did not want any ghost between them.

"Babe," he said. "What is the problem with the cross? It's only a cross and you're going to have to remove it anyway."

She looked at him said, "Our son sent it from Saudi and I never take it off."

He then understood. Their son, her only child, was her world. After that ordeal, the nurses thanked him and asked of his relationship to Carita. He was unwilling to answer. The head nurse began to guess.

"Are you her husband? A boy friend?" she asked but received no answer. "I'll just put you down as the significant other."

He smiled at that title. He gave her his telephone number and other information they required. The test would be performed at 8 a.m. but Carita would not be ready to return home until about noon. Carita had no idea the test would take so long and became very upset. She forgot about the anesthesia. She looked at Douglas.

He knew she was upset as she apologized for taking up such a large portion of his day. He calmed her down then told her he would return to the house, to call when she him ready to go.

Sometime in the early afternoon, Douglas appeared in her room. He kissed her on her forehead and she smiled.

"How soon will you be ready to go?"

"I don't know. They have not exactly released me."

"Are you hungry? We could stop and get some lunch."

Her appetite had not been good the last couple of months so she hesitated to accept his offer.

Knowing she had not eaten since the evening before, he insisted she get something in her stomach.

The nurses came in and gave Carita discharge procedures. They stopped at a drive thru and took the food orders home where they would be more comfortable. Douglas left to check on his mom and Carita lied down to rest since she did have to report to work the next day. Dr. Rea called later that evening to give Carita her test results.

The mass behind her liver was actually a tumor on the liver. Carita began to attribute the back pains to that diagnosis. Dr. Rea referred her to a digestive consultant, who requested the disc of the biopsy. His staff also made arrangements for her to have blood work completed by the time of the appointment.  Upon meeting the doctor, who was very cordial as well as professional, Carita began to feel relaxed.  He revealed his findings on the disc as well as blood test results.   She definitely had a cancerous tumor on her liver.  Carita remained in complete disarray for almost sixty seconds.  Cancer! Cancer!  It just couldn't be, she thought.  The family had just lost an elder earlier in the year to pancreatic cancer and Carita lost her husband to cancer.  She asked the doctor to consider sending her to Cleveland Clinic.  Although unable to prevent her husband's death, it was the third best hospital in the nation and the best in the area.

As Carita drove home in disbelief, she only thought about the disease.  What a large burden to carry alone.  She certainly could not tell her family at this time, considering the losses they experienced over the past eighteen months.  Her main concern was Todd and Douglas.   How would she tell them? Douglas asked her not to go to the doctor alone but she pleaded since it was only up the street from the house and would not be too much for her to drive. Her mind raced. She smoked for more than 42 years. As she approached the house and the garage door opened, she prepared to discard the remainder of her cigarettes. After all, she wanted to live. She thought of their son and granddaughter, the spitting image of herself, and of course Douglas.  He was her life and her love until the end of time. Now she had to tell him of an uncertainty that could end their affection and passion.

As she entered her open kitchen, adorned with baskets of fruit, she felt the need for a cool drink of water. While sitting in the rocker, she pondered the likelihood of not telling Douglas the truth. Douglas's plate was full.  He seemed concerned about his many disappointments in life and she did not want to be a burden. She laid her head back and tried to think of the best way to broach the subject with Douglas as well as the children. Once she closed her eyes to rest, she heard the garage door chime as Douglas opened it.  She had not expected him to come so early. Upon entering, he bent down and kissed her with such a beautiful smile.

"You look nice," he said.  "Come on, I'll take you to the doctor."

She smiled and looked at him in only a way a woman in love could.  She replied, "I've already gone."

"Already?"

"Yes," she replied. "His office is only up the street and my appointment was for 9 a.m."

"Oh, I thought that it was at eleven so I decided to surprise you and take you myself. So what was the verdict," he asked.

She gazed at him, ready to give him any explanation except for the truth. Her eyes slightly filled with tears. Her lips finally parted and she told him about the small tumor but that things would be alright.

He listened attentively but realized she presented half-truths. He knew she was hiding something. He had been with her long enough to know when she wanted to protect the ones she loved.

"Yes, but what about the tumor? What is it? And where is it? Re, don't you know that I know you. I want to know what the doctor said and not what you think I want to hear."

She put her head into his chest. Tears fell. "The tumor is on my liver and it is cancerous."

Douglas died inside. He reached out and held Carita as tight as he could. He did not want her to know the devastation he felt. He had to be strong for her. "Oh baby," he said. "I'm so sorry." He almost let down a tear.

She responded, "It's going to be alright, and I will be just fine. Sometimes God puts us through tests. It's just a test. Doug, we must have faith in God."

He held her tighter than ever and rested his head on hers. He kissed the crown of her head and promised to be strong.

They grabbed a quick brunch and did some shopping at Wal-Mart. He insisted on helping her put away the purchases. He had a few things that needed his attention but first he wanted to get Carita to take a nap. It had been a long day for her. He tried to give her a back rub but could see it aggravated her, so he promised to call later after she got some rest.

As he left, he could not get over her illness. He asked God, "Why her? She is such a good person."

He had to get to Lee Hilda. He needed to share and she was the only one who understood his feelings about Carita. Carita was like one of her own children and Mama Bear, as Carita called her, hoped they could have a full and happy life this time around. But the last year had been so full of obstacles for them both.

He entered his mom's house to find her potting around as usual. He still pondered the news he got from Carita. He hugged his mother. She was truly his favorite girl. Her silver hair served as an invitation to the best advice and wisdom one could ask for. He sat in the family room, in his favorite chair, placed his hand over the right side of his face so Lee could not detect his distraught emotions.

"How's your day going," she asked.

"Fine," he replied.

She left well enough alone. He got up and walked around the room as though God would give him an answer to the fix this dilemma.

"What's wrong, Douglas?" Lee asked.

As he sat back down in the chair, he looked toward his mom for comfort. "I just left Carita." His eyes begin to water before he could complete his sentence.

"Mama, she has cancer. Why her? She's such a good person. She raised our son with no help from me. She's been there for family and friends. She took care of her sick husband until he died and still went to work every day. Mama, it's just not fair. Mama, do you know what she said? She said, 'It's alright and I'm going to be alright. Sometimes God puts us through tests. We just have to have faith because he knows what he is doing.' Mama, I'm afraid for her. Mama what are we going to do?"

"Oh, my goodness! Not my Carita."

Lee had to regain her composure. Her son needed her strength and advice. They all loved Carita and now they needed to think about what was best for her.

"We all know Carita," said Lee, "she just keeps going. She's like the energizer bunny. That's who she is and will always be. We have to do what she wants and that is to trust and believe in God. We must have faith and know that she will be alight. I swear I don't know where she gets her faith from, but God knows best. As a family, we must support her as best we can. Have you told Todd?"

"No. I did not want to put too much pressure on her. She is not ready to tell any of the other family members. She really did not want to tell me.

She started with half-truths. I had to remind her that I know when she's lying. She did not want you to know. I gave her a back rub and insisted that she get some rest before I came to talk to you."

As Carita lie resting, she thought she needed to tell Lee and Aunt Anne. She feared that Douglas might have already shared with Lee. She reached for the phone and dialed the number. Lee answered.

"Hi Mama Bear. Are you busy?"

"Yes, I'm busy right now."

"He's there?"

"Yes. Let me call you later."

Lee called Carita as soon as Douglas left.

"Carita you were not going to tell me?"

"Yes, ma'am, I was going to tell you. I just didn't know how. I never dreamed that Douglas would tell you because I asked him not to. How is he?"

"Devastated and upset."

"Mom, you must trust me. I am going to be alright. God is just testing our strength and belief. He is our source and strength. He knows what he is doing. Everything is going to turn out okay."

The next two weeks were very busy with doctor appointments at the Cleveland Clinic. Douglas insisted on driving Carita. He did not want her traveling that far alone. Besides, he had to talk her into telling their son before additional procedures were done. Still, Carita insisted that she was not ready to tell anyone but agreed to tell Todd. In addition to her husband who fallen victim to leukemia, the family lost an elder to pancreatic cancer and two more members nine months prior to that death. She felt the family was not ready for this kind of news. Finally, she accepted the fact that time was falling short and she had no choice but to tell Todd. Douglas held her hand as she explained but it was not easy hearing the despair in his voice.

Had he not lived out of state, his parents could have told him face to face and not over the phone. He asked questions but promised his parents that he would be there as soon as they received all of the information for the removal of the tumor. He promised to keep her secret.

Chapter 13

There was much to do to prepare for the operation. Carita had to access the balance of her sick time at work and other time as well as check on her insurances, disability, hospitalization, and other criteria. She had several appointments before the final operation and it was crucial to have enough time for surgery in addition to time needed for recovery.

Douglas accompanied her to all of the appointments. Carita, being nervous, brought along a notebook.

"What are you writing?"

"Questions, for the doctor. Things we think of right now, we may forget by the time we get there. Can you think of anything?

"Not at present," he replied.

Douglas thought about what Carita may be going through in the weeks to come. He wanted to be there for her in every possible way. Although a strong woman, he did not want her to be strong at this time. He just wanted her to let him take care of her. He knew this could be a hard task since he remained in a situation that made no sense, even to him. He knew Carita would need him now more than ever. After all, she had been his best friend even through two bad marriages.

He watched her as she carefully guided him through the directions to the hospital. She knew her way around fairly well, considering it had been over a year since her last trip and there was a great deal of construction along the way. They managed to find the building for their appointment and, soon after their arrival, a nurse called Carita for regular weight and blood pressure procedures. After the doctor's arrival, he explained the information on the disk sent by Carita's primary care physician. The doctor told them they found a tumor attached to the right side of the liver.

Because it was cancerous, that part of the liver had to be removed surgically. It was the only way to be sure all of the cancer would be removed. Using this technique would also eradicate the use of chemotherapy and radiation. The doctor asked if there were any questions. Carita responded according to her list and Douglas asked about the points of recovery. Before leaving the clinic, Carita stopped to get blood work done. Her veins were small and phlebotomists always had difficulty completing the procedure before they collapsed. Douglas, aware of this problem, wanted to be with her but was requested to remain seated in the waiting room.

Once completed, they ate an early lunch then returned home.

Douglas wanted to hurry and get back. He promised Lee, he would bring Carita to her house. She just needed to look at her while she questioned her about health and wellbeing. Lee wanted to open her home if Carita needed any assistance at all. Carita just did not want to be a bother to anyone. As much as she wanted Douglas by her side, she knew he might not even be there.

Douglas suggested they stop and pick up lunch to share with his mom. This would give him the opportunity to shoot a couple of games of pool, while his two girls visited.

Upon entering the house, Lee hugged Carita for what seemed to be dear life. She missed Carita. They had not been on their Saturday luncheon rendezvous for quite some time. The girls laughed and talked about the latest fashion and, of course, shoes which had always been Carita's passion. Lee made her promise to keep her abreast on all of the procedures concerning her illness.

The next few visits at the clinic proved to be positive. Carita checked at work and provided the necessary forms for her absences. Douglas seemed so proud of Carita for following through with all of her appointments as well as following all of the doctor's instructions. And Todd called every day to check on his mom. He and his wife had already arranged to take the week off for Carita's surgery. They just needed copies of her diagnosis for verification.

While Douglas and Carita appreciated God's blessing, allowing them to be together while going through this tough time, Douglas received word that his daughter had some problems at home and needed his help. She lived in Maine, a ten hour drive away. Jena, Douglas's daughter had come to visit her dad, shortly after Douglas and Suzie started dating. With that, she and Suzie developed a relationship.

"She needs her father," Suzie said. "I don't see the problem. Why we can't drive just to check on her. She would not have called me if it weren't important. You're retired and what is a father for if he can't help his child?"

"Why didn't she call me," Douglas asked. "After all, she's my daughter and not yours. What could be so urgent? She has a husband."

Suzie convinced Douglas that this was a good opportunity to get away and he could visit with his grandchildren. Douglas was still hesitant. He did not quite understand the urgency. Her husband was there and she was good friends with his family. Why should he have to drive almost a thousand miles? He had been consumed with Carita and wanted to do all he could for her. She had become his priority. Now was not the time for him to leave her.

Suzie, knowing something was up with Douglas, began to be persistent about the trip. Why? Douglas could not figure that out. Since he lived with her, she tried to be in his daughter's life more so than her own mother. Jena was his baby so he had no choice but to go. The only problem was how would he tell Carita?

As he opened the garage, he hoped she was taking a nap. That would give him extra time to find a way to tell her. As he walked into the family room, she woke up.

"Hi hon," she said with a smile. "How are you today?"

He smiled as well. "Fine."

"I wasn't looking for you today," she stated.

"I wanted to check on you to make certain you were alright."

"I wish you and mom would stop worrying about me."

"It's only because we love you," he answered.

She grabbed him a cold drink of ice tea as he turned on the TV to check for his favorite programs. He sat in the rocker very quiet and without comment to Carita's new hairdo. He either did not like it or had not noticed.

"What's wrong," Carita asked. "Nothing," Douglas said.

She gazed at him. "Doug, we promised each other. Now what's wrong?"

"Carita, I can't take you to the hospital on Tuesday."

"Why?" "I have to go Maine to check on Jena.  She's got some things going on and she's needs my help."

"What things," Carita asked.

Douglas tried to explain but didn't make sense.  He only repeated what he had been told.  Carita decided to let it go. She could clearly feel Douglas didn't have the bottom line. Jena was married and had four children. Why would she possibly need for him to drive that distance?  She also knew Chickie Poo (Suzie) was going with him.  Carita figured it was probably Chickie Poo's idea to try to get her and Douglas's affair back on track.

"Baby, I'm sorry.  You know that being with you, at this time, means so much to me."

"It's, okay," Carita said, trying not to let a tear drop.  "She's your baby and it's only right that you check on her."

Douglas had a list of errands to complete.  There was an up upcoming seminar for the people who work with the mentally challenged.  He worked very hard with his team of children, playing volleyball.  They were champions in the district and wanted to hold on to the title.  Douglas couldn't let them down.  He just didn't know how he would fit it all in.  Carita suggested they have an early practice on Thursday to prepare for Friday's game.  That way, he could relax on Saturday and leave Sunday morning.  Douglas liked her suggestion.  He moved toward Carita, putting his arms softly around her as he tenderly kissed he lips.  He quietly sat her on his lap while rocking her in the rocker.  He knew she was upset with the news and did not want her to be too distraught.  He brushed her hair quietly as she laid her head on his shoulder.  He could feel a tear on his neck so he whispered to her.

"Don't you know that this cannot be helped?"

"I know," she spoke in a crackling voice.

After he thought Carita had fallen to sleep, he put her on the couch and covered her.  He then slipped out the door to begin errands for the trip.

Carita knew Douglas planned to leave for his daughter's on Sunday.  She showered and decided to drive over to Mom's, because it was Mother's Day.

She had sent her three aunts gift cards to their favorite restaurants. She had not spent quality time with Lee because of all the doctor's appointments. She didn't want to put anyone in a predicament so she refrained from just dropping in, but Douglas had left a message on her phone that Lee needed to see her. They decided to go out to dinner.

"Carita, I need to know what your plans are when you come home from the hospital."

"Mom Lee, I will be alright. Todd and Alexis will be home for a week after the surgery and I should be fine. Doug has promised to look in on me also."

"What about after they leave? Who will take care of you?"

"Mom, I will be fine. You and Doug worry too much."

"Why do you have to be so proud? That's the only problem that I have with you. Listen, we know that it may be a problem for Doug to come, so this is my suggestion. Either, you come and stay with me and Walter or I will stay with you for at least two weeks until you get on your feet."

"Mom, that's really not necessary but I will think about it. Now, let's enjoy our dinner."

They returned to Lee's to learn they had just missed Douglas. Lee wanted to show Carita all the presents she received. After much fun and laughter, Carita said good-bye to the family to make the drive home. She only lived about a forty-five minutes away but Douglas and other family members did not like her driving late at night.

After she arrived home, her cell rang. Douglas checked on her. He apologized for not calling earlier. He hoped she and Lee would have returned early enough for him to join them. He also needed to tell her he was getting ready to get on the road for Maine. He wanted to wish her a happy Mother's Day even though most of the day had passed. He sounded so sad. He regretted leaving her. He was most concerned about her driving to the appointment alone. He asked her to consider taking his mom with her. At least, she would not be alone.

"I love you. I'm really going to miss you. I hate that I am not going to be with you for your appointment. You need to remember to call me as soon as you get home from the hospital. Carita, I want you to be careful at work and get plenty of rest."

She noticed hurriedness in his voice as he told her he would call upon his arrival and said good-bye. She knew Suzie must have been coming to the truck.

She dressed for bed to relax as best she could. Her job was a trip. She and her co-worker Renee had their hands full. She had been on the job fifteen years but Renee had been there seventeen. Granted Carita was the older of the two women, but Renee was very positive and always helping to point things out to Carita.

The next morning, on the way to work, she worried if Douglas reached his half way mark. She also wondered about the conversation between Douglas and Suzie. It was a very long drive and she knew Douglas not to be very much of a talker.

She concentrated on all of the components at work that needed to be completed. She wanted to accomplish as much as possible. She had to be at the hospital for tests the next day. She wanted to make sure she fulfilled her responsibilities and not leave anything extra for her coworkers. Mom Lee called to see how her day at work went and to let her know Douglas arrived safely at Jena's. He planned to call her as soon as possible. Lee also offered to ride to the hospital with Carita. She also did not want her to be alone. Carita told Lee she would be fine and had someone to accompany her. Lee, rather upset, respected Carita's decision and tried to be in agreement with her. She just told her to drive carefully and to call as soon as she returned home.

Douglas called while she showered and left a voicemail. "Babe, I know that I am not there. But I am always with you. Please know that. I am you and you are me. Don't forget to call me as soon as you leave the hospital. Love you."

After conveying all of his love, he instructed her to get some rest.

Carita started her trip at seven in the morning. The appointment was at nine. Driving to the city was no joke. She knew, by the time she got there, traffic would be backed up. She felt, to some degree, lost. This was her first trip without Douglas. She had to remember the things they discussed as well the questions they generated. Despite the fact of the nurse's friendly and professional manner, Carita felt lost without her other half.

As the nurse entered the room, she hurried to schedule the blood tests and other procedures to be completed that before the end of the day. "Why do you seem to be in a hurry," asked Carita.

"Your surgery has been scheduled for next Monday," the nurse answered.

"No! No! No!  There are forms from my employer that still are not complete.  Insurances have to be notified and other family members needed to make arrangement to take off work. You have to complete this form for my time off work.  You can't just do this surgery without approval from my insurance companies.  This will be my only income while I am off and it has to be done correctly."

Because of the urgency in her voice, the nurse began to listen.  When the doctor entered the exam room, the nurse told him of Carita's dilemma.

"How long do you want to put this surgery off," he asked.

"At least two weeks."

"Two weeks. Alright. It cannot be any longer.  The risk is too great."

"I just need to make sure that all of the paper work is in place."

The doctor agreed.  Carita completed some of the blood work needed for the surgery before she left and again her veins would not cooperate.

Carita didn't bother with lunch. She got directly on the road.  She was tired and now she understood why Douglas always insisted on being with her when she made these trips.  She called Lee after she arrived home and told her everything went well.  Lee went on to tell her that Whitley called and wanted to know if she needed help during the time of surgery.  If so, she could ride back with Douglas.  She declined Whitley's offer because the ride back would place Douglas in an awkward position.  Carita told Lee that she scheduled the surgery for the middle of June.

Lee, knowing Carita all too well, could hear some apprehensiveness in her voice.  She knew Carita felt little unsure.  She loved Carita like a daughter but wished that she would not worry about things.  She tried to tell her that she and Douglas would eventually be together, that God had a way of working things out.

"Carita," Lee said. "You have faith, now if you just learn how to have patience.  Let God do his job.  He can't do it if you are always in the way."

She agreed and decided to try being a little more positive.  She elected to lie down and take a short nap before calling Douglas.  She was a little more wiped out than she thought. When she awoke, she called Douglas but the phone went straight to voicemail. She thought that perhaps he was in a meeting and would call her back. She tried again before retiring to bed, to no avail. She remembered he sometimes did not answer the phone if Suzie was in his face. The thought of this made her angry because, after all, she simply followed his request of calling to keep him informed.

Douglas was most upset. He had not heard from Carita and had traveled all the way to Maine to assist Jena with her predicament. The whole incident was bull. Jena had gotten herself into a dilemma, trying to do too many things at one time. She and her husband had some issues and needed counseling, not a father, but she was his baby girl and had always been able to depend on him.

Douglas thought his daughter and her husband should have been able to work things out without bringing him into the situation. He did notice, however, Suzie in the midst of their business. This led him to believe she played a part in creating the problem and convinced his daughter to have him drive to Maine. He became livid. He had no problem checking on his daughter. But, more importantly, Carita's health was his main priority. He had very little to say to his daughter and son-in-law. What he spent to make the trip could not be reimbursed. As far as Suzie, he had nothing to say to her at all. The night before, she snuggled up underneath him to make love. He felt very uncomfortable in his daughter's home, especially since they were not married. She kissed his lips, rubbed his stomach, blew into his ear, and tried everything she could to arouse him. Her attempt at loving making let him know that his daughter's so called problem was a part of her plan.

He gently pushed her away. "I'm tired," he said. How could he make love to her when he could see the deceit? Beside, thoughts of Carita consumed him? He made up his mind to busy himself with things he rarely got a chance to do with the grandchildren. This kept him from being so angry and worrying about Carita's condition.

When he noticed two missed calls from Carita, he scowled. He did not know how that happened. He waited all day for her to call. As he looked at the clock, he thought he might still catch her. The phone went to voicemail. She had already gone to bed and was probably asleep, he thought.

He called at nine the next morning, forgetting Carita could not take her cell phone into work. By the time she got home, she saw calls from him. By late afternoon, he became really worried. He did not know if Carita received bad news and avoided his call or if they just missed one another. He started to call Lee but he did not want to upset her, knowing she might drive to Carita's. He had meeting at eight in the evening and called Carita. Again, the phone went to voicemail. He left a message.

"Hey babe, we seem to be missing one another. I am really worried about you. I have a meeting in a few minutes. Soon as it's, over I will call again."

He just wanted to be able to hear her voice. He had to admit it. Carita had become his everything. The forty years had brought them closer than one could imagine.

Douglas tried to reach Carita, again. Finally, he heard her softness in her voice. "Hello."

"Babe," he said. "I have been so worried about you. How you are and what did the doctor say?"

Before she could answer the first question, he asked half a dozen more. She patiently waited for him to finish.

"Douglas, I miss you. My appointment was horrible. They had scheduled the operation for Monday and I totally lost it. You were not there and I had a hard time maintaining my composure. When are you coming home?"

"Baby slow down," he said. "Just how are you? Honey, do you have any pain."

"No," she answered, "just the usual back pain. I set the surgery for June 18th. The doctor said he would not permit me to put it off any further than that because the tumor would continue to grow."

They both managed to calm down while exchanging concerns. He told her he would call her later with particulars about his return home. Although he said he might be home the following Tuesday, six days away, her heart told her he may come on Saturday night.

Suzie could feel the difference in Douglas's attitude. She tried very hard to be loving and concerned. She planned a picnic on Saturday for the grandchildren and themselves. She felt this would give the troubled couple sometime to regroup and assess some of their problems. In the same instance, it might give her and Douglas the time they needed to smooth out theirs. Upon hearing the arrangements for the weekend, Douglas became very disturbed.

"Who do you think you are? What gives you the right to make plans of without consulting me? I may have had other arrangements such as leaving for home. This is not your family or your grandchildren."

He then walked away irritated. Suzie tried to explain. She only wanted to do something good for all concerned. Douglas just looked at her and grunted. He told her she needed to plan to leave early Saturday morning because he was ready to go. She hesitated as he spoke but his look indicated that she had no other recourse.

The trip home, needless to say, was long and quiet. Douglas had nothing to say to Suzie. Suzie was upset. Her plans to put their relationship where she wanted it to be didn't pan out. She became angrier as she knew Carita was their problem. *Who the hell did she think she was interfering with her man? After all, she was there for him when he went through that disaster of a divorce.* She needed a plan to get this woman out of their lives. She could not have anyone, especially Carita, messing up her good thing. She tried to exchange conversation with Doug on the road but he had very little to say. He had never been one for chitchat.

Besides, he concentrated on arriving home safely so he could check on Carita.

He told Suzie they would not be spending the night with Whitley. He just wanted to get home. He planned to just stop and rest for a couple of hours and get something to eat. Suzie had nothing to say. She knew he had his own agenda, with Carita. The situation was really a bitch and so was she. Whitley, glad to see her brother as always, and was only cordial to Suzie. She hated it when Suzie accompanied Douglas because it put their relationship on the spot. They could no longer talk the way they wanted. The two had been very close. The topics they shared were family matters and for their ears only. As they departed, Whitley reminded him to stop at their mom's to drop a package off.

Douglas was glad to see the Pennsylvania line. Home at last. It was two o'clock Sunday morning but he knew Lee would be awaiting his return. Whitley called her when they left her house. She told Lee about the package she had sent. Douglas did not stay long. He was tired and had done most of the driving. He promised Lee he would return later in the morning.

Sunday morning, Carita got up about seven and drank coffee. She did not want to miss the church service. Rev. Taylor was the morning speaker. She showered and prepared for the day. She had not heard from Douglas and became concerned. She expected his to return by now. She called Todd since talking to him on her way to church had become a Sunday ritual.

"Hey, it's me. I'm on my way to service. How are the three of you?"

"We're fine, mom, and you? I told Alexis this was our Sunday wake up call."

"I'm fine son. Do you guys have any special plans for the day?"

"No ma'am. Just the usual Sunday stuff."

"Well, you guys have a blessed day. I will talk with you later."

Service could not have been more humbling. Carita enjoyed a good word, needing to be filled for the week. She looked at her phone as she got into her truck. She saw two messages both from Douglas. The first message let her know he arrived at home and needed to see her. The second said he knew she must have gone to Sunday service and would try to catch her later. She hurriedly called him but the phone went to voicemail. She left a message, telling him she headed home from church. After arriving at home, she called Lee hoping Douglas might be there. Lee told her he had already left but she was not sure where he went.

Carita planned to prepare stuff pork chops with dressing and gravy, mixed vegetables, a salad, and dinner rolls for her Sunday meal. If Douglas didn't to eat dinner with her, she could always reheat it the next day. Since she did not know where Douglas had gone, she decided to complete her cooking and stop by her cousin's later on to round out her day.  For a moment, she felt lonely and lost until she heard the garage door chime.  As she looked up, Douglas stood in the family room.  She ran to him and gave him a hug.  He kissed her.  Both, so excited to see one another, fell onto the couch embraced in each other's arms.  They laughed and kissed once again.

"Oh honey, I'm so glad to see you. You had me so worried.  Now tell me everything about your doctor's appointment."

"Well…" Carita began, "they had the surgery planned for Monday, as I told you before, but I convinced them the doctor to give me a few weeks to get my paper work in order."

"I'm glad," Douglas replied.  "I would have been very upset had the surgery been done and Todd and I were not informed."

The aroma from the meal began to fill the house. Douglas asked what she was cooking.

"Stuffed pork chops with dressing and gravy, mixed vegetables, a salad, and dinner rolls."

"What if I had not come today?"

"Then, we would have this meal tomorrow. But my heart told me you would be here."

The smell and description of the cuisine made his mouth water and he could hardly contain himself.  Carita suggested he relax while she completed their meal.  She set the table, using some of her better china with cloth napkins and Douglas's favorite glassware.  When the meal was almost done, she bent down and kissed on his forehead.

"Dinner is on the table."

He smiled and went to wash his hands.  He enjoyed every morsel but was not surprised the meal tasted so appetizing as well as looking appealing.  Carita enjoyed cooking. It was one of the things that helped her relax.  He began to clear the table even though Carita insisted she could do it.

"It's the least I can do for such a fantastic meal," Douglas said.  "That meal was to die for."

His smiled and told her how much he really appreciated the meal and his kiss on her forehead let her know she was special.

After cleaning the kitchen, they sat down to watch some TV. They talked about their son and when he would be able to come for Carita's surgery.

Douglas noticed Carita pouting while they discussed the procedure. He did not want to upset her about anything. It had been a good day for them both.

"Babe, what wrong?" he asked in a quiet voice.

"Nothing," she said.

He held her face up to his. "We both know that that's not true." His eyes presented a color and seriousness she could not take for granted. She looked at him. "I'm just a little concerned about my family, you and Todd," she continued.

"What," he said.

"Doug, what if they should find other things or what if I don't pull through?"

He begin to kiss her on her cheek, in her ear, on her neck, on her nose, and finally on her lips. In a low but sexy voice, he said, "What if I told you I did not love you anymore? Would you believe me?"

She studied his gentle brown eyes. "No."

"Then why would you entertain such thoughts when you know you are a child of God and that he's got you?"

"I'm just frighten," she said, "not only for myself but the two of you as well. You're all I have and I worry about both of you."

He held her tightly. "Honey, you don't ever have to be afraid." He kissed her lips until his tongue met hers. He reached around her waist until his arm gripped the other side. They caressed one another and moved to the bedroom. His ears were pleasing to the touch as well as the taste. She began to stroke his head as he embraced her breasts and cuddled her body next to his. They fondled one another like there was not time for ecstasy. Their bodies relaxed and they became one. The pleasure of making love rose to a joyful bliss. Carita held onto to him tight, for she did not know when they would have the opportunity to be together again.

He felt her and held her once again. "Stop that, I will always be here for you," he said in an assuring voice. "You worry too much, Carita. We will always be together. This is not the last time we will be together."

"But," she said, "you have no idea how much I missed you."

"No, You have no idea how I missed you. The trip was not what I expected. It was actually a waste of my time and money. I was pissed the whole time I was there."

"That's not like you."

Douglas explained that she was his primary concern. "It was important to me that I am with you on all of your appointments; because Jena is my daughter, she took precedence but my presence was to no avail.  I could not get you out of my mind.  I didn't know what you were going through."

She never saw him so upset.  She kissed his nose and said, "Let's not think about it.  You're home and we're together.  Right now is all that matters."

They kissed tenderly and held each other as they drifted off to sleep.

Carita shopped for food she might need or want during her recovery, as well as picked up toiletry items to take to the hospital with her.  She had to make an appointment to get her hair done.  She wanted braids.  She knew the surgery could be extensive and she would not have the strength to take care of her hair.  She also made an appointment for a manicure and a pedicure.  She always kept her nails done but a pedicure was necessary at this time.  Feet were ugly things, she thought, so who would want to look at ugly feet during a surgery.  At least they looked better with a little polish on the toes.  She also arranged for all of the bills to be paid.  She did not want to leave anything to chance.

Douglas arranged for his truck to be checked.  He wanted everything to be in order since he would be driving back and forth to Cleveland, even though he could use Carita's truck.  He wanted to be able to share the expense of gas with his son.

Suzie knew Douglas's son was coming in but was not sure why so she started making a big deal out of not being able to participate in his home-coming.  Douglas tried to explain that Todd and his wife were coming home for family reasons and she did not need to concern herself.  When Douglas explained that to Suzie, she still had issues and Douglas had no choice but let her be agitated with whatever disputes she wanted.

Douglas, glad he would be able to make Carita's last appointment before the surgery, made a list of questions he and Todd complied.

Todd called his mom to let her know he would arrive Sunday evening. He and his wife planned to stay with their cousins Tessa and Randy so Carita and Douglas could have some privacy. Sunday afternoon Todd and Alexis, his wife, called to let Carita know they reached Tessa's home. She and Todd were upset that she had to be at the clinic at five in the morning for prep and processes relating to the operation, scheduled for seven. Douglas called to say he was on his way and asked Carita not to prepare a meal as she was not permitted to eat after six.

Upon his arrival, he hugged and kissed her then they sat down to just enjoy the company of one another. He conveyed to Carita that Todd should arrive by three in the morning. They planned to drive as a family to the clinic.

They knew three in the morning would come quickly and they needed to rest. Carita did not saying anything to Douglas while wondering what he told Suzie. Their time together was special and she refused to mar their relationship with such a negative creature.

He held her on his lap and tried to rock her to sleep in his favorite chair so she would be relaxed by the time they left for the hospital. He kissed her so she might know he was there for her and things would be alright. He told her she was one of God's special children and the operation would be a success. He laid her down in their bed next to him. He wanted her to be relaxed so he held her gently, caressing her body affectionately. He knew that making love did not always have to be physical. Carita was not only his love but his best friend and the virtuosity of making love was like having the knowledge and appreciation of fine art. He continued to whisper in her ear and kissed her affectionately until she drifted into loving slumber.

As she began to enjoy her nap, the time to get ready for the trip arrived. They both showered and Carita gathered her necessary items.

Todd, as usual, was on time and very anxious to get his mom to Cleveland. Douglas was elated they were going as a family. The trip was a little over an hour long and all were concerned about Carita.

They registered her and, soon after, she went to the prep area. As the nurse completed some of the pre-surgical preps, Todd requested to see a physician. There were several questions he needed answered. Todd proceeded to ask the doctor where and how the surgeon would cut Carita to reach her liver. He asked how long the surgery would take as well as the procedure for her recovery. When he thought all of his questions were answered, the orderlies took Carita to the top floor where another doctor awaited her. She woke several hours later stapled, wearing tubes, and sore. Douglas rubbed her hand and fed her ice chips.

"How do you feel?" Todd asked.

"Todd, why are you and Alexis standing on the ceiling?"

Douglas and the children just laughed. They knew the drugs for Carita's pain had kicked in. Alexis was concerned about both Todd and Douglas. She knew Carita was their heart.

Carita could not move. Carita floated in and out of consciousness. Her family was not ready to leave her but she finally convinced them that she would be fine. After all, they got up early and it had been a very long day. She knew all too well that it would be a difficult night and a very long recovery.

<h1 style="text-align:center">Chapter 14</h1>

Carita hated to see her family go. She needed them so badly. She was afraid and hurting. She felt helpless and only trusted her family. But in all fairness, she knew they needed rest. When she tried to move, she hurt. When she coughed, she hurt. Her voice cracked as she tried to talk and, the biggest thing of all, she had to urinate. She did not want to use a bed pan. She wanted to walk to the bathroom. Her getting well depended on her being self-sufficient. She did not want to become dependent on anyone. She was afraid Douglas may not be able to be there for her when Todd and Alexis returned home to gather up their daughter Aeleta. Carita's aunts offered to assist during her recovery but they were up in age. She couldn't have them wait on her. She knew it would be a long and difficult recovery but she had to be able to endure for her family's sake. She told Todd he could return home and perhaps come back once they released her from the hospital. He wouldn't hear of it.

Soon the nurse brought what was supposed to be dinner.

"Is this all," Carita questioned.

"I'm afraid so," the nurse responded.

Just as Carita thought, hospital food was still as bad as it ever. She had been placed on a soft diet, consisting of Jell-O, broth, and juice.

Douglas drove up with his mother, who insisted on seeing Carita. She and Carita had a bond that seemed to be everlasting. The only difference between Carita and her daughters was she had not birthed Carita. She grabbed Carita around the neck and kissed her for what seemed to be forever.  Douglas just stood back and smiled.  When Lee finished greeting Carita, Douglas gave her a beautiful bouquet of flowers.

"They're beautiful."

"I know.  They cost me a pretty penny."

"Still cheap are we?"

"No just thrifty."

They all laughed. Carita could hardly catch her breath.

Douglas and Todd talked about the prognosis with the doctor.  They all enjoyed one another's company and Douglas kept an eye on Carita. He didn't want to tire her out.  Todd and Alexis had an interesting conversation about tennis with his grandmother.  They decided to go to the cafeteria to get a light lunch so Carita and Douglas could have some privacy.

Douglas bent over and gave Carita a real kiss.  His eyes became very sad.  He told her he wanted her to be careful and take her time healing.  He promised to be there for her.  She knew, from the look in his eye, he had difficulties with Suzie.  She took his hand and kissed it while looking at him.

"Don't…  I know you're distressed right now and I understand.  God will work it out.  If you can't do something or keep the promise you have made, just tell me.  It will be alright."

He smiled and let out a sigh of relief. He wanted Carita to be well and continue to love him.  He kissed her nose while pinching her cheek to let her know he would always be hers.

Todd, Alexis and Lee returned.  After checking on Carita's diet and medication, Douglas and Lee said their goodbyes.

Todd managed to speak with the head nurse while Alexis kept Carita busy.  They really wanted to know the Carita's present the medication as well as the any future scripts.  If she needed help with the cost of medication, they wanted to be able to assist. They knew Carita would never ask for help.  Douglas also told Todd to find out what other provisions were necessary so he could contribute.  Lee had always told Douglas, the only problem she had with Carita, she was too proud.  Now he and his son found out what she meant.

Day by day, Carita continued to improve.  All of the nurses just loved her because she insisted on helping herself.  She gave them all little clichés to make their day as well tips for life down the road.  The doctors thought she was a phenomenal individual. She had just lost a spouse to leukemia the past year but kept believing in God and was willing to accept what challenges life brought forth. She shared her believe and trust with the medical staff and, believe it or not, they had a better day.

Douglas called to say he had trouble with the truck and would not be able to make it. He had to wait on a part that had to be shipped and was afraid he would not see Carita until she got home.

Although Carita accepted his excuse, she could feel there was something else going on. She suggested he use her truck, which he declined. When she asked Douglas if Todd could pick him up, he provided another excuse. She told Douglas she loved him and, if he could call, she may not miss him so much. He laughed and swore that he would. As they hung up, Todd came in with the surprise he promised. Carita's two aunts came to visit. Both planned to stay her first week of recovery so things would not be so awkward for Lee. Carita was their eldest sister's daughter, who had been deceased for some years. They were very close to her and wanted to be there during her time of need.

The day finally came for Carita to come home. It was difficult for her to walk but she gave it her best shot. Alexis brought the box of candy Carita requested for the nurses who had been so helpful to her. They were all sad to see her go because she had been such a good patient and made their day with some crazy sayings.

Upon arriving home, the aunts presented a meal cooked for a king. Carita was not able to each much for she did not have an appetite.

Douglas arrived with Lee, who brought her favorite fruit, as well as Shelly and Rod who brought her an editable arrangement. Douglas could see Carita was restless and suggested putting her to bed. He helped her undress and laid her gently on the pillow. Todd knocked on the door to see if his dad needed assistance from him. The both gently took her arms so they could slide her up to the pillow where she would be comfortable. Alexis came into the room where she could be close to Carita for the first time since the surgery. It was always their thing to lie on the bed together and have girl talks. She had missed that so much. This day, she had first dibs and she refused to give it up for anyone.

Aunt Lois prepared a wonderful breakfast so Todd and Alexis could begin their journey home. Aunt Anne saw to it that Carita had taken her meds and assisted her with showering. She saw to it that messages from her friends were relayed. Carita hated to see her son leave. He had been an inspiration. She was grateful that he and his wife loved her enough to take a week off work to be with her at this crucial time in her life. The two aunts called their older sister Ruby to keep her abreast of Carita's condition. Lee called every day to make sure Carita did not need anything and Douglas came daily to cater to her every whim.

The week ended and both aunts headed for home. Carita's friend, a nurse, came most mornings to assist her with a bath. Carita was watching TV when the garage door opened. She finally heard a strong hello and recognized Douglas's voice. He came to the bedroom and bent over to kiss her. He gently picked her up and placed her in his arms then carried her to the family room where he opened the patio door so she could get some fresh air. He continued to make a fruit salad for Carita. He knew she did not have much of an appetite but wanted to make sure she had enough nourishment in her body. They laughed and talked about getting his real-estate business going. He really did not want to plan anything until Carita recovered one hundred per cent.

Meanwhile, Suzie wondered what was going on with Douglas. He was always in a hurry and he had to do this or that. He was never anywhere to be found. She looked for him in several of his spots but no one saw him. While out and about, she ran into Nate. He bought her a drink and they sat at the bar.

"Looking for your man, I suppose," he said with smile.

"You know it," she replied.

"I'm right here," he said.

"Stop it," Suzie replied with a laugh.

"It wasn't funny when you needed money to get to Florida."

"Listen," she said, "I don't have the time to be playing games damn it. If you know something, let's hear it."

"Your girl has cancer. Yea. That's where your man has been, catering to her every need. I thought you were his woman and not his bitch. I understand that their son and daughter-in-law were here and they all drove to Cleveland as a family."

Tears begin to swell in Suzie's eyes. How could he do this to her? She could not wait for him to get home.

Once Douglas made sure Carita was situated, he got ready to go. He asked again to ensure she would be okay. He did not like leaving her alone. Her surgery was only two weeks old and she was still vulnerable. He made her promise to call if she needed anything. She reminded him that, later in the week, she had an appointment in Cleveland. He smiled and kissed her then told her that he had not forgotten. He made sure everything was on her nightstand so she would not have to walk any further than the bathroom. She heard the garage door close and settled down for a nap. She knew he would call in the evening, as always.

When Douglas arrived back at Suzie's apartment, she was drinking a beer. How he hated the smell of alcohol. He could tell from her body language she had an attitude. He wondered about its origin. He was so tired of these attitudes and tit-for-tat sessions that had become most redundant.

"Where you been?" she said, swinging the door in his face.

"Out and about," he answered.

"Really, she exclaimed. "Well, I've been to all your spots and you were not at a one."

"Listen," he said, "you don't need to check on me. I'm grown. I am not your son or your husband."

She looked at him with anger and said, "What do you tell your bitch when she's looking for you?"

Douglas whirled around in anger. "What did you say? Who are you talking about?"

"Your baby's, mammy. I know the bitch has cancer. And just what do you think you can do about it?" She glared at him. Who do you think you are? I'm your woman and you've seem to have forgotten that."

Douglas just stood and looked at her in disbelief then walked out the door. She followed him as though he would stop but he got in the truck and kept driving. He went to a small fishing spot where the trees and bushes secluded everyone's presence. He could not believe the ordeal he had just experienced with Suzie. He did not know what was happening with her. He was in love with Carita but did it show that much? He felt obligated to Suzie for being there when he needed someone. Something had to give but he did not know what.

Carita did her best to help herself. She had Todd bring up a walker that Tony used during his illness from the basement. He sat it by the bed and she used it as a lever to pull herself up when she need to use the restroom or get to the kitchen. She needed the help and someone to be with her but she did not like depending on other people, too proud to ask. She did the best she could on her own, many times falling and crying herself to sleep from the pain. She knew Douglas was concerned but it seemed as though he was not completing the commitments he had made to her. She trusted him and began to depend on him, too much to her own disapproval. Right now, she felt she did not have a choice. He told her that their relationship was a two way street and she needed to be a little more flexible when she needed or wanted him. He did not mind and had all intentions of being there for her. She did not want to pressure him. He had asked early in their relationship for her to teach him how to make her coffee. She just smiled and told him to not concern himself with her coffee. She could manage.

He just could not understand why he couldn't do that one little thing for her.

He came at the beginning of the week to check on Carita, who was still asleep. He entered the bedroom and sat down while pulling her up to give her a kiss. He knew she must have had a bad night for she was an early riser even with this illness. It concerned him that she was not doing well. He came to check on her while Suzie ran to the store. She gave him the blues about Carita and expressed what she would do if he continued to not be at home. He told her he was an adult, retired, and no one told him what to do. He needed to stay focus on Carita to help her get through this surgery. He knew she expected him to be by her side a little more but Suzie made it impossible, not to mention he had his meetings in the evenings. He knew he had to make a decision about his life. He grew tired of playing 007 and wanted a life with a woman he could depend on. He helped Carita to the bathroom so she could take care of her personals. While Carita showered, he decided to attempt to make her coffee. He wanted so badly to do more than just to come and check on her.

Carita did not feel well this morning, but was grateful that Douglas came. He helped her to the kitchen table, being careful not to hurt her incision.

"I made your coffee," he said.

She just looked at him in shock. "Thank you," she replied politely.

She noticed that, the last few times Douglas came to check on her, he seemed tense and in a hurry. Just as she tasted her coffee, Douglas announced he had to leave. Carita looked at him in disappointment for it had been two days since she last saw him. She smiled and clutched his hand.

"Can you give just a moment," she asked. Please understand, I am not trying to start an argument. I just have a couple of things to say." She took a deep breath. I've noticed, the last few times you been here, you were in a hurry. I feel like you have tossed me aside like a sack of potatoes," she pleaded. "Doug, if you are not able to keep your word just let me know. I understand and will make other arrangements but you must communicate with me."

Douglas, feeling pressured, just lost it. "You knew when we got into this relationship I was already involved with someone else."

Carita held her hand up.

Douglas continued, "Oh, it's alright for you to say what you want but I can't?"

Carita said sternly, trying not to let him know how much he hurt her, "If the other relationship is your primary concern than maybe that's where you need to be. You can return my things and please leave me alone. I'll be fine."

Douglas tried to ignore her by taking the garbage out. She flatly told him she could do that herself. She further indicated that his outburst was one of the reasons she did not depend on people. They always disappointed you. Douglas returned her items and reluctantly left.

Carita fell to the couch and just let all of what she tried to hold together out. She loved Douglas and knew he had to be feeling some kind of way to just let loose like he did. "Oh my God," she thought, not knowing what she would do. Her life and her love disappeared in moments' sweep of anger. Carita could hardly contain herself. The phone rang but she could not see any reason to answer. She knew it was not Douglas. She slowly walked to the bedroom and cried herself to sleep.

Douglas was angry with himself. He loved Carita but felt she did not need to be burdened with his issues. He should have never given in to her and gave the keys and garage remote back. Who would take care of her? Who would make sure she had the things she needed? How could he have let anger let him lose the woman he really loved?

Three weeks passed and Carita had not heard from Douglas. She had reached her wits end. She loved Douglas and thought he would call. She thought he knew her well enough to know when her emotions are offended she loses focus.

Although he had not heard from Carita, he worried about her. He did not know whether or not to call. Carita meant everything to him but she had been very emphatic about her request.

Suzie meanwhile knew something was wrong since Douglas spent more time around the town. She was glad. He spent most of his time fishing and going to the coach's meetings for the mentally challenged. When he wasn't doing either of those things, he shot pool. Todd was still calling to check on his mom, but did not tell her that he planned to come home for the weekend. He sensed something was wrong when his dad called and asked if he talked with his mother. He also noticed Carita had been very evasive when he asked about his dad. Todd seemed approving of the two finally getting together. To be very truthful, he wished for it his entire life. He knew his parents loved one another for a long time. He was grateful that they would possibly be together in their later years. Alexis wanted to bring Aeleta. She thought that might brighten Carita up. Todd knew Carita loved her granddaughter but, right now, he needed to get her to love herself more.

Arriving home, Todd found Carita potting around the house. She tried to keep busy but seemed to be in a deep depression. They hugged and kissed then he offered to treat her to lunch. She told him she did not want to waste his money, that she did not have much of an appetite. He kissed his mom and told her he needed a date. She took a quick shower and let him lead the way.

He knew the Pasta Palace was her favorite restaurant. He set the motion to make his mom smile. They completed the order when Todd looked around and saw his dad. He got up to go speak while Carita excused herself to the restroom. As she returned to the table, she spotted Todd talking to someone but could not get a glimpse. Then she saw Douglas. She looked beyond his head at the woman who one didn't appear to be his type. She gathered it had to be Suzie. Douglas excused himself to speak to Carita and Suzie became livid.

"Hi Carita," he said.

She gave Douglas a cool hello.

"How you have been," he asked.

She looked at him. "Do you really care?"

"I'm asking," he replied, so you must mean something to me."

"Really," Carita replied. "Don't have a snake waiting at your table?"

On that note, Douglas abruptly left.

"Ma, Todd said, was that really necessary?"

"Yes, she replied." And by this time, she really did not have an appetite at all as she saw Suzie march out of the restaurant and Douglas following her.

Todd tried to make Carita's weekend as pleasant as possible but needed to voice his opinion about his parent's relationship with one another.

"Ma," he said. "I am sick of you and dad. You two act like two little kids. I don't why you and dad can't cut the bullshit and move on."

"I'm moving on, Todd, she replied. After the scene in the restaurant yesterday, your dad does not have to worry about me. I'm done!"

"Ma, don't say that."

"Todd, I have waited for your father for forty years. I thought that the both of us had it all together, particularly when I had the surgery. I thought that he would be there for me, but I guess not. I love your dad. I really do but God does not have another forty years for me. And besides it looks like Douglas is where he wants to be."

Todd went to the bedroom. He really did not know what to say to his mother. From what his dad told him over the phone a month earlier, he loved Carita. He just did not know how to approach her. Todd became upset that Carita was ready to give up on Douglas. He felt that, if she gave up on his dad, she would give up on life. He called Alexis to let her know what happened and to see if she could give him any advice.

Carita once again cried herself to sleep. Douglas had left her again. She had not felt so distressed in years, but knew she had to go on. She did manage to have good conversations with Todd before he left and headed home. She assured him that she would be fine, even though she still had doctor's appointments to keep. He tried once more to persuade her to allow Douglas to take her but to no avail.

Carita managed to keep herself busy with a few orders for graphics and her ministries at church.

Lee continued to call. She was concerned about both her children. She dropped over a few times to assure Carita was alright, not only for herself but for Douglas as well. She tried to convince Carita to give Douglas a call. She knew he waited on her to make the first move. She hugged Lee and told her she truly loved Douglas but he was not interested in her and she had her doubts if he ever did love her. She however did tell Lee she still loved her and Walt, Whitley, Mike, and Ronnie.

"That will never change," she said.

Carita had appointment with her primary care physician, who was usually on time. But, this day, the office seemed to be running behind. As she sat reading a magazine, she heard a familiar voice. She looked up from her book and saw Mark Jackson standing at the appointment desk. When he saw Carita, he grabbed her for dear life. He had only been trying to get in touch with her for two years. She and Mark worked together on some graphics and he shared his knowledge and skills with her.

He was pleased to learn she had acquired her degree. He told her, early in their friendship, she was very good. She was one of the best graphic artists he had ever seen without a degree. He thought she had a God given talent. Just as the nurse called Carita's name, Mark made her promise not to leave until he came out from his examination. He had lots of information he wanted to share with her.

They grabbed some lunch in a small restaurant where they could have some privacy. Carita told Mark she tried several times to get in touch with him but all attempts were to no avail. He explained that he sold his business and moved west with his family. They owned a large graphic business and were looking for additional talent. He had come back to tie up loose ends.

Carita told Mark about the loss of her spouse and her illness. She was not planning on returning to her full-time position. It was far too dangerous. She knew that not all of the precautionary measures for her cancer had been finalized. Carita planned to take an early retirement. She had enough years on the job to do so.

Mark listened attentively and came up with an idea.

"Why not move west and join my family's business," he suggested. "We're looking for bright and new talent anyway."

Carita smiled and thought how gracious of Mark. Nevertheless, she could not leave her family. Although still angry at Douglas, she could not really leave him. She told Mark about her personal life and, at this time, she could not make any decisions about anything.

"When you're ready to relocate, my family and I would be glad to have you. We can assist with any arrangements you might need," he said.

They exchanged numbers, said their goodbyes, and promised to stay in touch.

Carita felt good that Mark remembered her and was thankful he thought she did excellent work. It felt good to know he appreciated her talent.

She continued to maintain all of her doctor's appointments and made sure she kept in touch with her son and other family members. She went out to dinner with several of her friends from time to time and kept busy with her volunteer organizations.

Todd and Alexis planned to bring Aeleta for a visit. She was the apple of her daddy's eye and Carita's only grandchild. She prepared for a grand weekend by preparing all of their favorite foods. They went shopping and she played word games with her granddaughter. She and Aeleta designed some graphics on the computer while Todd and Alexis went out for an evening with Tessa and her husband. She had just put Aeleta to bed when the doorbell rang. Thinking Todd forgot his key, she hurried to answer the door. To her surprise, Douglas stood at the door.

"May I come in," he asked.

She extended the door to him. "What can I do for you?"

"I came to see our granddaughter."

"I just put her to bed," she replied.

"Well, is she asleep?"

"I don't know," Carita answered, "let me see."

While Carita went into the bedroom, she finally realized this was something Todd cooked up to try and get them back together. She told Aeleta her granddad had come to see her. She gave her granddad a big hug and began to tell him of the day's events. Carita excused herself and went downstairs to the shop.

Douglas put Aeleta back to bed and left. Carita was devastated that he didn't at least tell her he was leaving.

Tessa and Todd were on pins and needles, worrying if their scam with Carita and Douglas would work. Alexis advised them not to get involved with the two elders.

"If they truly love each other, they will eventually work it out," she said.

"You don't know my parents," Todd told her.

After a fun evening with their cousins, Todd and his wife returned to his mother's. Carita worked on some orders in the lab. Todd came down to see what she was doing and asked how her evening went. She was full of conversation of what she and Aeleta had done with some designs. Carita could tell Todd anxiously awaited some details about his father but Carita did not budge.

"You didn't have any company?" Todd asked.

"Your dad came by to see Aeleta for a while."

"And," he said.

"And what," Carita asked.

"Did you guys talk?"

"Talk about what?" She looked at Todd like he was crazy.

"You and dad, what happened?"

"Nothing."

"Mom!"

"Look, Todd, your dad is not interested in me so will you please give it a rest."

"Mom, you're the one who needs to give it a rest. You will not give dad a chance, but always want me here to do things for you when you have a man."

"Where's the man, Todd?" she asked. "Todd, do me a favor. Stay out of grown folks business."

"You don't have to worry mom. I'm going to take my family and leave. I am tired of trying to satisfy your every whim."

He stomped up the steps like he did as a child. She knew, in the morning, he would be very apologetic. When Carita awoke, she got up to shower so she could make breakfast. The house seemed to be so quiet. She checked the rooms to make sure the children were asleep. To her surprise, they had left. Carita just sat on her bed and cried. "Why me Lord? Why me?" She did not hear from Todd and did not know whether they arrived home safely.

The week went slowly and her life seemed to be so empty. She heard through gossip that Douglas was thinking about marrying Suzie. She did not know how, knowing Suzie never divorced her husband. She noticed that Lee did not call as much and her son had not called at all. She supposed everyone had a busy life. Most of her friends still worked and their time for her was limited. Mark called to see how she was doing and wanted to know if she gave his offer any thought. They had a pleasant conversation. She told him she would be in touch with him. She began to contemplate. Douglas no longer loved her. She knew that. And Todd was just very put out with her. She called several times and left messages but he had not returned her phone calls. She could always visit her niece, who had been a nurse, to get her head straight but she would only call Todd. She wanted to keep this problem just between the two of them.

She thought deeper and deeper about Mark's offer. Her family was very small and everyone had their own issues. She checked her bank accounts to see if she had enough to move and be able to pay at least three months mortgage payments as well as the utilities. She had nothing to lose. No one loved her, so why stick around she thought? She needed to move on and really Mark's offer was plausible.

She called Mark to let him know she accepted his offer. She would fly out to make living arrangements. Mark's family and other members of the staff made Carita feel very welcome. It seemed that Mark told everyone about her and they were very anxious for her to be a part of the family, both personal and professional. She wanted to have her truck shipped and a few other things she may need. Now, she just needed to talk to Mark in private to put her plans in motion. She was very honest with Mark as far as personal life, and what she wanted to do. Mark disagreed with her and felt that someone should know she planned to relocate.

Carita felt as though no one loved her and this would be best for everyone. It was one of the conditions. Mark agreed. She would return to her to her maiden name. No one would look for her using her maiden name. She also wanted everyone to call her K. This way if her family would look for her, the letter K would not give her away.

She left the bank accounts at home open. She could draw off them, if needed, but moreover no one could find her through her banking. However, she opened a checking so she could begin to do business there.

Mark and Carita went apartment hunting so, upon her return, she would have a place to live and not have to depend on Mark or anyone. She found a partly furnished four-room apartment in a respectable part of town. Mark offered her a fantastic salary so rent would not be a problem. After she had worked out the details with the landlord and signed the lease, she was ready to go back east to complete her plans.

She still could not get over why Lee had not called and, as much as she hated doing so, she did not want to leave without seeing her. Todd still had not returned her phone calls even the one she made while out west. Carita was intensified by this newfound attitude of her son's. She felt sad but still pushed to move on. She needed to call Lee before bouncing over to the house but she feared she did not have a lot of time. She dressed and drove to Lee's house. Whitley answered the door. They hugged and kissed.

"I wondered where you were," Whitley said.

"Why," responded Carita.

"Mama has been sick and I've been calling."

"I never got the call," Carita explained. "What number you dial?"

Whitley gave her the book Lee used for numbers. It was wrong. That was the reason she heard not heard from Lee. Whitley and she went to the hospital to visit with her. Lee was so glad to see Carita. She had a million and one questions to ask.

"No, he and I are not together. Do I still love him? Yes. But sometimes, Mom, things are just not meant to be and we have to move on."

Lee smiled but really did not like what Carita said. She felt as though Carita was going away, never to return.

While hugging Lee again, she happened to look out the window to see Douglas and Suzie coming toward the hospital. Carita kissed Lee hard and made excuses to leave the room, giving Whitley some kind of look. She was barely out of the room when Douglas and Suzie walked in. Douglas looked at Whitley rather strange. He recognized the scent of the cologne and knew Whitley never wore that brand. Had Carita been there? He wondered.

Whitley hugged her brother and spoke to Suzie then made an excuse to leave. Douglas was sure Carita had been here and he had missed her. He hated that.

Whitley and Carita said their goodbyes and Carita had a few tears. She knew she might never see Whitley again.

Whitley assumed that Carita was unhappy because of Douglas.

Carita traveled home prioritizing her plans for her big move but praying her son would call. She made arrangements for her truck to be shipped. She packed it with items she would need in her new place. Basically, she left her home as it was. She took two of her favorite computers and some designs she had been working on. She packed clothes and shoes as well as other personal items. She cleaned out her safe so Todd would not have any records to find her. She looked around at her home. Tony had been so happy there and, because of God's grace and mercy, he allowed the last five years of their marriage to be happy. God allowed Tony a taste of the good life before calling him home.

Although devastated, Carita had to move on.

When she learned of the cancer in her body, she thought her life would not be worth living but Douglas proved her wrong. She thought that moving on would be with him. Fate, again, dealt them unscrupulous hand. And, once more, she had to live life without Douglas despite thinking she had a second chance. She touched the wooden chair rail in the kitchen. It had been one of the selling points of her home. The curio, displayed with her mom's Depression glass china, applauded the case to a rich anticipation. The family room had become one of Douglas's favorite spaces. The fireplace lit it up on a cold's winter night, seducing him to join his love in the amorous bedroom where their love filled the very depths of their souls. All that this house had been was for not, but she could not bear to let it go. It contained her heart, love, and soul. She looked at all the things that brought her pleasure and laughter then stepped out into a new world. She prayed it would be half as good to her as this one.

$$Chapter\ 15$$

Glad the plane was landing, Todd felt good to be back in the states. He had been to Saudi on temporary duty, teaching protected classified information for the government and taking care of a security briefing. He had done well for himself and his parents were so very proud of him, considering he was on his way to earning a doctorate degree. Alexis also held a degree in security information. Douglas and Carita believed that their advocating the importance of higher education enhanced Todd's chances of having a better life than them. Both had earned degrees but nothing higher than a bachelor's. Alexis and Todd in turn were stressing the same about education to their daughter.

It had almost been a month since Todd saw with his wife and daughter. He picked Aeleta up from school and took her to her favorite place to eat. After they arrived home, he presented her with the blanket he bought in Saudi and got her started with her homework. Todd decided to prepare Alexis' favorite meal by making it as romantic as possible. He dressed the table with her favorite fresh flowers and placed the candles in the perfect spot. He made sure the spinach was fresh for the tossed salad he prepared. His potatoes, for the twice-baked potatoes, were almost ready. He marinated the steaks in his secret dressing. He saw Alexis pull in the drive.

Once she opened the garage door, she became so excited she could hardly wait to get into the house. She hugged Todd and he her. They kissed and kissed some more. The aroma from her kitchen smelled heavenly but her eyes told him they could eat later.

Once Todd's life got back on a regular routine, he noticed he had not heard from his mom. He checked his phone and there were no voicemails from her either.  He thought that was strange.  She called him almost every day.  He called her cell and did not get an answer.

He thought she might be out and about and did not hear her phone ring.  He called the house phone to make sure and left a message on that phone as well.  Alexis told him she left several messages for Carita while he was gone but she had not returned any of them.  She feared the worst because Carita always returned calls, even though she might be upset.  Todd thought he would check with some family members later in the morning but, at the moment, he needed to check in regarding his job.  After reporting to his job and submitting all the required reports, Todd took the rest of the day off to find out what was going on with Carita.  He tried her cell again, to no avail.  Although he knew she only use the landline for the internet connection and fax, Todd decided to try that phone anyway.  Carita seldom used it for conversations but he took a chance and left another message.

He called Tessa who had not seen Carita since Todd and Alexis' last visit.

Tessa telephoned some of the other family members to see if they heard from Carita, to no avail.  Tessa hated to call Todd and tell him she had not been seen in more than a week.  Todd had numbers of some of her friends and decided to call them but that effort didn't yield any positive results.

Although he did not want to call his dad, that was his last hope.

Douglas told Todd the last he saw of Carita was when he visited with Aeleta.  He knew she had been to the hospital to see Lee but he missed her.  He felt for his son who sounded like he reached his whit's end looking for his mother.  Douglas knew the two had their differences but were still very close.  He told Todd to keep him updated on his mother.

Todd reached out to his childhood friend, Steve, who had become chief of detectives in Berkley.  He relayed everything that happen to him and that this was out of the norm for his mom.  Steve knew this be to true.  Ma, as he called Carita, lived in a small suburb outside the city and therefore Steve did not have jurisdiction.  He called in a favor from the Marlboro Heights Township police and they were willing to accommodate him.

They checked the house from front to the back and were unable to find any evidence of foul play.  Steve suggested they do periodic drive byes to keep a watch on the house. He then called Todd back to let him know his findings.

Todd, worried, called Tessa and Randy. He asked if they could go over to the house and investigate the situation. No one had a key but Todd and he lived five hours away. Tessa and Randy honored Todd's request only to find no answer at the house.

Tessa and Randy stopped by the bar. Tessa, frustrated, wanted a drink. Randy tried to calm her down but he knew how she felt about Carita. Carita had been like a second mother to her. Just as she took a second sip of her drink, Douglas walked in. He stopped to speak and asked Tessa if she heard from Todd. Tessa told Douglas everything, including how they tried to get into the house.

"Come on," Douglas said, "I have a key."

Tessa looked shocked but it made sense. She called Todd on the way. Todd, in turn, called Steve for criminal and security purposes.

Once they entered the house, Douglas called out for Carita. The house appeared in order as usual but remained very quiet, as if it had no life. Steve checked all of the windows and doors while Tessa and Randy checked all of the rooms. Douglas went downstairs to check the office then called the others. He noticed Carita's two favorite computers were gone. As Douglas examined the situation with Steve, he said only Carita could disassemble the computers. She was very passionate about all of her technical equipment and wouldn't allow anyone to move or use them.

"She does most of her designs on them," Douglas informed.

"How would she print out, none of the printers seem to be missing?" Randy asked.

"Carita always said printers are cheap. Besides, she has flash drives she can use if another system has the same program," Douglas answered.

"My, aren't we computer knowledgeable," Tessa said, smiling.

"Carita's a good teacher," he responded.

The only thing Steve could conclude was that Carita must have gone on a very important job and did not have the opportunity to call anyone. It just was not the norm for her to not touch bases with someone. The others agreed.

Although, she had not called Todd, why not call Alexis, or a family member, or Lee for that matter? Douglas thought. He began to beat himself up. If only they had not quarreled during the recovery from her surgery or at least made up. He knew Carita has some issues and concerns with her cancer but never had the chance to discuss them with him. He knew she would not tell Todd, for she didn't want him to worry and other family members were out of the question. Douglas decided to check her closets. Some of her clothes were missing. He checked her shoes and saw some of her favorites were gone. Carita loved shoes and had a closet full but she only wore certain ones with certain outfits, like most women, and the others during certain seasons. He checked them all and it seemed that most of her summer shoes were missing. Extremely puzzled, he decided to not mention this to the others at the moment.

Douglas called their son and the two decide to keep calling Carita. Todd told his dad he would be home over the weekend. Douglas let him know he would check the house daily and, if anything strange appeared, he would call Steve.

Carita's absence disturbed Douglas. Where would she go and why? What was the possibility of her never returning? He and she had been so foolish. They should be together, enjoying life, but he put another interest first and this situation was not really working out. He drove around with all kind of crazy thoughts in his head. He just did not want Carita to be hurt. She was his life but he never really told her. He finally stopped at one of his favorite fishing spots, where he could think and pray as well. If she never spoke to him again that would be fine, he just wanted her to get in touch. Just knowing she was safe would take a burden off his mind.

Todd accepted what Steve told him but he knew he could do nothing. This was unlike his mother. He knew she really loved him. Why would she leave and not tell him? Although she was angry with Douglas, Todd felt she would have a least called Lee. None of this made sense to him. Did she not know he loved her? He thought about their last conversation which ended up in an argument. He left without saying good-bye. He had no idea his job would send him to Saudi the next day so time did not afford him the option of calling her. "He was fit to be tied." He called his father, thinking that talking to him might make him feel better. Neither one of them could figure out where Carita would go.

Douglas wanted, so badly, to tell Todd about the conversation he and his mother had but did not want to upset him any further. He told his son he loved him and looked forward to him being home over the weekend. Douglas took his time driving. He really did not want to go home. He thought about returning to Carita's and waiting for her to return. This was truly home for Douglas but now it had become his retreat and comfort zone as well as his peace of mind.

Todd and Alexis came home for the weekend as they promised. To their surprise, Douglas was there. He just could not get it out of his mind that Carita was not home and he needed to be as close to her as possible. Upon seeing his father, Todd grabbed onto him. This was probably the most nourishing hug Douglas had ever given him.

He embraced his son with all of his love. Todd was Carita's baby and he knew she expected him to hold him close. Douglas knew that he and Todd had their differences but Todd was his son, his first-born, and he had been a joy to both his parents.

Todd called Steve to come to the house. Tessa and Randy were on their way over as well.

Douglas tried to make coffee but Alexis, who was no stranger to the kitchen, took over so her father-in-law could participate in the circumstances at hand. Steve, his wife, and Alexis, drank the coffee. Everyone else was tea drinkers with the exception of Tessa, who enjoyed a cold glass of Pepsi.

Once everyone had arrived, they sat around the table to try and sort things out. Alexis realized that she, Steve, and Randy would be the only ones thinking clearly. The others were too close to Carita to think and Douglas along with Todd was an emotional mess.

First, they needed to figure if anything was missing and make a list. Alexis and Tessa took Carita's bedroom. Douglas shared with them the items he thought were missing. Douglas and Todd went to the office in the basement to see if any additional equipment was gone. Steve and Randy checked the door and windows. They all found it strange that her SUV was missing as well. For the truck to be gone, she had to have only traveled a short distance.

Douglas discovered that three of the projects Carita had been working on were missing. Her easel, large case of canvass paper, stencils, pens, pencils, paints and other artist tools were gone as well.

Alexis recalled her mother-in-law favorite's outfits and they all seemed to be missing. She noticed most of her under garments and pajamas were missing too. Checking her outerwear, most of the summer and spring coats were gone. All of her make-up and cologne was gone.

While in the office, Todd asked Douglas if he checked the safe. Douglas had completely forgotten about the safe. They both were so upset that neither Douglas nor Todd could remember the combination. Alexis suggested they all sit and catch their breath for a moment. She took out a tablet and a pen and they begin to make a list of missing items.

After drinking some warm tea, Todd remembered the combination to the safe. The vital statistic envelope and all of her bank information was gone. However, the mortgage book remained in place.

They sat at the table and finished the list which Steve faxed to the station. If foul play were involved, detectives would be able to check the pawnshops for some of the items.

This really presented a mystery.

"First, we have to believe that Ma is all right," Steve said. "She would not allow harm to come to herself or any of us for that matter."

"But she was not well," Douglas said. "She still was somewhat weak from her surgery."

"I didn't know that," Todd said. "She never told me."

"She did not want you to know."

"You should have told me, dad. And while we're on the subject, just what did you do to help her," he asked while glaring at his father.

"Carita didn't want my help," Douglas said in a sad but forceful manner.

"I wonder why?" Todd walked toward his dad.

Alexis soothingly moved in between the two.

"This is not the time guys. We all need to focus on Carita. First of all, it looks like mom's leaving was her own decision. Nothing in the house has really been disturbed. The things that are missing are items only valuable to mom. So we need to ask ourselves where did she go and why?"

Steve agreed.

At this point, Todd looked at his dad, feeling like some of this was his fault.

Douglas spoke up. "I guess I could take some of the responsibility for her leaving. I wasn't exactly helpful to her and I knew she was hurting physically, mentally, and emotionally."

"Where do we start, Steve?" Tessa's husband asked.

Steve suggested they run a check on the truck. "If it's on the road, we can have it stopped. We can check through UPS and the regular mail to see if she had anything mailed or shipped in the last two weeks from this address. We should get to the bank and find how much money is in her accounts. This way, we will be able to tell the date of her last deposits or withdrawals."

Todd remembered she had one account out of state but he did not have access to it. He then remembered he did not have access to any of her accounts. "Now what?" he asked.

"It will be alright. I am on all of your mother's accounts. I can get access." Todd looked at Douglas in astonishment.

"Why would she give you that privilege," asked Todd.

"Because you wouldn't accept the responsibility," Douglas responded.

As Todd walked hurriedly toward his dad, Tessa grabbed his arm. "Todd this is not the time. It is not about you or your father but Carita. Besides, she would never approve. She loves you both."

Todd calmed down, somewhat.

Douglas stood strong. "No, let him come on. Let me show him what an old man will do to young snot."

"Dad," said Alexis, with a long draw, "not now."

With all that had to be completed, Todd knew Steve's time was valuable. He suggested they hire a detective agency.

Douglas told Todd he would take care of half the expenses. During the time he sold real-estate, he met a multiple of people so he assured Todd he would hire the best firm he could find. Todd thanked him because Carita meant the world to all of them. Tessa suggested they get a list of her friends' numbers and addresses then check with them to see if they knew anything about Carita's whereabouts. Douglas suggested he and Todd visit Carita's primary care physician, Dr. Rea to check on her mental and physical state.

Todd and Alexis took emergency leaves from their jobs to deal with the situation and left Aeleta with her other grandparents. The group completed all of their assignments but it served no purpose. When Douglas checked the bank accounts, he found no unusual spending and everything was intact. He was somewhat disturbed that the mortgage had been paid up for three months. When Todd checked the utilities, he learned they were paid up too. Steve had his squad check the mailing and packing establishments and came up with nothing. They even talked with Carita's volunteer organizations as well as her church ministries. The group virtually got nowhere.

Douglas and Todd went to Carita's doctor, who made a special appointment for them. They introduced themselves and began to tell the doctor of their dilemma. After listening to the pair, Dr. Rea thought Carita may have gone back to Cleveland Clinic. She had her staff check but found nothing.

Todd and Douglas shared all of the procedures they had enlisted to locate Carita with the doctor. The doctor told them Carita had been doing as well as possible physically, due to the surgery and recovery. She had however noticed a difference in her behavior. Although encouraging to the doctor and staff as usual Carita seemed to have lost some of her own self-esteem. When asked if there was a problem, she just laughed and said, "I am getting old."

"I knew she had a problem sleeping," the doctor said, "but she refused to allow me to prescribe something for her."

"She was always afraid of becoming depended on pills. She did what she could to sleep without them," Douglas said.

The doctor promised to get in touch if Carita contacted her. She was positive that, if Carita left the area, she would call for her records because she was very conscientious about her health.

Todd thought it would be a good idea to call his cousin, Ruth, who had become a doctor. He shared what was going on with his mom and asked her advice as far as her health. His cousin gave him several theories regarding Carita's health. She promised to check the pharmacy to see if Carita purchased prescriptions before she left and found that Carita bought enough medication for three months. She also told Todd and Tessa that Carita would not travel to a hot or humid location. Her asthma couldn't stand it, even with medication. It would probably flare up. Todd's cousin became as upset as everyone else. She checked her schedule for the next three days and booked a flight to fly to join the other family members. Carita was her only aunt and had been a driving force of inspiration in her life. She had to do something even if nothing came out of it.

The group met at Carita's home to share all the information they had obtained. Alexis seemed very distraught and upset that they had not come up with anything. She began to cry.

"Do you all think we took her for granted or just she got tired? Dad, do you know how much she loved you? You had a second chance. What happened to that? She was so elated to think she had survived the cancer and had a second chance at life with you. I know that part of her life was you. And, Todd, you treated her awful because your plan with Tessa did not work. I told you we should have a least awakened her to let her know we were leaving. Now, what?"

Douglas put his arms around her wishing he could cry too. He missed Carita. He felt her disappearance was partly his fault, allowing her to get away with the attitude she maintained. If only he had just moved on with her. He found every excuse in the book to stay with Suzie despite his lack of love for her. Now, the real love in his life was gone and he did not know how to get her back.

Todd stepped forward to take his wife in his arms but Douglas just put his arms around both of them to let them know how much he loved them and they would get through this together as a family.

Tessa looked at everyone. "Well family, we have to accept that Carita is gone and we don't know why. We do not even know if we are going to be able to find her; but I am willing to go on if you are. One thing we haven't thought about, wherever Carita is, it's warm."

"What do you mean," said Todd.

"All of her winter clothes are here.  She took all summer stuff and lightweight coats."

"We need to have someone check all of the airlines that travel to warm climates or least make a list," said Alexis.

Steve told them, after they made the list, he would have it faxed and put a special detective to work on the possibility of air and train travel to warm climates.

Since a considerable amount of people knew of Carita's disappearance, Todd grew cautious about leaving the house unattended.  While the others went over phases and other possibilities, Todd asked to speak with his father in private.

"Dad," Todd said, "how stable is your relationship with this woman you're living with?  Is it all that?"

Douglas thought about it for a minute.  "No son."

"Dad, why don't you stay here?  I know that mom would want you to. And besides, it will give you a chance or clear your head since she's not here."

Douglas promised Todd he would think about it. Todd stipulated that Suzie could not come, not even for a visit.

Steve thought everyone should get some rest.  They had the next day to try out new ideas. They were also scheduled to meet with the private detective agency Douglas hired to see if they meet everyone's approval.

Douglas was driving back home so he could think but knew he needed to stop and see Lee. The day before she asked about Carita and he did not have the heart to tell her of Carita's disappearance.  Now, he did not have a choice since he leaned toward staying in what should have been their home. Had he contemplated marriage with her, like she asked months earlier, this might not be occurring.

Lee was watching sports, as usual, when Douglas arrived.  He kissed her the cheek, sat down, and started a conversation.

"Mama," he said, "I need to seriously talk to you.  May I turn the TV off?"

She looked at him in bewilderment. He never made that request. "Certainly," she said.

"Mama, Carita is missing."

"What!" She screamed and covered her mouth at the same time. "When, how, why?"

Doug went on to tell her the scenario. He also told her everything the group had done and their plans of continuation.

"I knew something was wrong when she hugged me at the hospital. It was more of a good-bye hug than a hello." She wiped a tear. Carita had always been one of her favorite people.

"When was this?" Douglas asked.

Lee told him the day and the time.

"I knew she had been there. I smelled her cologne. It was my favorite."

He told Lee of Todd's plan for him to stay at the house. Lee agreed that someone should stay at the house for several reasons.

They chatted some more while Lee prepared Douglas a light supper. He kissed her on her forehead and told her not to worry. Lee asked him to tell Todd to come over the next day. He was her second eldest grandson.

Douglas took his time driving home. For the past few days, Suzie had been busy but had not gone without noticing how little he had been around. He worried about Todd. Despite his mom missing, he was very vulnerable to hurt and pain but was still capable of being a man. Carita always wanted them to bond and become a little closer, but they only seemed to fight over her. Ridiculous, he thought to himself.

As he walked into the apartment, Suzie stood over the sink.

"Where you been all day," she questioned.

"Out and about," he answered.

"Yea right, probably with your baby's mama," she alleged.

He ignored the comment and put the TV on. Then he thought. They had not contacted the news media. He called Todd.

Todd agreed but only after Douglas settled in the house. Todd thought giving the news media a story such as this may do more harm than good, not only to his mother but to other family members. Suzie than questioned his phone call.

"Who were you talking to?"

"My son, why?"

"Really," she said. "What does he need, some money?"

Douglas just looked at her because, now, she was really beginning to get on his last nerve. This was family business, no place for her to stick her nose. He got his hat and walked to this truck while she made unwelcomed comments. He got in the truck and started driving. To his surprise, he ended up at Carita's house. He put his truck in the garage and entered the house. It seemed so quiet and lifeless without her, but maybe it would not be so bad. He showered and put on his pajamas. Carita had bought different items for Douglas from time to time so he had some clothes available. He walked around the house, hoping to see her face or just to hear silly laugh of hers. He knew that Carita would return.

The next day brought new chores. Douglas decided to check around the area at different activities for the retired. He especially needed to know where to go for a game of pool. He made up his mind to stay at Carita's for a while. He needed the break and Todd needed him to do this for the two of them as well as Carita. He checked the listings on the computer. He opened the door to the office and got a chill. He could hear Carita's laughter as she taught him some things in Microsoft. He booted the computer she had set up for him.

Later that day, he went to check on Lee then shot a game of pool. He went to the apartment to talk to Suzie. As he entered, Suzie was talking on the phone with her daughter. Douglas ignored the conversation and went upstairs. He really did not know how to approach the subject in a kind calm way but need to tell Suzie he was moving.

When Suzie finished with her conversation, she came upstairs to find out what was going on with Douglas.

"Where have you been for two days," she demanded. "I have been calling you and you didn't pick up or return my calls."

"Sit down. We need to talk." Douglas looked at her. "I do not know how much you know because you seem to know everything, but Carita is missing. My son and I and other family members have been trying to figure out where she has gone."

"Gone; where!" Suzie yelled. "But I thought you said she was missing.

"Well that's true but we think she just took up and left and didn't tell anyone."

"Why should you care," she screamed. "The bitch was nothing but trouble for us. Maybe we can get our relationship on track. Good reddens."

"I never thought you would be so cold at someone's misfortune. I really do not know you. Well, anyway, I'm moving into Carita's house."

"What!" She exclaimed. "How am I supposed to get everything packed? How long do we have?"

"I said. I'm going to move."

"What do you mean," she asked.

"Just what I said. Me and me alone. I will be over to check on you from time to time." "You bastard!" she hollered. "You no good son of a bitch!" She got ready to hit Douglas.

He grabbed her arm. "Listen," he said, "this is my son's mother and a family matter."

Angrily, he walked to the spare bedroom and carried as many clothes as he could carry in his arms. He had a few boxes in the truck that he used for shoes and other items. Suzie pleaded with him not to go but he told her he would be in touch when she was in a better frame of mind.

He stopped by Lee's to give her the latest developments. While at Lee's, Todd called to let Douglas know the detective agency had nothing new to report.

Douglas arrived at Carita's and he needed to figure out where he would put all of his things. He did not want to move any of hers around in case she came back. To his surprise, Carita had emptied drawers. The closets in the spare room were vacant as well. That made it easy for him to settle in.

Douglas began to adjust to a new life and a better relationship with his son. He was at peace. The year passed quickly and they received no word from Carita. The holidays were sad but all managed to get through. The second year seemed to be even worse. Douglas did not see Suzie that often but she called him when her husband passed. She thought they could spend some time together. Douglas, knowing where this would lead, gave his condolences and declined her invitation.

Often times, Douglas went to the office so he could feel Carita and perhaps look around to see if they had missed something. They continued to employ the detective agency but they really had not reported anything in the last two years. Douglas decided to go to the office and look up some things on the computer. As he waited for the PC to boot, he noticed several pieces of large software missing. Although Carita kept most of this information on her main PC, she also made a hardcopy and stored it in a file cabinet. Douglas checked the hard copy to find what was missing. He made a list for Todd. He remembered how to get online and emailed Todd the list of the missing software.

Todd called about fifteen minutes later to let Douglas know that most of the missing CDs were large designs programs and some of them were very expensive. "Oh my God," Douglas said. "All this time, we've been looking in the wrong places. We should have been checking out graphic and design businesses."

Todd agreed.

Todd called Steve and Tessa to meet at the house. They discussed Douglas's findings and started a new plan of action. Tessa searched graphics on the internet while Steve checked a five hundred mile radius in the area. They called the detective agency and told them to begin searching graphic design businesses on the east coast, in warm climates.

Todd took a month off work to explore the west coast with his dad. They begin to look for graphics with logo and designs similar to Carita's work. They even looked for handwriting resembling hers.

"This is our year," Douglas said. "Carita will have been gone for three years but we'll have her back in a little while Todd. She is alive."

"How you do know, dad," he asked.

"Your mom used to say she and I were connected. That when I was going through and stressing, she could feel it. I believe that now. All I can feel is joy in my heart and I know that she is alive. You'll see, son. We will find her."

*Chapter 16*

Carita boarded the plane in devastation. Leaving home – all she knew as well as the two men she loved so much – seemed more than she could bear. The tears stored in her eyes started to drop. She worried if she did the right thing. She believed Douglas would never leave Suzie and Todd hated her for not being able to at least understand his dad's dilemma. She thought he viewed her as selfish and uncaring. But, he was mistaken. Leaving was the only thing to do. She always told Douglas she would never place him in an uncompromising position. She always felt that, when something didn't work, you needed to keep it moving. Here, at age sixty-two, she was changing her entire lifestyle. According to her, she had no choice. She loved her family and knew they loved her. Somehow, she had issues with telling and showing them the depths of her love. Therefore, she took a deep breath and told herself, "It's for the best." She closed her eyes only to see Douglas's face with the smile of approval he always wore to display his pride in her. She could feel Todd's hug and hear him saying, "I love you mom."

Mark picked Carita up from the airport. He was glad to see her and elated they would finally work together. Her truck arrived at the office two days prior. She had everything packed in it so Mark employed two of the janitors from the company to assist in unloading the truck at her new apartment. Mark also took her by DMV to reregister the truck. This way, she did not have to continuously worry about being legal or the pair finding her through its prior Ohio registration.

Things were just everywhere in the apartment and Carita was not use to disarray. She called a cleaning agency to assist her with placing things in order. They sent a woman, just a little older than Todd. She was friendly and willing to help wherever needed. Tameka went right in, putting things in place. It only took two days to get Carita's new living space together. Carita liked this woman because she saw them as the same. She liked to keep it moving. Although Carita was supposed to start to work the next day, she called Mark and told him Monday would be better for her.

Carita remained unhappy about some of the things in the apartment. The proprietor painted, as she requested, but the place did not feel like home. She needed a new bed. The walls were bare, needing color. She also needed curtains and other things. She called the agency and requested Tameka's help. While waiting on her to arrive, Carita made a list of all she needed to make her new home a little more comfortable.

The two women shopped all over town. Tameka's suggestions proved to be in very good taste. Her new bedroom suit and other furniture were scheduled for next day delivery.

Carita and Tameka begin to design and place the newly bought items in their respected areas. The apartment started to look like something out of Better Homes and Gardens. The women ran out again to pick up some greenery and a few other attributes to make the apartment exceptionally appealing.

They were both pleased with their efforts. Carita suggested they stop working and get something to eat. Tameka, being a native of the area, knew all the good restaurants and suggested one on the other side of town. After they ordered Carita asked Tameka to tell her a little about herself.

Tameka was born in the south, married, and moved to the area at an early age. Her marriage did not last, so she worked to support herself and a son. She and her former husband were still friends so things were not too bad. She smiled as Carita listened attentively. She sensed she found a new friend. After they ate their dinner, she offered to show Carita the grocery store so the fridge could be stocked. Carita dropped Tameka off and found her way home with very little problems. Tameka planned to come the next morning to complete their decorating.

Mark called to check on Carita the following morning and invited her to breakfast with his family. Carita declined. She wanted her home to be in order when she started to work.

Tameka arrived promptly at nine as promised. Carita made a pot of coffee and the two got started. Later in the afternoon, someone knocked at the door.

"I dropped in to see if you were able to have dinner with me and the family?" Mark looked around. "My goodness, look at what you have done to this place. I'm not surprised. You're very talented. You need to be careful though, the landlord my want to go up on your rent."

They both just laughed.

Mark knew her graphic arts ability was impressive so her home decorating seemed to be just another outstanding skill she acquired. Again, she declined to eat out with Mark and he looked somewhat disappointed. Carita smiled and told him she would be in early on Monday morning.

His pride was somewhat hurt but Carita put a smile on his face by saying there would plenty of time for them to have dinner. Once he had left, Carita sat down and shook her head.

"What was wrong," Tameka asked.

Carita told her Mark tried to make more out of their relationship but she was not ready to get involved with anyone.

"Miss K, you're right," Tameka said with her smile and slow southern drawl. "I think he likes you."

"He's a nice guy but not for me."

Carita and Tameka finished their chores and called it a night. As Carita drove her home, she asked Tameka to consider cleaning for her once a week. She knew that, once she got involved with her job, she would be very busy. The company had a lot of competitors. Her surgery still being new, she also didn't want to take the chance to aggravate anything before she could find a doctor. Tameka thanked Carita and agreed to consider her offer.

Once Carita returned to her new home, she thought of Douglas and began to cry. She missed him and their son. Redoing the apartment had consumed her time so she did not think about her two loves but, now, she was all alone. She showered then grabbed Teddy, the only thing symbolic of her and Douglas's love other than Todd.

On the Sunday before she started her new job, she just laid around. She went into the spare room she turned into an office. She decided to install her two new printers and work on some graphics. She had an idea for some of things the company produced and thought it would be in her best interest to get started.

After an hour of work, Tameka called, invited her to dinner. Carita accepted. She met her son, a very bright and respectful young man. He talked about plans for continuing his education, a plus in Carita's book. Although only fourteen, he appeared to be headed in the right direction. Tameka prepared fried cabbage, fried chicken, mashed potatoes, and cornbread. She was a very good cook.

She invited Carita because she didn't want to see her alone on a Sunday and to fellowship. She also wanted to let Carita to know she accepted the offer. Carita was grateful because her incision from the operation disturbed her. From time to time, this problem occurred. She knew she had to find an oncologist as well as a primary care physician. She was grateful that Tameka could help. She could not have completed everything alone.

After listening to the young man's plans for his classes in school, Tameka offered Carita desert. She chatted about her family and childhood. Carita listened with interest. Soon it was time to say goodnight.

Once Carita got to her new home and settled in, the phone rang. Although it sounded like her old one, she knew it wasn't. She had the number changed and purchased a new phone but held on to the old one, just in case. She decided she needed to change the ringtone, which she did immediately. It was to no avail for she cried herself to sleep again thinking about Todd and Douglas.

Carita awakened thinking of the scripture that says, "Joy comes in the morning." She was not at all sure if this was true. It was a new beginning without the love of her family. She prayed that she could make it through the day. She had asked Tameka about churches in the area. Church and God had always been in her life and she could not be without them now. Had it not been for God, she would not have been able to go through her surgery and recovery.

Once she arrived at the job, she was ready to get started. The manager for her department introduced himself and suggested they get acquainted. Carita felt some apprehension from this man and thought the air needed to be cleared.

"John, I feel a little apprehension from you. Please understand that Mark and I are old friends but I do not expect any favoritism. I am here to do the best job that I can."

John calmed down and gracefully apologized for being unprofessional. They went over company policies and, after signing the paperwork, John asked for her name because she wrote K on all her forms. She smiled and said, "That's it. K."

He smiled back then asked how she felt about working on a large department store campaign logo. Carita told him it would be a pleasure as well as a challenge.

"Great," he said before returning to his office.

Carita knew she had gained a new friend after she let John know she was not expecting any special treatment.

Carita had brought some sketches she toyed with the night before with her. Carita began to work on the logo for Shutrump Department store and got lost into her own world. Before she knew it, lunchtime arrived and Mark stood at her desk, inviting her to grab a bite to eat. She consented but asked if she could freshen up just a bit. She excused herself to the lounge. The two-piece peach suit she chose to wear to work looked very stunning and stylish with her light cream silk blouse. Her light brown stockings showed of the cut of her opened toe pumps. Her brown hair, now with streaks of gray, complimented her complexion.

Mark waited patiently in the foyer of the building. Once she arrived, they proceeded outside. The car pulled up to the curb then the attendant opened the door for Carita. As they drove along, Carita wondered where in the world they were going. Soon, they arrived at the country club. Carita was pissed. She did not want Mark to think he and she had a relationship other than work. What would her co-workers think? She just arrived. Besides, her life was so unsettled. She left her family to make a better life for her, not to confuse it even more.

Evidentially, Mark and his family were well known at the club. They held a table for him.

"I took the liberty of calling our order ahead," he said.

This upset Carita even more.

The maître d' showed them to their table. Mark begin to converse about the club and the quality of food they served. Carita listened in spite of what she had to say. Soon, their meal arrived. Mark ordered filet mignon, baked potato, salad, and tea. One look at his heavy lunch made Carita full.

The operation left her with less than an appetite.  She took a sip of her water and sat back.  Mark looked at her with a raised eyebrow and wondered why she was not eating.

"What's wrong," he asked?

"Nothing," Carita replied.

"Then why aren't you eating?"

"Mark," Carita said as calmly as she could, "I expect nothing other than a work relationship. You have brought me to a country club fit for a queen and what will my co-workers say? I don't want or expect any favors. I want to be able to pay my way. I don't want to be romantically involved with anyone for any reason. Is that understood?"

Mark looked at her with question. Any woman would jump at the chance to be in her position but Carita was not just any woman.

"Yes," he said.

"Then you'd better hurry.  You only have twenty minutes to get me back to work."

Mark was hurt and devastated but he understood where Carita came from and admired her for it.

John checked with her on the assignment and was pleased at the progress she made.  Employees could not remove files or take their work assignments off the premise because of competition. Carita knew how to email her graphics to her home computers. She planned to work on them at home since she wasn't sleeping well because of the pestering incision.

She left work and stopped by a restaurant near by the apartment. She asked to see the manager. She informed the manager that she was new to the neighborhood and, from time to time, would be calling in her order for supper.  The manager was pleased to meet new customers.

"I usually work second shift. I'm Vince. Just call and ask for me when you decide to have carryout.  I will be glad to work on your order personally."

Carita gathered her meal and headed for home.  While the apartment was breathtaking, it was still not home for Carita.  Home was back east with her son and Douglas. She had to move on but couldn't get pass worrying about them. How was she going to know they were alright?  She decided to invest in a private detective who could give her monthly reports.  She also had to find two doctors as well as a beautician and a church. She quickly made a list of things she needed to do as well and calls she had to make. She ate her supper and went to her office in the apartment to finish the morning assignment she received. She emailed the sketch to the computer at work. The only thing she needed to complete was the color and a few other items. Carita thought she might go in early for that. It was nine o'clock before she knew it and five came very early. She showered and turned the TV on, hoping to go to sleep.

At her desk the next day, she made a list of things to do during work or afterwards but decided she did not want Mark involved. He knew enough of her business already.

John was surprise when he arrived about eight and saw Carita. They drank coffee together until his eight thirty appointment arrived.

Before returning to her workstation, Carita chatted with a co-worker who told her some of the company's sketches and other valuable information were being obtained by competitors and the executives were trying to find out who was releasing the information. The company hired a detective agency.

John checked with Carita again. Amazed that she completed her sketch, he looked very pleased while reviewing it. He needed to have it approved by his superior and it would be on its way. Carita asked John if she could have a moment of his time. She inquired about the private detective agency. John gave her an entire background on the detective agency then offered her the number and name of its best agent. She thanked him and returned to her area but not before Mark could get there with the news of how pleased his father was with her graphic. Carita thanked him and went to see if John had any additional items that needed work.

The day at work was going well and Carita took a break to call Tameka. She asked Tameka if she could meet her at Bolos, the restaurant around the corner from the apartment.

The two women ordered their meals and Carita begin to express to Meeka what she needed accomplished the next day. She wanted the very best primary care physician as well as an oncologist. She also needed someone to style her hair. Meeka, as Carita started to call her assistant, shared with her the name of a very good beautician and would arrange an appointment.

Carita was pleased that Meeka did not ask any questions and was ready to assist Carita where she could.  Carita dropped Meeka off and told her to be ready at seven in the morning.

John was so pleased with work that he gave her an even greater challenge. Dore's Fashion House had been operating for two years but did not have logo. John arranged for the owner, himself and Carita to have a business lunch.  Stephanie, the owner brought some of her ideas and sketches. Carita looked and immediately got an idea.  Of course, she did not share the idea with them. She promised to review Stephanie's ideas and get back to her by the end of the week.

As they drove back to the agency, John asked Carita if she would have dinner with his family on Friday. She graciously accepted.  He also asked if she called the detective agency.  She thanked him and, once she got to her desk, she made an appointment for the next day.

As Carita entered the agency, she got a strange feeling.  What if her family used the same agency to look for her?  She knew they had several offices with one on the east coast.  Then, she thought no. Both her men were tight and, although they loved her, she couldn't see them spending that kind of money.

She stepped to the receptionist and asked for Hal D.  She wondered what the D stood for.  The receptionist told Carita to have a seat and Mr. Dukes would be with her momentarily.

"Ah the D stood for Dukes."

Mr. Dukes appeared younger than she anticipated.  He could not have been that much older than, Todd.

"Hello, I'm Hal Dukes."

"Pleased to meet you," Carita said reaching out to shake his hand.

"Mr. Dukes what kind of investigating is your agency involved with?"

"Well it depends on the client and exactly what is involved."

She explained to Mr. Dukes she wanted a report of her son and Douglas every two weeks.  She gave him both addresses. Neither party was to know they were being investigated and no one at the agency. She gave Mr. Dukes all the additional information he required and left her private cell number with him.  He promised to be in touch within a week.

Arriving home, Meeka greeted Carita with a meal fit for a queen and had completed all of the phone calls and appointments.

Carita checked with John to confirm dinner with his family on Friday. They discussed the sketches from Dore's Fashion House.

He thought Carita was doing a fantastic job. He had never seen anyone so quick to learn all of the things Carita placed her in drafts. Many of her pictographs were early symbols of communications in early Africa. Some of her designs related to the hieroglyphic inscriptions used by the Egyptians. John knew Carita was good for him and the company. The design for Shutrump had gotten Genero Graphics traveling back to the top.

Carita had an appointment on Friday afternoon so she arrived at work at six so that she could complete the design for Stephanie. She wanted to pull her weight. Shortly after she arrived, Mark came in. He looked surprised.

"Why are you here so early?"

"I have a doctor's appointment and wanted to make sure that I carried my fair share"

"Is there anything I can help you with or that I should know?"

She looked at him as though he was crazy and smiled. "No. It's just a regular checkup."

Carita left work to meet her new physician and things seemed to go well. Dr. Mays asked to contact her old physician and Carita told him that would not be necessary. She had copies of all her records and would fax them to him later during the day.

He thought she should see an oncologist and referred her to his friend Dr. Bennett. He did not like how she had problems with her incision. Carita felt that she had established a good relationship with Dr. Mays and hoped to do the same with Dr. Bennett.

John had given her the directions to his home but Carita had to call once, when she missed a turn. John had a modest home in a very nice neighborhood. He had three children: two boys and a girl ranging from the ages of ten to five. Jackie, John's wife, was a slim young woman, who worked as a financial consultant. She stood about 5'5 and wore her hair straight on her shoulders, giving her a model's look. With John's height and striking physic, they made a stunning couple. Her eyes gave away to any excitement as they sparkled when John told her that Genero was on the rise again.  She seemed to be a lot of fun and enjoyed hearing about other people's work experience. The children were well behaved and very respectful.  They asked Carita all kinds of questions, which she did not seem to mind answering at all.  In their own way, they reminded her of Aeleta. Jackie's dinner was pleasant as well as appealing and Carita was glad she joined them. Jackie was also interested in learning how to prepare other menus and asked Carita for suggestions. She made Carita feel welcome. Both she and John told Carita to call if she needed anything and not to hesitate to ask.  Carita said her good nights and left for home.  She felt a little calmer since she made more friends but she still missed home.

After she reached her apartment, she saw that Hal Dukes had called and left her a message.  He suggested they meet at the café, the following morning, for coffee if she could.  Hal seemed to sound stressed so she did not know if this was good or bad. Carita could hardly sleep. She thought something might be wrong with her family.

In the morning, she rushed to take a shower in addition to throwing on some jeans and a top so she could be at the café on time.  She had been careful as usual about her makeup and just pulled her hair back.  Hal was there when she arrived.  He stood to greet her as she reached the table.  He gave her a full report on Todd.

"He's was doing very well at his job but his superiors had noticed somewhat of a little declined in his productivity.  They are attributing that to the disappearance of his mother.  Douglas however is living at Todd's mother's house and is seeing very little of his friend named Suzie. He is however spending his time tracking all the leads he can on his son's mother. Miss Smallwood asked Hal, how do you know these people and who are they to you?"

She just looked at Hal and said, "I am not at liberty to say.  Just please continue to report every two weeks and, in time, I may be able to share.  In the meantime, tell me about your agency and how did you get it started."

As Hal started to tell the story of DDA (Duke's Detective Agency), when a man approached the table.  He was tall with skin the color of black coal and smooth as silk.  His salt and peppered mustache told all of his wisdom and experience.

"Here you are," the gentleman said. "Having breakfast with a beautiful woman, when you need to being acquiring customers for the agency."

Hal just smiled and said, "This young lady is a new client. I thought I would treat her to breakfast while bringing her up to speed on her case."

"Oh," the older man said. He asked to sit.

"Ms. Smallwood this is my dad, William Dukes." A lot of people refer to him as Willie D."

He seemed to be a very suave man. He asked Carita how long she had been in the area and if she was pleased with the work the agency completed so far. The younger Mr. Dukes went on to explain to Carita that they had five branches of DDA. The most affiliated branches were the east and west coast. The east coast primarily looked for missing people or assisted in cold cases. The present agency with Hal and his dad just reported on cases when the clients wanted an agency or person watched and or investigated. They all conversed about the area and the dozens of events it contributed to for the community to participate. The older Dukes continued to say that he had known Mark and his family for quite some time and they were very nice people. He asked Carita if she would be interested in attending some events in the future and, of course, she consented.

Carita worked harder than ever at Genero. All of the assignments given to her were expedited with professionalism and competence. She started to be become distinguished and well recognized. Her effectiveness landed John a better position with a handsome raise, of which he seemed very appreciative. Mark offered to take Carita for a victory celebration but, of course, she declined. It seemed that everything she touched turned to gold. However, this still did not help the pain in her heart.

Young Hal continued to report to her. She worried as Todd had taken very ill. Douglas had gone to be with his son to see what he could do to help. She needed to hear Todd's voice but she did not want the number to show. Hal managed to procure a throwaway cell and Carita was able to hear Douglas's voice but not Todd's. She almost let herself go. She kept the phone for short period and, after hearing Todd's voice, she threw it away.

After Hal did this favor for Carita, he began to question her even more. Hal even told her he thought his father was interested in her then asked what she would do if he questioned him?

She looked at Hal and said, "My answer is this. You better convince him that it is not policy or procedure. If he wants to have a relationship with me and if you want to keep me as a client, you will not mention a damn thing about my case."

Hal just smiled. He liked Carita. He looked at her as a mother image. He would never do anything to hurt her and would not tolerate action of that sort from anyone else.

William Dukes called Carita to attend a play and have a late dinner. He was very charming as well as knowledgeable. He talked about his children and other family members. His wife had passed several years ago and he never remarried. She enjoyed William's company and accepted an engagement for the next week. There was no question that the elder Duke had fallen in love with Carita.

The two quickly became an item about town but she still had ties that she did not want to break.

Carita became a top at executive at Genero. She contemplated starting her own graphics business. She knew the business and evidently had the skills. Her expertise and talents assisted Genero to become the top graphic agency in the area. She could be her own boss.

She discussed her plans with William that evening at dinner. They had been dating over a year and she felt that she could trust his judgment, somewhat. Hearing Carita's idea made him very enthusiastic. He was all about the money. He put a few things on the spit as he sometime enjoyed doing for Carita. He agreed that it would be a good move. He loved Carita so. She was attractive, bright, intelligent, innovative, and so many other things. But she would not let William get close to her. As they sat in the chase lounge chairs, he held her hand.

"Hon, why won't you let me get close to you? I love you. You know this. You can have my heart, body, and soul," he said. "I just want to be next to you and I want you to be happy. Who hurt you like this and why won't you let me wipe all your tears away?"

She looked at Willie D and smiled then said, in her usual manner, "I'll be alright."

Meeka brought the salad from inside to the patio. Carita had referred her to the Dukes when their old housekeeper moved back to her hometown. Carita let the Dukes know she had first dibs on Meeka. After dinner, Willie D asked Carita if she would like to go for a ride. As they rode along on the other side of the ravine, Carita spotted a little house for sale. She asked Willie to stop so that they could look at it. The purchase price was small for the area. Carita assumed it evidentially needed some work completed on the inside. Willie promised to check on the house the next day.

He called her at work to let her know all of the particulars.

"K," he said, "you don't need this house. All you need is me. We could get married and you can move in with me or I'll even buy you another house if you want."

Carita was flabbergasted. She told Willie that they would discuss it after dinner. Instead of going home, she called about the house. She had written the number down in case something like this happened. She saved money from her prior position as well as the retirement fund she had not touched. She could go back through her prior employer who would write her a check for the amount needed and they would draw the money out of her retirement account. This way, if Douglas and Todd were still looking for her, they would not be able to get any information.

She met the real estate agent at the property and they went inside. The house appeared perfect. It had a large sunken in living room, with a logged fireplace. A walk up three steps put you in a bright, state-of-the-art kitchen housing a small family room leading to the patio. To the right of the kitchen sat a dining room. Off of the dining room where two bedrooms. Carita imagined how she could better design this house.

The next day, she called her former employer and had the retirement department draw a check the next morning. Willie called to find out what had happened to her and she told him she had not felt well and ended up going to bed early. Carita was fine, knowing the house was in her possession and Willie could not negotiate marriage to her. They met at the café for

Carita had grown tired. She had been stressed all day. He stood up to kiss her on the cheek.  He went on about the house and all of the reasons she should not be connected to it.  She just listened.

Finally, she said, "I bought the house."

Willie D was quite upset when he found out that Carita purchased it.

"I don't understand why? I am able to buy you a nice home that is new and all you had to do was move in."

"I needed to do something for me. After all, I work. This way I can see my investment firsthand of all the hours I put in at Genero."

Willie was even more upset because this meant that she was not ready to accept his proposal.

Carita drew graphs of how she wanted her new home to be designed. She hired a decorating firm to initiate all of her plans and ideas.  She and Meeka went shopping for new furniture and all the other attributes Carita felt she needed.  She also assigned a company to clean the outside of the house and place greenery in her designated places. The corner where the house stood didn't look like the same place.

Willie D was still proposing marriage and telling Carita she could either sell the house or rent it out. She told him she wanted to get her business started and be able to bring something to the table. Against his better judgment, he accepted her reasoning.

While Carita worked on the house, Willie D and Hal looked for a building that suited Carita's purposes for the business. The building they found seemed perfect but the sale price along with equipment and other elements the business would need was somewhat out of Carita's reach.  Carita was having dinner with Hal and his father when Willie could see Carita was quite disturbed.

"What's wrong," Willie asked? "You have said very little all night."

Carita just smiled. "I really want that building and now I have to look all over again because I can't afford it."

Hal replied, "Miss K, why don't we join in this venture together. Allow dad and me to buy the building and you can buy the equipment you need, hire personnel and take care of all the other aspects. This way you could just pay us a monthly rent payment until the building is paid off."

Leave it to "Little Pup" as Carita sometimes called Hal. Willie D just gleamed at the idea. This way, he felt he could keep Carita close to him. It was not that he did not want her to be successful, or to depend on him, he just didn't want lose her. She had become the love of his life. She was everything in a woman that a man could want. The only thing puzzling Willie was Carita never talked about family. He did not know if she had siblings, if her parents were still living, or even if she had children? He could have a background check on her, for his access to information was limitless. He knew, if he opened that door and Carita found out, there would never be a future.

Close to two years later, Carita had become very successful in the graphics business. She had named the business Pebble's Publishers. She was not up to where Genero was but she was well on her way. She had an office at the house in case she did not want to go in. On a particular day, she noticed a box that had never been unpacked. She went through it and found old logos she worked on years ago, that she had forgotten. Graphics had been her beginning, when she was back at home. Her heart ached. Todd had become a little older and she had not been able to send him and his family holiday and birthday presents much less call. She thought about all the people who loved her, who she did not tell good-bye. How was Douglas's life going? Had he finally married Suzie or was he still in her house? How big was Aeleta? It was too much.

She was crying when she heard the door opened. It was Meeka coming to do what chores remained. She noticed the tears and ran to Carita saying

"Oh, Ms. K, what's wrong?"

Carita smiled. "Memories. It was just too much."

"Want to share," asked Meeka?

Carita shook her head no and removed the box and its contents to the master bedroom. While checking things around the house, Carita received a call from Little Pup.

He was frantic and need to see her right away.  Carita had thought that it was just a scenario, which the young man was going through. She was not prepared for what she was going to hear.  He insisted they meet at a small pub outside of the city.  Hal found out, through an informant, that Carita's family stepped up their game to find her.  Hal had a friend on the police force in the city nearby Carita's old hometown.  Not being known by Steve the chief of detectives and Todd's childhood friend he was sharing information to a policeman, which was making extra money for informing to DDA.

Hal ordered her a coffee and cream. By this time, everyone knew that she did not take sugar.  He kissed her as they had grown to be good friends — almost like mother and son. Willie D was glad for that. When Hal told Carita the news, she was traumatized.  She never expected her family to continue to look for her.  She felt that Douglas would have gone on to be with Suzie and Todd would continue his life being a good husband and father.  Her eyes swelled with tears. She was beside herself with worry, for not only them, but Willie D, as well.  She could not bear to hurt him.  He had been her rock, but because she was bound to a love, she could not commit to him.

"Miss K," Hal said. "What is going on? Can you a least tell me something?"

She smiled through her tears. "Never fall in love. It may be years before you can understand what it may do to you."

Somehow, Hal believed Carita but he also knew she would never hurt Willie D. That was his main concern.

*Chapter 17*

Carita had been working so hard that she had almost forgotten about the information that Hal had given her. Although he did not want to take vacation at this time, his dad insisted. He told Carita, if anything would come up, to give him a call and he would handle it personally. Neither one of them wanted Willie D to know anything about her case. Hal explained all of the particulars to Lloyd, a new agent he trusted but who also sometimes seemed very aloof.

As Douglas and Todd boarded the plane, knots continued to go back and forth in each ones' stomach. Todd was determined to find Carita and Douglas continued to pray for her good health. He knew in his heart that God kept her from all harm. They decide to go to LA. It was a place Carita always wanted to visit and was not very humid. Once they landed and got to their hotel room, Todd reviewed their agenda. He gathered all information he received from Rob, the agent for DDA – east coast. He had been very helpful and gave Todd, the name of a west coast DDA agent. Since they planned to start their search in the same town, where the agency was located, Rob gave them Hal's name and told them he was the best agent there was as well as being part owner in the agency. He assured them that Hal would be very accommodating.

Carita prepared for a small dinner party to celebrate her two years with Pebble's publishing better known as PP.  Since the party was being catered, Meeka was in charge of making sure things went alright.  Carita had grown very fond of Meeka and vice versa.  The guests begin to arrive and Carita mingled as best she could.  She never did like social events of this kind but it had been Willie's idea and most of those attending were his protégés.  It was times like these that she missed Little Pup.  She watched Willie as he began to brag and boast about different things. She overheard one conversation where he told a potential client he gave Carita her start.  Carita felt livid but decided not to say anything.  Once everyone arrived, Meeka announced that dinner was served. Willie looked at Carita with love and admiration.  He knew that after a few more dinner parties such as this he would be able to talk her into marriage.  The dinner conversation consisted of politics and stock market for the men.  Most of the women were interested in how Carita got her start in the design business.  They were very impressed with her home décor, and wanted her to give them the name of her designer.  They were all surprised when she shared with them she had done the layout as well as the color coordination and other essentials.  Some of the couples played cards while others sat on the patio listening to jazz. Carita could not wait for them to leave.  This was nerve wracking. Willie came to stand by her as she looked at the sky from her favorite spot on the patio.

"What are you doing," he asked.  You look like you were praying."

She smiled at him. "I was."

"What were you praying for love?" he asked

"These folks leave," she said.

Willie D looked shocked.

"K," he said, this party is for you and people like our guests can take you places."

"Who the hell said I wanted to go anywhere," she replied.

At this point Willie D did not know what to do or say. He got another drink and continued to play his role.

Carita sat on a rock and continued to pray.  For some reason, Douglas remained heavy on her heart. Todd did too.  She wished Little Pup was here. She wanted to call him but she could not interrupt his vacation. Soon the guests begin to leave, telling Carita they had a great time. Carita smiled and gave them all hugs and kisses but was grateful the party had ended.

Willie D sat at the table waiting on Carita after the last guest left.

"K," he said he stood. "I don't understand your attitude."

She glanced at him with fire in her face, tongue and just everywhere. "Excuse me," she retorted.

"I did the party for you to help you go places."

"Oh," she rejoined, "Where the hell am I supposed to go? Is that why you told Tom Bolding you gave me my start?"

"That's what's bothering you? Guys talk," he said. "It's just a way of staying in."

"I didn't know you were ever out," she said.

"K, I don't want us to argue. I love you," he said.

"Love is not the answer to everything, Willie D."

"I don't see why you're so upset. Things went well. You'll be the talk of the town."

"I don't want to be the talk of the town. I want to do things on my own!"

"Oh, I'm tired of this," he yelled. "Since you want to be your own sister, you got this."

He left in a stupor and Carita did not seem to care. All of a sudden the fresh air came in from nowhere and she could breathe.

Meeka completed assisting the catering company and was dead tired. Carita suggested she spend the night and go home in the morning. Carita awakened the following morning and put coffee on while she showered. Meeka was quick to dress and make breakfast. The girls discussed the events of the party while continuing to clean the house. Carita's phone rang off the hook. She knew it was Willie D and refused to answer it.

Meeka gazed at her and said, "Ms. K, was it that bad?"

Carita replied, "No, but stay out of it Meek."

Douglas and Todd made a list of graphics agencies in L.A. that they wanted to visit. They had no idea the job would be so tedious. Todd created a schedule allowing them to get to at least five agencies a day. He made a call to DDA and asked to speak to Hal, only to find out he was on vacation. He decided not to leave a message. Todd had a composite drawn of his mom from a picture taken during happier times. The composite was to look as close to Carita's features at the present.

The artist, a police sketch artist who worked for Steve, did a very good job. He also had a copy of her handwriting from cards she gave Todd and Douglas. Douglas had found some copies of old logos Carita produced as well as graphic letters for her business back home. He believed that, if they found any similar sketches, they might be able to find her.

Todd was glad they arrived over the weekend so they might begin to execute their plan. Alexis and Tessa both called to check on the guys and to make sure everything went well. Alexis was extremely worried about Todd. He had worried all these years about his mom and blamed himself for her leaving. Douglas tried to spend all the time he could with Todd and shouldered just as much of the blame. Through the ordeal, the two bonded. If Carita had known, she would have been so proud.

Carita took Meeka home and spent some time with her son Clinton. They went over some homework together and Carita showed him an easier way to create his graphs in Excel. She shared a variety of techniques to complete different homework assignments. Clinton was so grateful. Carita was like an aunt he didn't have.

Carita hated to go home alone and decide to stop at the office to check things. There, she could reminisce about the old days. True, she enhanced her work as well as her quality of life but she was still not happy. She always loved Douglas and the only child she birth served as an affirmation of that love. "Why did I leave," she said to herself. "How are they, really?" She thought, "I've got money, position, and a man who says he loves me and

I'm still not happy." She concluded that she was angry with herself for not sticking the situation out back home.

"By this time, maybe we would have been together," she continued to ponder while twirling in her executive chair until coming to her senses when the phone rang. It was Willie D.

"I'm outside. I've been trying to get you all day, but you weren't answering your phone."

Carita was silent for a moment. "Guess what," she said. "I'm still not answering my phone." She hung up on Willie D. left the office and drove home.

Sunday morning arrived and Carita made the usual preparations to attend services at St. Peter's Baptist church. She always went to the first service. This way, if she had worked to be done, she was filled with the word for the week. The church was having its annual revival, joining St. Paul's in L.A. for worship. Carita decided to drive to the city. After all, she would spend the day and dinner alone anyway. At the last minute, she decided to call Meeka and Clinton to see if they would like to ride with her and have dinner. Meeka was delighted and assured that they would be ready when she arrived.

Douglas attended church every Sunday since Carita's disappearance. So as they ate breakfast, Douglas decided that he and Todd needed a divine intervention and should go to Sunday service somewhere. The waiter suggested St. Paul's around the corner. It was in walking distance and they would arrive in time for second service. As Douglas and Todd approached the church, they were amazed at the number of people departing from the first service. They entered the church climbing the steps on the left hand side. At the same time, Carita and her party started down the steps on the right hand side of the building. Neither party looking up they missed each other by just a tenth of a second.

Carita wanted to treat Meeka and Clinton to breakfast after church. She also suggested they attend any movie he wanted to see. After the breakfast, they went to the mall and picked up items for Clinton regarding his school projects. Carita also treated him to a couple of outfits he wanted. By the time they completed their shopping spree, it was time for the movie.

Douglas and Todd decide to catch a movie as well. They reviewed their plans for the next day and needed a new light on all subjects. They chose the same movie theater where Carita had gone but were in a different lounge.

After the movie, Meeka, Clinton and Carita chose an Italian restaurant. Meeka found Italian food to be Carita's favorite. The group was making their selection when Carita heard a familiar voice from behind. She was certain it was Willie D. She continued with her order and felt that, if it was Willie, he would make himself known. Meeka laughed about something that happened to her in her childhood, during their conversation, and Willie D happened to look her way.

"What are you doing here," he asked?

"My son and I are with Ms. K."

At this point, Carita turned around so that he could get a glimpse of her face. She also could see he was with a very young woman, even younger than Hal. Carita smiled at her and said hello. They continued with their meal but Meeka was concerned for Miss K. K eyed Meeka and voiced that she was fine.

"It is what it is, Meeka," stated Carita. "All that glitters is not gold."

They finished their meal but waited longer than usual for the bill. When the waiter returned, he explained that the gentleman at the next table paid for their meal. Carita gave the waiter a one hundred dollar bill and asked him to bring back the correct change of the meal as she wanted to reimburse the gentleman. As she and Meeka got ready to leave, she stopped at

Willie D's table. He looked up at Carita and grinned as though he had done something wonderful.

"Did you ladies enjoy your meal?"

"Immensely," Carita beamed but I thought you might need this change. She politely laid $65.89 on the table and told the young woman to have a good evening.

Meeka and she drove back to Pebble Beach in complete quietness until Meeka broke the silence. "I just can't get over you Ms. K. Mr. Willie really does love you," she said.

"Meeka," Carita answered, "most people don't know what love is. Willie is one of those people so let's not discuss it."

Carita dropped the couple off and returned to her home. She needed to get some rest. She had a big day ahead of her. There were several graphics that needed completed for exhibition and she had a new artist coming in. Carita sat in her chair and thought about the events of the day. She wasn't angry at Willie D, but very much disappointed. It was okay. It was not the first time a man disappointed her. She just had no reason to run this time around. She grabbed Teddy. It had been such a long time since her Teddy had sat together. She thought of her love for Douglas. You would have thought, after all these years, the love she had for him would have gone away but there was still a passionate sensation in her heart filled with an amorous love affair that seemed never-ending. She held onto Teddy for dear life and cried herself to sleep.

Douglas felt distressed as he looked out the window at the city lights. He whispered, "Where are you, Re? Do you know how much you have been missed? I have loved you all of these years and I never thought I would lose you. When you told me that you had loved me for forty years, I took it for granted. You have been through so much. I really thought I was going to lose you with the liver cancer. God smiled upon you and you lived. What did we do to you, Carita? Why couldn't you have talked to me? I love you, Carita. Where are you?"

Todd awakened to see the distress look on his father's face. He knew how his father felt. He knew, if something happened to Alexis, it would be hard for him to go on. He watched his father's head drop and put his hand on his dad's shoulder. "Dad, joy comes in the morning."

Carita went to the office, which was busy as all get out with the exhibit. Of course, Willie D showed up to apologize for the previous day's events. Carita asked him to step in the office.

"Willie D," she said. "This is not the time or the place."

"I just want to explain," he stated.

She looked at him and said, "Not on my time" then opened the door to show him out.

During the exhibition, the office seemed like a mad house but Carita received several offers for some of her logos.

Willie D stayed around to meet some of the graphic personnel. He hated not being able to talk to Carita. After such a busy day, he decided it would be best to leave Carita alone. He walked her to her car and told her he would see her in the morning. Carita did not reply because she really did not care when she saw him.

Carita stopped at the old restaurant and Vince had his famous lasagna ready for her. He missed her patronage since she moved to the other side of town. Carita continued home excited about the day but tired as a dog.

Todd and Douglas begin their campaign. They were able to do six agencies instead of five, as planned. They had become good friends with the waiter, Dan, who he gave them some ideas about Pebble Beach. He suggested that they try that area after doing LA. He claimed there were many graphic agencies because it was such a picturesque area. Todd thanked him for the tip. The next day Douglas and Todd went out again, to no avail. Douglas felt disheartened so Todd suggested they look in the Pebble Beach area. He told his dad he would call DDA in the morning to see if he could reach Hal.

Although Todd did not reach Hal, he finally inquired as to who was handling his cases. The receptionist referred Todd to Lloyd. Lloyd remembered the case being important to Hal. He listened to Todd attentively. He suggested that they try Pebble Publishing and told them the owner's name starts with a K. "She only uses the initial," he said. No one has ever known her name. Todd thought the young man didn't know what he was talking about but still shared the information with his father.

Douglas looked at his son with enthusiasm. "We couldn't get a break like that, Todd. What are the chances that this Ms. K is Carita? My nickname for her before you were born was ReRe. She would never use that; she's too smart. How much do you want to bet the K stands for Carita"

"Are you serious? Dad, can we at least go there and try?"

"I don't see why not. Our other plans are almost exhausted."

Douglas smiled. He knew he son was also weary and exhausted. He even drove as Todd went over some of their notes. He also called Steve to let him know they made some progress. They arrived at Peebles Publishing around ten in the morning. They were greeted by Kelly, who assumed they were potential customers. Todd was very professional in his approach. Douglas looked around the office. He felt something. The smell of cologne reminded him of Carita.

"Could this truly be her business? What did she look like now?"

She was always very attractive and he knew her well enough that she would continue to be so. Todd presented the old photo of Carita as well as the composite of today's look to Kelly. Kelly's heart jumped but she tried not to show her emotions.

"My God," she thought. "That's Ms. K. What is going on?"

She just smiled at Todd and began to ask questions. Todd was feeling like they were in the right place but Kelly was not telling him what he wanted to hear.

Usually when Carita came to work late, she used the front door so the personnel could see she arrived. She had become a mother image to some of the workers and they worried about her. On this particular day, she had a change of heart and decided to use the back door leading to her office. She got herself organized then went to open the door from her office to get her usual cup of coffee and stopped in her tracks. The man standing in the hall favored Douglas. As she looked beyond his body, the younger man resembled her son. She quickly closed the door and rang Kelly's phone.

Kelly politely excused herself and asked Todd to have a seat. When she came to the office, Carita put her fingers to her mouth letting Kelly know not to make a sound.

"Ms. K," she exclaimed.

"Kelly," Carita said, "Who's that man?"

Kelly went to explain as simply as she could what the man had told her. Carita knew her son and her love had found her but she needed more. She had Kelly to offer them tea to see if it was really them. Carita knew they would not take any sugar because both of them were health nuts and only used honey. As Carita suspected it was them! She had given Kelly instructions of how to direct them. She did not know if it would work. She and Douglas had always felt connected. If that were true the pair might be back tomorrow.

Kelly ran back to Carita's office as soon as the pair left. Carita looked at her and said, "If you want your position here at Pebbles, you will not mention this scenario. Give me the papers they gave you."

Carita looked at the picture taken at Todd's wedding and the composite they attained. It was very well done. Carita sat down as she grew week in the knees. "Oh my God. What now?" She did not know that they still loved her.

Todd examined his dad's face and eyes. His face actually had some color. Earlier in the week, he appeared very dark around his eyes.

"Well dad," he said.

"Carita's here I can feel her. She alright. Just a little confused."

Todd did not want to question his dad for he waited for this moment for three years. Todd suggested they stay at a hotel several blocks away from the Carita's publishing house. As they drove up to the hotel, they could not comprehend all kinds of commotion.

As they registered, they learned that Oprah was in town filming a show about finding lost love ones. Todd was stunned. What were the chances that he and his dad could get on that show? He had to find Carita. He knew that both of his parents loved one another and needed to be together. Todd called Rob (DDA – east coast). He told Rob of the opportunity and how he needed an in.

"What about Hal Dukes," Todd inquired.

Rob told Todd that he was on vacation but Hal knew a lot of people. He would try to get in touch. Fortunately, Hal was back from vacation and gave Todd a call. He accepted a dinner engagement with Douglas and Todd to see if he could not be accommodating. Todd and Hal met in the lounge for a drink and Douglas planned to join them later. They discussed the weather, the area, sports and world events.

Hal keep looking at Todd, for he reminded him of someone but he just could not put his finger on the person.

Douglas joined them and they ordered their meal. Hal had some influences with the hotel and others who were putting together the show for Oprah. He assured that what he could not manage, his dad could. Hal went on to inquire about who the pair was trying to find. Todd brought the composite and the picture out. Hal almost collapsed.

Todd went on to tell Hal a scenario of what he and his dad were attempting to do. They communicated to Hal the importance of finding Carita.

Now, Hal understood why Ms. K was so secretive. The only question in his Hal's mind was what about Willie D. He loved K in spite of his father being an ass for the past two weeks. Hal was in a dilemma. He finished his dinner with the men and promised to call them first thing in the morning. Hal had a lot of thinking to do. He could tell that Todd was very hurt and concerned, just as his father. He remembered how shy K appeared when she first arrived. He could not tell Miss K because that would put her on the defensive. He now understood why she did not want him to know anything about her. He also had to consider Willie D. He had a right to know but, with his attitude lately, he would try to get Carita out of town.  Hal had to pray on this situation.  Ms. K had been good to everyone she encountered.  Because of her outlook on life, a lot of the people in Genero Graphics, as well as her own company, received a second chance at life.  Even Willie D had a better demeanor toward people.  Carita deserved whatever God had for her.  She needed her family just like everyone else. Even if it meant he and Willie D might lose her, she deserved to be with people who loved her.

Hal D went to see Al, the producer of the Oprah Show, to see how he might be able to assist him.  While making the inquiry, he had the opportunity to confide in Oprah with what he thought may have happened to this family.  They planned other alternatives in case Hal's original plan failed.  He knew Ms. K would not give her family up second time around.

Hal called Todd, the next morning, to inform in that the arrangements were completed. They were to meet with Oprah's executive producer at ten a.m.

Todd and Douglas were at the set promptly.

They were greeted by excited staff members.  The producer went over questions, different scenarios, and the segments of the show so Douglas and Todd were well prepared.  They were advised, to be back on the set at two for make-up and other essentials.

Carita felt pleased and content over how well the exhibit had gone.  The attention the company received overwhelmed Carita.  All in all, it had been a good week, month and she was finally going to have a good year.  She was still however concerned that Douglas and Todd were in town.  She wanted to call Hal but she didn't want him to think she was checking on Willie D. As she was going over the company's sales for the past week, the phone rang.  It was Willie reminding her of a board meeting.  He continued to say that he would like to have dinner so the two of them could talk.  Carita agreed to meet Willie at the restaurant later in the evening.  After checking other financials for the company, Carita decided to call it an early day.  The excitement of the last two days started to take a toll on her.  She was not as young as she used to be, or thought.

She stopped at the store to pick up some fresh fruit, vegetables, and crackers along with her favorite cream cheese. She made herself a tray and settled down to watch the Oprah Show. Oprah came out and shared the theme of the show with the audience. She went on to say many people had lost love ones under different situations and circumstances, leaving loved ones heart-broken, especially if the loved one was unable to bring closure to an issue in the relationship. "Today's guests have been looking for their loved one for three years," said Oprah. "But the difference with this pair is they feel their loved one is still alive."

She called for the pair to come on stage. The audience clapped as Douglas and Todd appeared. Carita looked closer at the monitor and saw Douglas and Todd. She was astonished. She listened conscientiously as they told their story of why they thought Carita left. Each one bore the burden of responsibility, for not being conscientious enough during her surgery and recovery. They pleaded for Carita to come forth. Todd shared with Oprah, the old picture of Carita and the composite. Oprah showed it to the audience and of course, the cameras picked it up. She left a number for Carita to call and reminded the audience and the TV viewers that there would be a series of questions, for anyone calling claiming to be Carita to answer. The questions were composed by the father and son. Only the real Carita would know the answers to these questions.

Carita felt devastated. And, just as the feeling intensified, the phone rang.

Meeka, who was also watching the show wanted to hear what her plans might be and Hal was only minutes behind Meeka with the same concerns, both stating they wanted to make sure she was alright and voiced they were on their way to the house. Carita turned the phone off, for she did not want to hear from Willie D or anyone else for that matter.

"What about dad, Hal asked?"

"I don't know Carita answered. I don't know what to say or what I am going to do. This is my son who I have never stopped loving. I have always and will always love his father, but I had no idea that he still loved me."

She shared some of her thoughts with the two; but she still had not come to any conclusion. Hal told her that whatever she decided, he would support her. He told her he would never share the truth with his dad. After all, cases were confidential and with that policy, it would keep him out of the woods. Carita thought all night about what she really wanted to do. She missed Todd and, of course, her love of forty years. Once again, she and Teddy slept arm in arm as though he could give her an answer.

When she woke up, she took a shower and remembered her phone was off. She turned it on to retrieve messages. Oh No! She had forgotten that she had a dinner date with Willie D and his messages were most disturbing. She did not have time to worry about his idiotic issues. She hurried to the office to pick up her materials for the board meeting and left before the staff asked her a million and one questions.

Arriving at the meeting, Willie just looked at her then asked what happened. She made some excuse of working on project and lost track of time. He accepted her excuse for her knew that Carita was very much into her business and it had always been a habit she maintained. The meeting started and Carita started to think about Douglas. Willie asked her opinion on a dispute before the board and she could not respond.

Angrily, he said to Carita, "If you're not going to pay attention than you might as well go."

Carita glanced at him. "You're right." And, to everyone's surprise, she gathered her belongings and left.

Once she arrived at home, she began to think. She loved Douglas and her son. What a fine man he turned out to be. She got the number to call Oprah. The phone had rung several times and, just as Carita was about to hang up, someone came on the line. She identified herself and reason for calling. She heard commotion in the background and, all of a sudden, it became quiet. The man on the other end of the line told her he had a series of questions he would ask. He proceeded to inquire about when, where, and the time of Todd's birth. He also asked what music played while you were in labor, Douglas's birth date, the family's homestead address, and both men's social security numbers.

Once she answered them, she heard a scream in the background then Oprah's voice on the phone. She asked when she could meet with them to be on the show. She was going to have to fly to Chicago because the segment of the show airing the day prior was just for that time frame only.

Oprah told her someone from her staff would call her back with all of the final accommodations.

The studio quickly called Todd and Douglas, who had returned east, to tell them a woman called and answered all of the questions. They were hoping that it was not a farce.

Tears trickled from Douglas's eyes as hugged his son with affection. He felt that as though a burden had been lifted. He glanced at Todd and said, "I told you she was not dead and this would be our year. What time do we leave tomorrow?"

The studio told Todd and Douglas not to share the news with anyone but, of course, they had to tell Lee, Tessa, and Alexis.

Carita was frightened. She did not know if she had done the right thing. She went through her closet to plan her wardrobe for the trip. Carita received the phone call about two hours after she spoke with Oprah. She was truly pleased. This way she could get out of town without another argument with Willie D but it was too late. He was at her door. She let him in. He really did not know how to approach her or what to say. He could feel a little strain between them. He tried to apologize for his attitude in the board meeting. She told him he was right and not to worry about it.

Willie was surprised at her mindset.

She quickly explained that she was going through some things only she could resolve. Willie tried to take Carita into his arms but she stepped back from him and said, "Now is not a good time." She went on to tell him she was going away for a couple of days to get her mind together. Willie was disappointed they could not make it a holiday for them both but Carita told him she would rather that they did not. He left after kissing her on the check.

Carita called Meeka to let her know she would be out of town for a couple of days and to check on the house. Carita knew in her heart she may not come back and took the time to write Hal and Meeka a long letter explaining everything and telling them of her affection and appreciation for all they had done.

Carita arrived in Chicago in the early evening. Once in her hotel room, she took a long warm bath. Her phone rang and it was Charlotte from the Oprah show. She told Carita that Oprah requested her presence at dinner as she was excited and could not wait until the show to meet Carita. The two meet in the lounge of the hotel. Oprah was so kind and gentle and made you feel like she had known you all of your life. After hearing Carita's story, she told her of the love Douglas still carried in his heart for her.

Carita asked, "Did he tell you that?"

"No but, if one just looks at him and mentions your name, you can tell his heart just melts. I have been around long enough and I am able to tell about these things.

The women talked until almost midnight. Oprah reminded Carita that she needed to be at the studio at 10 a.m.

Todd and Douglas were nervous. Douglas looked in the mirror several times to make sure his tie appeared straight. Todd was worried about his dad. After their phone call from the studio, he had left the house and remained gone several hours before returning. Alexis told her husband that he might have just wanted to be alone. The whole ordeal had been overwhelming for everyone involved.

When the show aired, Oprah re-introduced Douglas and Todd and gave the audience a short synopsis of the story. Carita was in a room off stage, hoping the two-piece mauve suit she wore was appropriate. Her hair, cut into a pixie was now salt and pepper. She remembered when Douglas had asked her not to color it because he thought that it was so pretty.

The door to her room opened and her palms begin to sweat. Her legs were weak from pacing the floor. She could hear the audience clapping. Tears begin to swell her eyes.

As she walked onto the set, Todd grabbed her and said, "Ma," and held on to her.

Douglas came behind him, hugging her and was just so filled he could not speak.

Carita just broke down and cried.  She tried to explain, she was only doing what she thought was best for them.  Both men were hanging on to her so tightly she could hardly breathe.  Douglas kissed her with such passion that she knew they had not lost their love.

The audience needed some Kleenex. Oprah, who needed Kleenex as well, had the producer go to commercial.  When everyone regained their composure, Douglas took Carita's hand and bent down on his knee. The audience went wild and Todd's mouth just dropped opened.  Oprah began to cry again.  Carita could not contain herself.  She looked beyond the road of forty years, and realized, all the accomplishments they achieved had not been lost but was once again theirs.

**To *everything* there is a season, and a time
to every purpose under the heaven:**

Many women and men as well have struggled to keep love; for it has been the very essence of our souls and our whys that makes sense. We have felt that it has generated the faith, family and friends' clique, when in truth love is and has been our quality of life.  It is without question that love is an endowment as well as a second chance from God.

I lost my husband to cancer and was told a year later that I had liver cancer.

What do you do?  What do you say? Where do you go?  Love sometimes depicts not only the quality of life but is the diverse objective of wanting to continue life.

Had it not been for my experiencing the quality of life, wanting to live and a forty year love affair, which fate would not entertain in those early years, I would not have been able to appreciate life and all that love has to offer.

It is with that knowledge, privilege and the second opportunity that I share this special part of my life with you.

Continue not to let the battle of love go and look at it as the chance that God gave us for a better quality of life.

The author is available for speaking engagements.  Please contact PJ at pjauthor320@aol.com or call 330-759-3669.

*A Lifetime Love Affair*

*Synopsis*

At some point in our lives we have all felt the fire of love and the shatter of heartbreak.   This intriguing romance depicts the lives of Carita and Douglas who are engulfed in love's flame only to be separated by the injustice of fate.  Douglas knew Caritas's characteristics of love and inspiration made her the exceptional woman in his life. Carita thought his return home would restore their passionate love; but the cruelness of jealousy and time detours their relationship for what seems to be a lifetime.

While the ambers of their love continues to burn, the couple separately endures the travels of life, finding it to be difficult as well as disappointing, interjecting one roller coaster ride after another.  Although destiny will not be cheated and neither will it change, it is not until a series of unfortunate circumstances occur that once again unite Carita and Douglas.  Through drama, secrets and commitments their love affair after forty years is once again renewed.

## About the Author

PJ was reared in the Pennsylvania by her maternal grandparents and learned at an early age any desired goal would take stamina and dedication but is well worth the effort in the end. As a child she was very independent and considered obstinate, but with each new challenge, she gained knowledge that laid a foundation for the bumps in the road which were to come. She is the mother of one son and, sadly, has recently become a widow. After graduating from college, starting her own printing business, and losing her husband, PJ was diagnosed with cancer and started writing as therapy for the soul. Now in remission, she speaks to those who also have encountered misfortunes, giving them hope, love and just a bit of  laughter. She hopes every reader enjoys her first novel and will be waiting with anticipation for her second which is in the works.